The Runaways

Center Point
Large Print

Also by Max Brand®
and available from Center Point Large Print:

Curry
Valley of Outlaws
Hired Guns
Sacred Valley
Gunman's Rendezvous
Twenty Notches
White Indian
Peyton

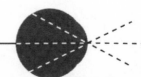

**This Large Print Book carries the
Seal of Approval of N.A.V.H.**

The Runaways

MAX BRAND®

CENTER POINT PUBLISHING
THORNDIKE, MAINE

This Center Point Large Print edition
is published in the year 2011 by arrangement with
Golden West Literary Agency.

ISBN: 978-1-61173-246-7

Library of Congress Cataloging-in-Publication Data

Brand, Max, 1892–1944.
The runaways / Max Brand. — Center Point large print ed.
p. cm.
ISBN 978-1-61173-246-7 (library binding : alk. paper)
1. Large type books. I. Title.
PS3511.A87R86 2011
813′.54—dc22

2011030018

Chapter One
AN UNWILLING SONGSTER

There are two ways of taking a high note. The natural way is to squint up your eyes, get your mouth as wide open as you can, close your fists, and let it come. The other way is to keep your head down and your eyes wide—to try to smile and force out the note while you feel a sort of sick look coming on your face. That was the way that the minister wanted us to sing in the choir.

When Aunt Claudia sent me upstairs to put on a clean shirt with one of them big, stiff-starched collars on it, I knew mighty well that she would want me to sing for her guests that afternoon, and that I would have to sing the minister's way. Well, it made me pretty sick.

I got up in my room and put the shirt on. The edges of the collars always sawed into your neck when you put the shirt on. I seen that I wouldn't be able to turn my head very much that afternoon without sawing my neck about off. That didn't make me much happier.

Just then the front doorbell rang. I could hear Aunt Claudia's voice bubbling and dancing up and down the scale. So I knew that the Porsons had come. Well, I knew that it would be a while before I was wanted. Aunt Claudia would have to settle them down, and ask how they were, and what they'd been doing. Then she would have to paw over Jack Porson, who was only a year older than me. She would have to say how much he had grown, and how like somebody in the family he looked, and all that sort of rot.

All of this would take a lot of time. So I sat down by the window and looked out. I started thinking what a mighty lot of trouble and sorrow there is in the world. I mean, how much trouble there is for people. I could see the Simsons' cow lying down in the shade of a tree over in the lot, chewing her cud and twitching her hide to make the flies leave her. Only they just buzzed up and settled down again on her. She was so plumb lazy and contented that she didn't bother turning her head to lick them off or switching her tail to knock them off. Just then a rooster hopped up on the top of McGregor's back fence, flapped his wings, crowed, and then stuck out his head to see who had noticed his voice.

Well, you could see that there was happiness in the world for things like the rooster and the cow that didn't go bothering themselves all the time. But mostly folks is bothered a lot doing things that somebody has said that they ought to do. It is a queer thing how many "oughts" and "ought nots" there is—in school, in church, or in Aunt Claudia's house. It didn't make any difference. One was about as bad as the other.

6

Just when I was thinking of all this, a loafer came down the street playing a violin. He had a white dog along with him to do the begging for him. That fellow, he could play a violin pretty good, with a lot of quivers and things in the top notes. When I heard him first, he was playing "Ben Bolt" so sad that it made your Adam's apple ache.

He was a pretty slick player, all right, but it done you good to see that dog carry on when anybody stopped to listen—or just walked along, wanting to hear the music, but not stop and pay for it, you know. That dog would run up in front of whoever it was, and stand up on his hind legs, and walk backwards in front of him, sort of hopping along. It must have been pretty hard for a dog like that to stand up that way. I saw the minister come along, and I had to smile when I seen that poor dog try his trick on the minister. But the dog was right, and I was wrong. Pretty soon the minister reached into his pocket and tossed a coin that the dog grabbed right out of the air as slick as you please. Then he ran and dropped it into the hat of his boss.

The minister stopped and said something to the violinist just as he got to the quivery, quavering end of "Ben Bolt." I saw the beggar shrug his shoulders and the minister roll up his eyes. He shook his head mighty sadly and walked away down the street, pitying the beggar. He was a great hand at pitying folks, the minister was. Except when he was rehearsing the choir, and then he laid his pity on the shelf for a rest that it had earned, I suppose. Well, I guessed by this that, most likely, this loafer with the violin was a lost soul, or something like that. Of course, it made me take a lot more interest in him and even his dog, too. I just noticed that he had sort of reddish hair and that he was kind of big around the shoulders when a door opened downstairs and let out Aunt Claudia's voice, still bubbling and running up and down scales to show how plumb tickled she was to have the Porsons there that afternoon.

It made me sick to hear her because I knew that she hated Mrs. Porson. I don't know why, unless it was that she had to wear glasses, and Mrs. Porson didn't. I turned around and made a face. It's wonderful what you can do with your face when you let yourself go. I had done a good deal of practicing, so that I could make any boy on the block want to fight in a minute. It comes mighty handy, being able to do a thing like that. In school, for instance, if there's some sassy-looking girl on the far side of the room with her nose stuck up in the air, it does you a lot of good to let her know what you think of her without having to use no words.

I could see by the mirror that I had worked up an extra good expression, and I was so busy studying it that I didn't hear Aunt Claudia coming up the stairs. When she busted in on me, I hadn't wiped off all the look that I was wearing. It brought up Aunt Claudia standing, as they say, and she flattened her shoulders against the door behind her.

"You young scamp," said Aunt Claudia in her most swearingest voice, "how dare you look at me like that?"

"I wasn't looking no way," I answered.

"Humph!" exclaimed Aunt Claudia. "I thought I sent you up here to put on your clean shirt. You ain't got the necktie on it, yet."

"I didn't know," I said, "whether you would want me to wear a bow tie or a . . ."

"Stuff!" said Aunt Claudia. "Did you expect that you would learn what I wanted by sitting there like a great lump? Come here to me!"

She gave me a yank, picked up a big, beautiful blue tie, put it around my neck, and fluffed it out. Then she stood back and squinted at it, and nodded and smiled sort of critical, not admiring me, you understand, but the picture that she was going to make out of me. She grabbed the comb and brush and begun to tidy up my hair.

"Ouch," I howled, "that's a sore spot!"

"Stuff!" exclaimed Aunt Claudia. "What a great softy you are! I wish to goodness I could understand why your hair is all bristles in back. Now, Sammy Moore, I want you to do your best this afternoon, because Missus Porson is a great lover of music and a great judge of it. She has got classical taste. Do you hear me? And I shall be dissatisfied if you don't sing perfectly."

I knew what that meant. Whenever they say "classical," you know it is something mostly without no tune and up around high C part of the time, the rest being down where you got to squawk it with your chin away inside of your collar.

"All right," I answered. "I shall do my best, Aunt Claudia."

"Sammy," she said, "you are a dear boy . . . when you want to be. Now you come along. And if you impress Missus Porson . . . the horrid, critical thing! . . . you shall have a great big piece of apple pie tonight for your supper."

"A quarter of a pie?" I asked, not wishing to lose no good chances.

"Yes, I suppose so," she agreed. "But only if you do extra this afternoon."

If you ever tasted one of Aunt Claudia's apple pies, you would know why it was worthwhile to do extra good when she wanted you to. She had a way of cooking up green apples and sugar and crust so's it was half sweet and half sour. It sent a tickle from right behind your eyes clear down to your toes. So I promised faithful and I made up my mind that I would sing fine.

When we come in, Mrs. Porson smiled at me

and said: "How are you, Samuel, my dear boy?" Then she jabbed her elbow into Jack's ribs, and he gasped and got up, and wished that I might be feeling pretty well. I said that I was and shook hands with them both. I thought that was all, when Aunt Claudia stepped on my toes—with her heel. That reminded me to hope that they was both well, which they was, they said, except that Uncle James had been throwed from a horse and broke his hip the week before.

I had never heard about any Uncle James before; neither had Aunt Claudia, but she wouldn't let on. She began to exclaim: "Poor man!" Then she got reminded of one of *her* cousins that had broke both arms and a collar bone, once. It was pretty hard to come over Aunt Claudia in a thing like that; she had so many relations, and she could remember them all most amazing.

After that, they had a real good time for a while. Aunt Claudia told how they took care of the two arms and the busted collar bone of her cousin, and Mrs. Porson told how they fetched Uncle James home, and what a lot he had suffered. This talking give me and Jack Porson a chance to look each other over. It was easy to see that he didn't think much of me. It was because my big white collar always made me look sort of sick and thin. I could see that he was a lot fatter than he had been the year before when I seen him last. And I picked out the exact place where I would hit him hard if the time ever came.

He said to me with his lips, not making any sound: "I can lick you just as easy as ever."

He was referring to the last time he came over when he tripped me up and sat on me before I could get up. I had to tell Aunt Claudia that I had run into a swarm of wasps and that was why my face was swelled up so terrible bad.

I made as good a face at him as I could. It was a real whopper, because he sat up stiff in his chair and give me a pretty evil look, I can tell you. Just then both the ladies had come to splints; there they busted off talking sort of by mutual assent, the way ladies have of doing when they see that they can't talk each other down. They looked over at us boys, sort of smiling and nodding— with tears in their eyes, they had both been having such a good time talking so fast.

"But I must hear your dear little Samuel sing!" says Mrs. Porson. "I have heard such a lot about his thrilling voice."

Aunt Claudia was so pleased that she could hardly speak. But she pulls down her mouth as long as she could and says: "Poor child! He has such a frightful cold, I don't think he could possibly manage to sing a single note. Could you, Sammy dear, to please dear Missus Porson?"

Of course, I didn't have no cold. Aunt Claudia had to run down everything that belonged to her.

If somebody come calling and said how pretty the pattern in her carpet in the front room was, she would say how bad the color was fading and that the dyes was not what they used to be. She never set people down to her table without apologizing for every dish, because the oven wasn't hot enough, or the wretched cake had fell just as it came out of the stove. She would even apologize for her green apple pie.

It was enough to make you ashamed the way that woman carried on about my cold, how my throat was terrible delicate, and how I was a frightful anxiety to her all the time, although she hoped I might one day grow up and retain my art and become a comfort to her old age.

Have you got any aunts? Well, you never could have had an Aunt Claudia. When I stood up to sing that day, I was really feeling sort of sorry for myself and weak. When I hit the first note, my voice wobbled something awful. Aunt Claudia brought me out of that mighty quick with a look out of the corner of her eye. You can bet that I thought about the apple pie and didn't let my voice shake at all.

Well, I sang pretty good that day. Particular because it made Jack Porson feel so mean to have me shining and showing off like this. Every time he caught my eye, I would see his lips say: "Gee, what a guy!" That didn't bother me none; it tickled me, rather. I sang a lot of them classical songs. I suppose you have heard most of them. They're all about islands of dreams where you are going to go to hunt up somebody that you never happened to meet lately. There was a song called "The Curse of the Dreamer" that was so full of language, it used to send a chill right up and down my spine. It was about how a man lost his girl, and how he set in and told her how bad she was for leaving him, and how she would suffer, and how terrible hard fate was going to be on the gentleman friend that had run off with her. Right at the end the music gets mighty sad, and then you find out that the girl hadn't left him at all. It was only a dream—you see? But what he said to that poor girl while the dream lasted was something awful.

Just as he was waking up out of the dream, I heard the fiddle squeaking out in the street. Aunt Claudia give the window a wild look. She could hardly wait to finish the piece and hear Mrs. Porson talk about how I had "interpreted" that song; Aunt Claudia just tore for the door and sailed out to light into that tramp.

Chapter Two
THE TRAMP

Looking out the window, I could see that he was a real tramp, all right. He was dressed up pretty good and neat, but there was a streak of red clay along the inside of the cuff of one of his trousers. I knew that he must have hoofed it all the way from Port Hampton, which was about fifty miles away. There was no red clay like that between our town and Port Hampton.

Aunt Claudia said: "Sir, your music will be more appreciated if you take it to another street in this town."

The white dog sailed over the fence and stood up in front of Aunt Claudia, wagging his tail and laughing at her out of his little, bright black eyes.

"That is a fighting dog!" cried Aunt Claudia. "That is one of those nasty bull terriers! Call it away from me this instant! Heavens, what a person to allow wandering around the streets of our town. I suppose it will be the death of someone before it's done."

"Come back, Smiler," the tramp ordered.

Smiler sails over the fence again.

"The lady doesn't like us, Smiler," said the tramp sadly. "We must go away."

"*Humph!*" exclaimed Aunt Claudia. "I suppose

15

there is a place for every one of God's dumb creatures . . . but not in my front yard."

"Ma'am," said the tramp, with his hat in his hand, "I am going right on. I was misinformed. I was told that the mistress of this house was a great lover of good music."

"And who, pray," asked Aunt Claudia, "might have given me a name like that?"

"A lady on the same street . . ." He waved to one side of him.

"Missus Rice?" asked Aunt Claudia. "Was it a Missus Rice?"

Mrs. Rice was the widow of the baker. She was pretty rich and always gave money to the school and the poor families across the track. She was terrible important in our town. She wore double spectacles and walked with a cane and had a stiff black silk dress.

"Yes, ma'am," said the tramp, "that is exactly who it was. She said that she thought you would appreciate my art. . . ."

"You step around to the kitchen door, will you?" said Aunt Claudia. "I think that I've got a snack of something for you. But mind that dog of yours don't scare my chickens . . . because I won't have it! It spoils their laying for days."

Aunt Claudia come back into the house, walking pretty proud. She got noticed by Mrs. Rice about once a month, and she was set up, I can tell you. She give Mrs. Porson a family

16

picture album to look at, and stopped only to point out the group picture of Cousin Minnie's children before she went on out to the kitchen to feed the tramp. I got caught with a terrible coughing fit right afterward, and went out to listen. I heard the tramp apologizing for interrupting the singing. He said that the wind had been blowing toward the house, and that he hadn't heard. That was a whopper, because, when I open up, they can hear me two blocks away. But when Aunt Claudia wanted to believe anybody, the facts never bothered her none. When she didn't want to believe anybody, all the facts in the world wouldn't have proved anything to her. I come around to the door and looked through. Aunt Claudia was sitting down with her back to me. The tramp was sitting sort of sideways and saw me right away, but didn't let on.

He was telling Aunt Claudia about his life, which had been pretty sad. He had been the son of an opera singer. Nothing had been too good for him until finally his mother died of a fever. He was left in the world with "only a few trifling thousands to complete my musical education." When that was spent, he had to fall back on his fiddle to piece out, which was only natural.

Aunt Claudia pitied him a lot and hoped that he would soon be in better shape. He let on that he was saving enough money to rent a hall, and then he would start in to give concerts. Aunt Claudia said that she didn't mind giving a boost to a good cause and that there was ten cents for him. He thanked her for it, saying that if the world had more people like her in it, life would be like walking in a garden of roses.

Here she busted in: "Young man, did I see you give that piece of ham to the dog?"

It took a fast eye to see that trick, because he was mighty quick with his hands. Smiler had just opened up and swallowed that piece of ham like it was a gulp of air.

"It slipped from my fork," said the tramp, finishing his lunch and standing up.

So I went back to the front room. There was no more singing that day, though. Because when Aunt Claudia sat down to the piano and started to nod to me, Mrs. Porson started talking about it being time for her to start. I knew that she wouldn't be going for a long time, so I winked at Jack, and we went out in the back yard together.

I hoped that the tramp might be around, but he was gone. Jack Porson didn't seem interested at all in what I had heard at the kitchen door. He kept a sort of a fishy eye on me, and in another minute he gave me a shove.

You would think that he would have let things alone as they were, because he had given me such a beating the year before. He was just as sassy as if he had licked me fair and square the last time out. Well, I hit him in the stomach the first pass I

18

made at him, and after that it was easy. He tried to kick me as I was coming in, but I managed to get close, and then I fair ripped into him. Finally he couldn't stand it any longer, and he dropped on his face, holding his head in his arms.

Fat boys are like that. They ain't apt to have any nerve. I asked him if he had enough. He said that he had, but that he would lick me to a pulp the next time he came over, and that he would start in and train for me. When he sat up and I saw his face, I knew that I was headed for plenty of trouble without Jack Porson being mixed in it at all.

His face was so fat and soft that I had cut him up pretty bad. He had two black eyes and his nose was all blood, and there was a tooth missing from in the front of his mouth. He was still dripping, and the blood was running down from another cut in his lip, so that he looked pretty bad.

I wanted to clean him up. But he said that he would take care of himself. He went straight on into the house the way he was. You can see that he wasn't no sort of a man. He was just a mean, low-down welcher that wanted to have me get a licking.

I knew that, after one look at him, Aunt Claudia would be ready to give me one of her best. Well, there are different kinds of lickings. Dad used to lay into me with a lot of muscle, but he was always so mad that he couldn't pick out the places that hurt the most. Aunt Claudia said that she always believed it was a sin to whip a child when anybody was in a temper, so her eyes were wide open all the time. She picked tender spots every lick.

Knowing what was coming, I decided that the whipping wouldn't be any worse if it come a little later. I lit out for the swimming pool as hard as I could split so that I would be out of hearing before she begun hollering for me.

It's a queer thing that when somebody calls you, you sort of got to go home so long as you can hear it. If you can't hear, you feel a lot better, and pretty soon you forget what's going to happen when you do get home. Then you go along and have a mighty good time, mostly. Aunt Claudia had a fetching sort of voice; it ended up with a squeak that traveled like a bullet. She would call—"Sam-meeee!"—starting down low and ending up high. When the wind was with her, I could hear her eight blocks away, and even when it was against her, I could hear her a good three or four blocks.

With one dive I took the fence and cut across the fields. Every minute I thought I heard the beginning of her siren call. I legged it out longer and longer and pretty soon I was taking the big barbed wire fences, sailing.

When I got to the top of Gunther's Hill and I rounded over to the other side of it, I knew I was out of earshot of Aunt Claudia. I sat down and got my wind. Then I peeled and slid in Gunther's Pool.

I just lay there on the flat of my back with my head in the shadow of the willow tree and my toes wriggling out where the sun was the hottest. I just had to keep my hands flapping a little to keep the current from floating me down—which was about all that kept me from falling to sleep. However, sleeping ain't half so much fun; the best part of being asleep you never know anything about.

"How's the water, kid?" sang out a voice on the shore.

You know how sudden a voice comes clapping into your ears when you're lying in the water? I rolled over, and there I seen the red-headed gent that played the violin left-handed. He had his dog with him and everything.

I told him that the water was pretty good.

"I don't think that I'll go in," he said. "I'm worn out with travel. Do you live around here, my young friend?"

I could see that he didn't recognize me. You could hardly blame him, having seen me only once. Besides, being peeled and in clothes is a lot of difference. So I just said that I lived pretty close.

"Ah, well," he remarked, "there are some cold-hearted people in that town."

I allowed that was right and asked him how he had found out. At that, he lifted up his head and stood there sort of sad and noble.

"Why should I tell my troubles to a child?" he queried. "Ah, well!"

"Have you lost your suitcase?" I asked.

"My uncle, the wealthy Sir Oliver Radnor," he replied, "was parted from me in Ashton by mistake. I found myself alone on the train. However, it is impossible to persuade the townsmen. I was about to walk back to Ashton. . . ."

This yarn didn't hitch up with the one that he had told at Aunt Claudia's house about being the son of an opera singer. I could see what he hoped was that I would ask him home to supper, and maybe then he could get something out of my father, if I had one. So I rolled over on my side in the water and winked at him.

He stopped right in the middle of a sentence with a little frown. "Where have I seen you before, youngster?" he asked, a little sharp.

"Back in the last house," I answered, "where you was the son of an opera singer."

You would think that he might get a little red or something like that, but he didn't. He just grinned at me as much as to say: "How do you do?" Then he peeled down to his undershirt and took the air in the shadow of the tree.

Looking at him then, you could tell that he was pretty strong by the way his chest stuck out and

22

his stomach stuck in. He had a thick neck, a pretty deep chest. His arms were big, but over the muscles there was a little soft layer of fat, like there is on the arms of women that don't do much work. He had red speckles over his shoulders and down on his wrists, and there was a big white welt along his left side by the ribs. I would have give fifty cents to know what had made that white place on him. But he wasn't the kind of a fellow you could rush with questions. I saw that I had better take my time a little.

Chapter Three
ROLLING STONES

By that, I don't mean that he was offish, because he looked very pleasant. He had a sort of a way about him that seemed to mean that he expected people to be a little respectful—which was queer in a tramp. He didn't make his own cigarettes, either, but took a smoke out of a silver-looking case. He snapped his match into the water, and, while he was watching it sizzle, he asked: "Do you smoke?"

"Everybody does at the swimming pool," I answered.

"Come ashore and have one, then," he invited. "My name's Lefty."

I swam in and started up toward him, but the

white bull terrier stood in front of me with a growl that meant business. I didn't want to ask no questions; I just dived backward, and, as my toes went up in the air, I could feel how close his teeth snapped at them.

"Your dog doesn't like me," I told him.

"He is only a little nervous about having people come up to me without asking leave," answered Lefty. "Sit down, Smiler."

Smiler sat down and grinned at his boss, but he kept the fishy corner of one eye pegged down on me all the time.

"You can come out now," Lefty said. "He won't bother you. This young fellow is a friend of mine, Smiler," he said to the dog.

Coming ashore beside that dog was a good deal like picking red-hot coals out of the fire. When there is a growed-up man around, you got to act sort of easy and natural, no matter how you might be feeling. My legs felt terrible naked when I stepped past Smiler's nose to get one of Lefty's cigarettes.

I sat down on the edge of the sun and the shadow, so's I could dry off without getting chilly. Lefty said: "You live with the lady that loves music, I guess?"

"I guess I do," I answered.

"Do you like music, too?" he asked.

"Her kind of everything I hate," was my reply.

His eyes slid over toward me gradual, then

flickered up and down me quick and powerful, like the headlights of an automobile.

"She is a hatchet-faced old cow, isn't she," he said.

It is sort of comfortable to be asked opinions by a growed-up man. I told him that what she looked like was nothing compared to what she was inside.

"She is a maiden aunt, I suppose," said Lefty.

"She is all of that, and then something!"

Lefty gave me a grin that froze sort of halfway on his face. He looked all at once as though he seen something my way that scared him. I looked beyond me with a sort of sick feeling that maybe Aunt Claudia might be sneaking up behind. There was nothing in sight. Then he asked: "Were you doing that singing in her house?"

"Me? Oh, yes," I replied.

"Could you," asked Lefty, "sing 'Ben Bolt'?"

When I told him I could, he picked up his violin and played it. I sang it through which is easy because no hard notes was put in it. That was why Aunt Claudia never bothered me none to sing it, because she mostly liked me to try things where I had to squawk for a while up near the top of my throat. And that violin had a way of coming right in on the note with you and boosting you along, or else, where you were sailing along in the nicest, saddest parts, the violin would be saying things quite different, but very harmonious, if you know what I mean. Half the time I was almost forgetting what I was singing, I was listening so hard to the funny tricks that he was doing.

When I got through, he said: "You need a lot of training. Who has been teaching you?"

"The minister," I answered.

"I thought so. The fool has been forcing you on the high notes. Don't force yourself, kid. If I never see you again, just remember that. It doesn't sound well, and it will ruin your voice sooner or later."

He got out a knife, then, and began to whittle a twig. I watched him at first because it was such a fine knife with an ivory handle onto it; in a minute I was watching because of the things that he was doing with the blade. He slit the bark off that twig, and he began to gouge into it as though it was dough or clay. First thing you know he had shaped out the hull of a boat, long and low and racy-looking. He drilled out a couple of holes in the deck, stuck in two twigs for masts, and fetched a big leaf for one of the masts. Then he put it in the water.

It was no bigger than a handful, altogether, but it was mighty graceful on that smooth water. When I blew at it, it slid along with its image beside it very slick, and went clean out into the center of the pool, washing a tiny little ripple on each side of it.

Lefty and I smiled. It was so pretty and so small

that it would have been spoiled if you had laughed out loud. I said that I would go in and fetch it out again, but Lefty said: "Never do any work that a dog can do for you. Go bring it to me, Smiler!"

That white dog got up, walked down to the water, dived in, and took the boat in his mouth.

"Careful!" said Lefty.

It was funny to see that dog wag his tail in the water to show that he understood. He shifted his grip on the boat, took hold of the end of it, and came swimming in with it, wagging his tail as if to call attention to what an extra good dog he was. When he got to the bank, the leaf that was the sail fell out of the boat. I stooped to pick it up, but he stopped me with a terrible growl. I never seen a dog that could say so little and yet mean so much when he twitched back the corners of his lips.

Lefty took the boat from him, and, while Smiler stood by wagging his tail, admiring his boss, and cussing me out of the corner of his eye, Lefty told me to come up.

He took Smiler right by the muzzle and held him so hard it hurt.

"Now sock him good and hard!" said Lefty. "Double up your fist and hit him as hard as you can!"

I doubled up my fist and got ready to hit him. He knew what was coming. And he didn't budge, just looked up to me very quiet. I dropped my fist and told Lefty that I couldn't sock the dog. It was too much like hitting another boy that was being held for you.

"All right," said Lefty. "That was the way I taught him to follow me . . . by licking him. I used to have an old brown dog along with me with just about as many tricks as Smiler, here. One day Smiler came out and gave my brown dog a grab and a shake. That was the end of him. I managed to catch Smiler . . . which wasn't much trouble, because in those days he didn't know how to run away. He made quite a fight of it for a while, and then I beat him to a pulp. I didn't think he could walk. When I got about a mile away from that town, I looked back and there was that white pup trailing along behind me. He's kept on trailing for six whole months and never backed up from anything all that time."

It was interesting to hear about the dog, of course. It was more interesting to see by this that Lefty was a regular tramp. He had had another dog before this one to beg for him, and he was still keeping at it.

Most of the tramps that I had seen were ragged and didn't use a razor more than once a week. Lefty could have stepped right in the way he was behind a counter in a gents' furnishing store, or any place like that where a man has to dress up real fine. Why, I wondered, did he want to be a tramp?

"But," Lefty continued, "if you don't want to be the boss, I'm not going to make you. Only, that Smiler will walk right over you until you show him that you're the master."

I asked what difference that would make, when I would probably never see the dog after today. Lefty looked straight at me for a long time. Before he answered, he blew out a little puff of smoke and punched a hole in it. Then he said: "Because I've taken pity on you, kid. And you're going along with me."

It took the breath out of me. I had heard, now and then, about tramps running away with boys. I edged away from him a little and looked at the top of Gunther's Hill and wondered if I could run to the top of it before Lefty could catch me.

He didn't seem to notice. He had half closed his eyes, the way that a man does when he is seeing something almost too good to be true.

"When I was about your age," said Lefty, "*I* had a voice, though it wasn't a patch on yours. It was good enough to cart me all over the world. I've gone where I liked, and, when I ran out of money, I used to just take off my hat in the street and sing. Well, the windows would fly open, and the money drop like rain. It didn't matter where. Marks, francs, Mexican dollars . . . music is a language that the whole world understands, and I've had my share of the fun. Same as I'm going to show you how to have your share of it! Yes,

I've made up my mind. You're a pretty good kid. There's no reason in the world why that old goat of a minister should make capital out of you, or the hatchet-faced dame give you a whacking when you get home."

When I saw that he didn't mean to take me by force, it made me look at the idea again. Of course, you can see for yourself that I wasn't having such a lot of fun at home there with Aunt Claudia.

"But I would have to go back and get clothes," I said.

"No, you're fixed the way you are . . . if you want to come. Of course, it would be a lot of trouble sneaking you out of the county and a lot of danger to me. But I've taken a liking to you. I don't know why. If you say the word, I'll take you along with me."

Chapter Four

THE JOURNEY STARTS

You never can tell what you'll think of in a pinch. I saw my spot in the Sunday choir all vacant and the lead soprano in the singing gone, too. They would have to let Jimmy Roscoe take my part, and his voice squawked terrible whenever he got out of the high register. It made me laugh out loud to think of it. Also, I wondered if Aunt Claudia would miss me or just be glad.

I said: "I'll go along! Let's start now, if you want."

He rolled his eyes up at the top of that hill and said that it wasn't a bad idea, because Aunt Claudia impressed him as the sort of a woman who spent less time wondering, than going to see what was wrong. He dressed up again, tucked his violin into its case, and off we started.

We tramped along for about two hours, cutting through the fields until we got to a lane that we followed until the sun was down. We finally camped in an old barn with some hay of about ten seasons back stacked on the floor.

Lefty started a little fire in the woods near the barn, and told me to keep it up while he went off to the next village to buy some chuck. I couldn't go with him, because by this time Aunt Claudia had probably sent in an alarm call for the police.

It was dark when Lefty went away, but, before he started, he said: "Smiler, watch the boy. Take care of the boy, Smiler."

Smiler came over and lay down where he could keep part of an eye on the fire and the rest of his attention on me. You never saw such a dog! When I started to get up to look around to get some more wood for the fire, Smiler stood up, too; his growl said just as plain as words: "You stay put, kid! You stay right there where you were left. You belong to the boss. I don't know why he wants you along, because I'm sure that I don't like you

31

a bit, but, if you think that you can walk away from me, you're mistaken!"

Anyway, I didn't try. I just sat down again and reached out my hand over his head, slow, so that he could see that I wasn't going to hurt him. Then I petted the back of his neck, but he didn't like it a bit. He just sat there with a growl humming in the back of his throat. His neck was arched up, as hard as iron.

It was like being left in the woods with a wolf. I wouldn't have been surprised if the dog had taken a flyer at my throat any minute. And the woods got blacker and blacker all the time. Only off to the west, through the trees, I could just see a smudge of red made by the day dying very gradual. The birds were done talking for the day and only let out a few squeaks when the wind came walking among the trees. The trees seemed to get bigger and bigger and taller and taller until they were reaching right up into the sky. Then the stars came out—just over the tip-top branches that kept brushing back and forth across their faces.

After a while, I began to feel eyes behind me. You know, you read in books that eyes can be felt. That night they were drilling into the small of my back. Sometimes I could almost see a pair of big yellow ones, like a panther's, in the shadow across the clearing. I tried to tell myself that the dog would know if anything like that came around, but that dog didn't seem to have eyes or ears for anything or anybody except just me.

The fire had burned up all the twigs and grass that I could reach and was burning pretty small. Now and then a bit of flame would get a new start and jump up to show me all the trees standing around, wagging their heads in the wind.

Lefty was away only about an hour, but it seemed a lot longer time before I heard a *crack!* The dog sneaked a bit back from me and pricked up his ears. I got ready for almost anything to jump out from among the trees at me. Then I heard the step of a man walking along, whistling the first bars of "Ben Bolt" to let me know it was Lefty. He was thoughtful, that way. It didn't cost him much, and it eased me a lot. Mostly nobody but the women ever think to put the frills on things that way.

He came in so cheerful and full of news that I forgot about how still and ghostly it had been alone in the forest. He raked the fire together in two jiffies and got it blazing. After that, he gave me some nice sausages and showed me how to roast them by spitting them on little sticks, then holding and turning them near the fire. He had brought a pot along that he made coffee in. Nobody would believe how terrible good those sausages could smell when the grease began to run out of them, and they began to turn brown and pop open, or how fine that coffee smelled when it began to simmer.

While we were eating, he told me how he had gone into the village telling people that he and his wife were making a tour in an automobile that had broken down back in the forest and that they intended to camp out that night. Somebody wanted him to take back a mechanic from the garage, but he said that he was a pretty good mechanic himself.

After that he got some of the news—how Sammy Moore had been missing from the town of Gunther that evening, and now there were parties out hunting all over the country for him. They had sent down a lot of men with lanterns and nets to drag Gunther's Pond for him, because it was thought that maybe he had got stunned diving into the water and hitting his head on a stone. The last reports were that nothing had been found of him, and Aunt Claudia was disturbed enough to offer a reward of fifty dollars for information.

It set me up a lot to know that people were fussing around and hunting for me. I was most surprised to learn about Aunt Claudia's fifty dollars because she was that way that she couldn't speak of ten dollars, even, without catching her breath before and after. She paid all her bills by the week, instead of by the month, because it used to scare her to see such terrible big sums stacking up against her.

It scared me, too, because I knew that, if she

was offering fifty dollars for me, she would give me a whacking that would be worth remembering for years and years. She would start in to get the whole fifty dollars' worth out of me, and she knew exactly how to do it. It made me ache just to think about being caught and handed back to her. I suggested to Lefty that we put out the fire and start on the march again.

He only laughed at me. When I said that a hunting party might stumble onto us at any time, he agreed. He said they might if we were moving about, too. If luck was against us, I would be found. If the luck was not against us, I would not. There was nothing we could do to help one way or the other. He said that a lot of worrying was saved by leaving things to fate.

Lefty talked, very grave; it made me feel pretty grown up to have a man like that talk so seriously to me. He was always very thoughtful of me, just like I was his own age.

When we had got through with our supper, he hauled out about a pound and a half of mighty good hamburger steak, giving a little handful of it at a time to the dog. His tail nearly wagged off; between bites he would look up into Lefty's face as much as to say: "How come that any man as wonderful and as good and as great as you could ever be made? And how could you ever take any notice of a poor dog like me?"

I said I would like to feed him a little of that

meat to make him more friendly, you know, and Lefty said: "Sure, here you are! You feed him the rest of it, if you want."

It tickled me to do that. I took the paper of meat and made up a ball of some of it and offered it to the Smiler. Well, sir, that dog just turned up his nose and wouldn't look at it. He stayed there watching the meat very mournful. Now and then he would look at his boss as much as to say that he didn't see how Lefty could do such a thing as to let all that good meat be poisoned by a snake like me.

I can't tell you how small and mean I felt. Then Lefty took the meat and started feeding again, and Smiler went on wagging his tail and eating. Mind you, that for all the things that dog had done all day, he never got a word of thanks, or hardly so much as a pat. But while Lefty was giving him that meat, he would say now and then: "You are a pretty good dog, Smiler. Yes, sir, a pretty good dog, I have to admit."

Well, sir, it tickled that dog so much to be spoke to kind, that he would leave off eating to listen. Before he would taste another bit of that meat, he would lick Lefty's hand. It put the tears in my eyes. I said to myself that, if a dog could love a man as much as that, there must be a good deal in the man. Anybody would have felt the same way about it.

We slept in a heap of the hay that we carried

outdoors because Lefty said that you could always sleep just twice as good under the stars as you could under a roof. Maybe you could, after you got used to it. All that night, I would sleep five winks at a time and then stay awake forty, shivering, and watching the cold faces of the stars—but mighty glad to be there instead of in Aunt Claudia's house.

We got up before the sun and went down to the creek. We chased each other around until we were hot, then we peeled off our clothes, dived in, and swam around. It was cold, but it was licking good sport. Lefty could swim like a fish.

After that, he cooked our breakfast, which was eggs roasted in the hot ashes and coals of the fire. There was never anything so good! Just with coffee and salt and eggs—that was our breakfast, but it beat almost anything that you could imagine. Then we hit away on our day's tramp.

Chapter Five
CAUGHT

That early in the morning, even people in the country were not up at work, so, for a time, we used the lanes. We even went out on the main road, keeping to it until an automobile, honking for a corner, made us dive for the bushes. We watched it go by, and then headed across fields again. Lefty didn't like the rough going, so, when we came to the next lane, he said that we would risk it again. Risk it we did, though I felt pretty scary, you can bet. No matter what Lefty said about fate and luck, there was no sense running our heads right into such a lot of trouble.

On some of those lanes the dust was so thick that a horse hardly made any noise. We hadn't been half a mile down that road before we turned a sharp corner—and there was a farmer driving his horse right at us. He hadn't made any more noise than a ghost, and the bushes had shut him out of our sight. Matter of fact, he might have run right onto one of us if he hadn't pulled up very sharp.

He gave me a look that sank right through to the bone.

"Well, Master Moore," he said, "I see that you're coming out in my direction. Maybe you're looking for work?"

I couldn't have answered him in a hundred years. And I couldn't help noticing that, while he had a lot of sacks in the back of his buckboard, he had a fine new shotgun lying in the seat beside him. There was no doubt about who would have the upper hand if it came to an argument between him and us, unless Lefty carried a revolver, which I hadn't seen yet. Besides, those big, bony hands of that farmer looked like they could manage that shotgun pretty easy. They were a sporting lot, the farmers in that section. They liked to take a pop at the birds as they drove in for town.

Take him, all in all, there was too much of that farmer for me. As I said, I could not have answered him a word, but Lefty clipped in as easy as you please.

"Yes, sir," said Lefty. "I've found the young rascal, and I'm tracking him right in to Gunther. I can use that fifty dollars' reward that is offered."

"You are taking him *to* Gunther?" said the farmer.

"Exactly! I only wish you were going that way."

"That is the way that I'm going," said the farmer.

Lefty took off his hat and stared at him. It would have done you good to see how baffled and bewildered he looked.

"Going toward Gunther?" asked Lefty like an echo.

"That's exactly it, young man. Unless the town has moved overnight, I'm going to find it right there." He stuck out his chin and pointed with his whip. He was a man that looked pretty sure of himself.

"Why, sir," said Lefty, "if that's the case, the young devil has let me walk him right away from . . . What do you mean by it, you scamp!" He grabbed me by the nape of the neck so hard that it didn't take much acting for me to double up and let out a yelp that you could have heard a mile away.

"Leave him be," suggested the farmer. "I think that his aunt will give him what's what when she gets him back home. You can have a lift, right into town, if you want . . . look out for that dog of mine, or he'll eat your pup!"

A big mongrel that looked half wolf and half mastiff came zooming down the road. When he saw Smiler, he made a beeline for him. The white dog gave his master a look, and Lefty said: "Heel, boy!"

Smiler trotted back behind Lefty and sat down as quiet as you please.

"Take him into the rig with you," said the farmer. "That'll get him out of the way of my dog. Get back, Tiger, you old fool. I never saw such a dog."

But just the same, you could tell that he was mighty pleased. Who doesn't like to have a dog that can lick almost anything in sight?

There was hardly anything for us, except to climb into the buckboard. Lefty got into the seat with the farmer and me. Smiler got into the tail of the wagon, and the big dog followed along behind, slavering at the mouth, he wanted to sink his teeth in the Smiler so bad. We started off at a good trot. My heart went down in my boots when we turned out sharp onto the big main road.

Lefty had enough nerve for a whole army. He kept right on talking along, smooth and easy. He was a musical student, said Lefty, walking across this beautiful country as a sort of vacation to build up his strength—he had been broke down so terrible.

"You don't look it," the farmer said, very flat.

"Overwork," said Lefty. "The nerve strain of violin practice is very great."

That seemed to hit the farmer in the right spot. He warmed up.

"Ain't that a fact!" he exclaimed. "My house is right close to another house, and my neighbor's daughter is took bad with wanting to learn how to play the violin. There is a forty-acre field in betwixt us, but with the wind favoring her a little, I can tell you what, she makes life mighty miserable over at our place, that girl does. She's got a violin that she can make squawk just like a sick duck. Most amazing part is that her ma and pa likes it and always trots her out to play for folks that come to the house. And yet they ain't people that got anything wrong with their ears! But most parents is that way. Peculiar about their kids. Personally I never had no kids, and I ain't never hankered for them any."

My, he was a mean man. You could tell it by the set of the big cords of the back of his neck. I was glad that I didn't work for him.

Then he turned around and popped out at me.

"Look here, youngster, what made you run away?"

It made me mad, it did, to be talked to like that, and I barked right back at him without thinking: "Because I was tired of the house where I was living!"

He give me a look that was like a swat with a stick. Then he turned back to Lefty.

"There you are!" he said. "There's the gratitude that kids have for them that raise them and slave for them. No, sir, give me a dog, first. That's the breed that I raise."

He whistled, and Tiger ran up alongside the wagon, jumping up in the air so's he could see farther across the fields. You could see that when his boss called Tiger, it was usually to send him after something.

"There's a dog," said the farmer, "that can run like a hound and fight like a lion. He hunts his own feed. When one of my dogs gets too old to hunt his own feed, I finish them off and use their hide for leather. A dog that ain't wise enough and able enough to fend for himself, in my eye, ain't any dog at all! Now that white pup that you got . . . I suppose that you got to buy food for that?"

Lefty was mad. I could see that even from behind. The big muscle at the base of his jaw kept working in and out as he set his teeth to keep his temper back.

But he said, very soft: "Oh, yes, I feed that dog. I buy raw meat for him."

"Do you now? Good enough for a man to eat, I suppose?"

Just then an automobile came scooting by. The farmer jerked up in his seat and pointed his whip over his shoulder at me. All the people in the automobile turned around to see me and popped out their eyes and made Os with their mouths, as much as to say: "Oh, he's going to catch it fine!" I never seen such a crowd of people. They made me sick.

The farmer had got onto a thing that he liked to talk about, now, and he went right on with it. He said: "Good enough for a man to eat, that meat you buy for your dog, I suppose?"

"I suppose it is," said Lefty, very patient.

"Blast me!" exclaimed the farmer.

It busted right out from him. He was so mad that he couldn't stand himself.

I wish that he *had* been blasted. I never seen a man that I hated so quick and easy and complete as I hated him.

He went on: "And will you tell me what good that dog is?"

"I'll tell you," said Lefty. "That dog does what I tell him to do. And, also, he will lay down his life for me and ask no questions."

"He will lay down his life," retorted the farmer with a sneer. "And what in hell difference does it make if he will lay down his life for you? What good will it do? What could he save you from except a house cat, maybe?"

"Sir," said Lefty, with a sort of bur-r-r in his voice that I had never heard there before, "I suppose you are not familiar with the breed. They are fighting dogs, sir."

"Fighting fish!" exclaimed the farmer. "Didn't I see him sneak out of the way behind your heels?"

"I ordered him to do that," replied Lefty.

"What chance do you think that he would have ag'in' my Tiger, yonder?"

"My dog is big for his kind," said Lefty. "Yours, yonder, is in good, hard condition and yet weighs all of a hundred pounds. He has size in his favor, you must admit."

"He has," said the farmer, grinning, "and that ain't all that he has in his favor. He has grit in his favor, and a fighting head on his shoulders."

"If he has all of that," said Lefty, "I wouldn't mind pitching in Smiler against him. Though I don't let him fight with ordinary dogs." The farmer was staggered, but Lefty went right on. "I'll bet you ten dollars, though, that he chokes your Tiger down."

I thought that he was trying to bluff the farmer out. It made me pretty scared for poor Smiler—against a brute like that Tiger. The farmer had the same idea. He popped out ten dollars, quick.

"Cover that!" he said.

Lefty covered it quicker than you could wink. "Is your dog ready?" he asked.

"My dog is ready!"

"Smiler," said Lefty, "go take that big, clumsy fool, will you?"

Smiler whined and dived over the tailboard. Tiger opened a yard of mouth to swallow him alive, but Smiler did a flip while he was sailing through the air and grabbed that big dog right across the nose—and glued onto him. There was nothing for Tiger to do. He growled and thrashed around and turned himself over on the ground to shake off Smiler. While he was doing that last trick, Smiler shifted his grip quicker than you could wink and sank that long fighting jaw of his right in Tiger's woolly throat. After that, Smiler just closed his eyes, contented, and worked his grip deeper and deeper.

The farmer reached for his gun. "My heavens," he cried, "he's killing my dog!"

But Lefty grabbed the gun first. He said: "If you try to kill the terrier, I'll break you in two."

It sent a wriggle through me. I was so proud of Lefty; I could see that he meant it, and that he could do what he promised. The farmer didn't let out a peep.

There was Tiger lying on his back in the road, just giving a little wiggle.

"I'll take the ten dollars," said Lefty, and he did what he said. Then he jumped down off the wagon, took Smiler by the neck, and hit him in the ribs. When Smiler opened his mouth as much as to ask—"What's the matter with you?"—he was dragged off the other dog.

Chapter Six

THE MANHUNT

Smiler hated to be pulled off like that. When Lefty spoke, though, Smiler stood back and didn't say a word to anybody, just licked his lips, very regretful. Lefty went on working over Tiger, squeezing his ribs and working his big hind legs back and forth until the poor dog was breathing once more.

Suddenly the farmer snapped out: "Leave that dog be!" There he stood in the wagon, his face drawed a mile long with meanness, the shotgun over the hollow of his arm.

Lefty got up and dusted his hands clean. "Very well," he said, "let your dog die, if you want."

The farmer said something about not caring whether he lived or not if it couldn't take care of itself. Then he sat down in his seat and drove off, without saying any more to us about giving us a ride on to town.

We watched him around the next corner of the road, and then we started running. We kept at it until I was nearly black in the face.

Lefty pointed out that we would have to hoof it right along, because, as soon as that farmer came to town, he would spread the news, and they would probably send out searchers to look for me. I suggested hitting out in a different direction from the one in which the farmer had seen us traveling when he first came along. Lefty said we couldn't do that because our one hope was to get me down to the nearest railroad. So we *had* to keep along in that direction, and he only hoped that we might win through.

You can see how exciting it was. If they caught us, I would get the worst licking you ever heard of from Aunt Claudia, and Lefty would go to prison. He said that the law was terribly strict about kidnapping, which was what he would be charged with. I said then he shouldn't go on with me.

"What difference does it make?" asked Lefty. "Either we get through or we don't. Luck is with us, or against us. All we can do is to try. If they are going to get me, they'll get me with you or without you. And there you are!"

You couldn't argue with him when he began to talk like that. He had that superstition, and he stuck to it.

We worked along until noon, then we laid up in the woods. Lefty said that he reckoned we were about four miles from the railroad. After dark we could make a dive for it.

I was glad to stop there in the shade. Partly because of the heat of the sun, and partly because I was fagged out. Then we got to the edge of a creek, and I took off my shoes. My feet were a sight. Lefty got out a little paper with some powder in it and fixed me up fine. He brought some soft white cloth out of his pocket and bandaged both feet. I can tell you that I felt like a different boy.

I asked Lefty how could he manage to carry so much around with him. He said it was all in knowing how to fold things. Most people crumple a handkerchief up so that it looks as big as an apple in a pocket. If you fold it down neat and flat, nobody could tell that there was anything there. That was the way Lefty managed. He had a little bit of nearly everything about him—just in papers, envelopes, or folded things. To look at him, you'd never know that he had anything at all in his pockets. He said that if he was to lose everything he had in his pockets, it would cost him a month of work to get another collection together. I believed him.

We laid up there in the woods all through the afternoon, but it wasn't a dull time. Lefty could have made things hum even on a desert island. He said that we had to eat. When I asked him what he had in his pockets to eat, he answered: "The best half of any meal . . . salt!"

It made me smile, to think of eating salt, but

afterward I saw what he meant. He made some little snares for birds out of notched pieces of wood that he whittled out of twigs faster than you could think. Then he looked around to find little runs in the grass. He put some of the traps there and picked out places in the trees for others. It was slick to see the way that he worked it. You would have said that he knew just where the birds were likely to be.

I knew there was no use suggesting there was danger of us being seen, if we moved around among the trees so often. He would only have said that we had to trust something to luck. That was his way. It was an exciting way of looking at things; you just gambled on chance all the time.

After he had set those little snares of his and baited them with bread crumbs, we sat about. He wouldn't let me go near any of the traps for a long time. He told me even to stop *thinking*.

"What in the world good will that do?" I asked him.

He frowned and told me not to bother him with so many questions. I could see that what I had asked was working on him.

"I'll tell you why," he said at last. "It's because the birds might be able to *feel* your mind working!"

He went on to tell me how he had been lying in a room, once, sound asleep, and all of a sudden he woke up with his heart beating fast. He sat up and looked around him, but there was nothing stirring and nothing to be seen. He lay back and tried to sleep again, but pretty soon he could feel danger sneaking in on him. He got up and sneaked around that dark room on his hands and knees, with a gun in his hand. There was nothing to be found. Then he decided to take a look in the next room. He threw open the door quick and shoved his gun in ahead of him. Just as he did that a revolver exploded in the room. By the flash he saw the face of his worst enemy. All that saved Lefty's life was the man's aiming breast-high instead of knee-high.

Lefty said that was a good example of what he meant—that if we knew more about our minds, they could tell us lots of things. All that most of us could understand was when our minds was telling us things in words, that was only the beginning of what our minds could talk about. He said that a man's mind was not only with him, but it was in every place that he had ever been, and in a lot of places where he never *had* been but would go before he died, and that mind was collecting information all the time and wire-lessing the news back to the central mind that always stayed with you.

This was pretty hard for me to understand.

"Some people are sensitive to these things, and some aren't," said Lefty. "I'm pretty sensitive. I get lots of messages, like that one that I was telling you about. It saved my life that night, and it's not the only time that it has saved my life. Everyone gets them, more or less. Why, you've been blue lots of times without knowing why you were really sad?"

I admitted that was right.

"It's because you are getting messages that trouble is ahead for you and your mind is trying to tell you about it, but the words of that language can't come home to you. You feel things in a general way."

It was a ghostly way of thinking about things. I couldn't agree with Lefty about it. I could see that he felt about it the same way that Aunt Claudia did about religion. There was no one talking to him any more on that line. I asked him, instead, what happened when he saw the face of his enemy.

He gave me a long look as though he wondered whether or not it was worthwhile to tell me. Then he said: "This is what happened. I tried a snap shot at him as I was jumping back through the door. I missed.

"I slammed the door and made a pass for the violin. That was all that I was interested in. I didn't use the other door because it led out on the stairs and I thought that that was where he might try for me next. Instead, I dived out the window, landed on the roof of the porch, and jumped down into the garden. I got away into the town, where I was pinched for going around half dressed. But it was worthwhile getting pinched . . . I was never so glad to see the inside of that jail."

You can imagine how I stared, because I thought of him as just the opposite of a man who would run away from anything except work.

"Would you mean," I asked, to make sure, "that you were afraid of this man?"

He nodded. "I mean just that," answered Lefty. "I'd rather meet a dose of poison than that man!"

I kept my mouth shut and digested that for a while. I was beginning to get a sort of scent of trouble that was lying ahead of us if I kept on with Lefty. I saw shadows of guns and men bad enough to make even Lefty run. However, it was fun, too, to look ahead to chances that you couldn't figure up. I decided right there that I wouldn't change places with anybody. I was scared, too, on general principles. I asked Lefty if he would tell me the name of this enemy of his. But he only answered: "You ask more questions than you're worth."

After that, it was time to look to see what the traps might have caught.

We let one little brown bird go free. Lefty watched it fly away and said: "That bird will bring us luck. I've got a feeling in my bones that it will."

When he had gathered the other birds that had been caught, he said: "An army is a walking stomach, and so is a tramp. We've got to have food."

We got the fire going and began to roast the birds, turning them on spits. With the salt and the water from the brook, they were prime. Just as we finished, Smiler jumped up and made a point, his head and tail stuck out in a line.

"Somebody's coming," said Lefty. He scattered that fire to pieces in one swoop. We stamped out the sparks, and the wind tossed the last of the smoke away off among the trees. All that happened before we heard voices. I wanted to run for it, but Lefty wouldn't let me. We just crouched in the brush with the dog sitting between us, wrinkling his nose and jerking his ears.

"He smells some kind of news that he likes," Lefty said in a whisper. "I wonder what it could be?"

Well, in another minute we saw them. There were five men scattering through the woods and coming straight at us. Three of them had rifles or shotguns. When we saw the big farmer in the lot, we didn't have to be told that they were after us.

I heard one of them say that he had seen smoke over this way. That made me look up reproachfully at Lefty, but he didn't change color a bit. He just said: "That's the first trick for them, but the game isn't over yet." Then he said: "The devil, we're going to lose. There's that dog."

It was Tiger! His throat was all black, where

the dust had caked over his wound. He looked almost as frisky as ever, and he was scenting along the grass like a bloodhound. I never saw a dog that looked so big and so mean.

The five of them found the fire and talked about it for a while. Our farmer said that the fire had just been put out and he pointed to the way that the grass had been burned off. Two of the others said that the way the wind had scattered the ashes made them think that it must be several days old. There hadn't been any strong wind since yesterday, at the latest.

We breathed a little easier, but the farmer said: "We'll beat up those bushes, before we go on."

"There goes Tiger," said one of the others. "He'll tell us what's there."

Yes, sir, that big brute of a dog came crashing right into the thicket where we were. When he saw us, his eyes flared like red fire. Then he got a whiff of Smiler that Lefty was holding by the neck. When he seen the white dog, Tiger turned around and jumped out of that thicket as if he had been kicked.

"There you are!" someone sang out. "Tiger says that there is nothing in there. Let's go on, or we'll never catch them."

Tiger wasn't interested in that bunch of bushes any more. He began to pretend to be busy among the trees right on ahead, but he and Smiler both knew why it was, I suppose. We were glad to see the five of them go on. Our farmer was mighty mad, saying that sort of searching would never find anything.

When we couldn't hear their footsteps or voices any more, Lefty said: "That goes to show you. A mean man can't persuade people, even when he's right."

You can see how steady and brave Lefty was. That was all he had to say about our being in such a tight squeeze. A lot worse for him than it was for me, too, because all I would get was a hiding, while it meant prison for him.

We kept on there in the thicket until the dusk of the day. It was full dark before we got to the town. We skirted around and came down the track to a siding where a freight train was being made up. Lefty sneaked me under a car, showed me where to get on the rods and how to stretch out and be pretty comfortable on them. When I was fixed, he gave a little whistle. Smiler slid in and jumped up beside his boss without being told.

Chapter Seven
A NEW RÔLE

You could hardly have picked out a worse trip for a first ride on the rods. I've learned, since, how to jump the iron ladder of a freight car while it's on the run, but in those days I hardly knew what a freight car was like. Well, I learned that night while I lay stretched out on the rods.

That was a train of empties. It made a noise like all the tin cans in the world doing a jig, and it went smashing along faster than a passenger express bound overland with time to make up. It was on a rough road, too. There were bumps and jumps in that track that jogged the wits out of me. Up from the roadbed, there was a steady, flying cloud of cinders and grit and dust. There was a head wind doing about thirty miles an hour, and there was the train doing about fifty, which made an eighty mile wind driving that stuff in your face. If you opened an eye even so much as a wink, you could be sure that you would be about blinded.

After I had lain on those rods for ten minutes, I knew that I had enough. I hollered out and told Lefty that.

He sang back at the top of his lungs so that I could hear: "This trip is just starting, kid, and, if you don't hold yourself on, it'll be the finish of you. You've got to depend on yourself!"

That voice ripped into my mind, and I forgot all about my little aches for an hour or more. When the troubles came back again, they kept on getting worse every minute. I could feel my face getting almost raw. There were bruises all over my body where I had twisted around on the rods finding new places to lie and always getting sore again, surprising quick.

After that, there came a time when I knew that I couldn't hold on much longer, when I decided that to hold on for even another minute was a lot worse than simply to die. If I dropped off the rods, the wheels would take me in half a second. Then I would be ended, and my troubles, too. So I would see myself letting go and flopping off— and then I would see myself lying on the track and the big wheels coming. . . .

I turned my head around and looked back. I could see the wheel that would get me and clip me in two. It looked terrible big and bright, it was wobbling a little as it came along, as though it staggered with its speed. It looked anxious to get somewhere—and that somewhere might be me!

It was the idea of having to lie there and wait for that wheel that kept me on the rods. A good many more suicides would come if it weren't that you had to pull the trigger of the gun with your own finger. Once I let myself go a little, when I was sure that I was all tired of life, but the minute one leg dangled down, I began to fight and scramble to get back again, with my heart racking and rushing. I was scared to death and kept on shaking for a long time after I was stretched out in place again. That showed me how much I loved living. It's always surprising to see how much a man loves life—and a boy just ten times more.

The noise began to bother me more than

anything else. It began in waves; it would start at the engine and you would hear it reaching back, crashing along. Right over your head it gave an extra bump and an extra roar, as though all the tin cans in the world were dropping over Niagara Falls. Then it galloped on past you, that wave of sound, and jumped out of the end of the train. Maybe for a split part of a second there would be something almost like silence and you would hear the *whish* of the wind and the groaning of a wheel, somewhere, that was tired of going on with the night's work.

I got so tired that I was sick, and just then all the noise stopped except a terrible big humming, like ten billion bees roaring and buzzing along.

I looked down. Bars of darkness were flicking past my eyes, uncommon fast, but beyond the bars there was silver water. The train had slowed down for crossing a big iron bridge. I was so light in the head that I pulled myself together and got all ready for dropping off, because I thought that I would have one chance in two of dropping through to the water below—that looked so peaceful down there.

"Steady, kid!" said Lefty.

That brought me to.

After we got over that river, there was a shaking and thundering of brakes. We eased down to a stop, gave a shudder and shriek, and stood still with nothing except the engine wheezing and blowing up ahead of us. What do you think Lefty said?

"A nice, fast trip, Sammy, what? You ought to go over this section of the road in winter."

Trying to think of something that was really any worse than that ride made me laugh, although it wouldn't have taken much to make me cry, either. The minute I started laughing, I rolled off the rods and just lay on the ground, shaking.

Lefty picked me up by the nape of the neck and gave me a shake. I reached out and touched the back of Smiler, and he gave me an unfriendly growl. Then I heard Lefty say: "A good, clear night and a good, flying start. They'll never nab you now, son, if we have any luck at all. Take a breath of that air. Like wine, I say!"

Not a word of sympathy to me, not a look at me, when I was so groggy that I could barely stagger along. That was Lefty's way.

A lantern came swinging along beside the train.

"Here comes a shack, kid," said Lefty. "Can you run?"

I told him that I could barely walk.

"All right," said Lefty. "You start for the woods, there, and I'll tend to the brakie."

I could only hobble along at about half walking speed. From the edge of the trees I looked back and saw Lefty saunter up to the brakeman as cool as you please.

They say that a brakeman can smell a tramp a mile off. I heard the shack swear, and saw him swing his lantern to brain the hobo. It was just holding a light to get himself knocked down, for I saw that long left reach out, and then I heard the *whack* of that brakie's shoulders as he hit the ground.

He didn't get up quick, either. He must have wanted to have a good look at the stars while he was in that position. Lefty came back to me, and I said: "Jiminy, Lefty, but you're a great fighter."

"Rot!" said Lefty. "Forget that chatter."

He went along whistling to himself, and anybody could see that he was pretty pleased with himself. We held around through the trees, me hobbling pretty bad on my sore feet. Every now and then I stumbled and fell flat. Lefty would yank me up without a word. Finally he kept his strong hand right under the hollow of my arm. So we went along.

"We're going to hit the hay in a real town tonight, son," said Lefty. "I've had enough of this rough life to last me for a while, and so have you."

We got to a town. It was a fine, brand-new, shined-up sort of a town with the pavement all macadam and very bright under the street lamps. Every block there was the skeleton of a new house standing, or scaffoldings up around new walls. Or else you would smell where the ground had been dug up just lately. Anybody could see with half an eye how that little town was booming. Lefty was very pleased with it. He said that it all smelled to him like money in our pockets.

All at once he stood still and gave a quick look around him. And then he stepped into the shadow of a front yard. Behind a big lilac tree he took a goggle-shaped pair of dark glasses out of his pocket and put them on.

"I forgot," said Lefty, "that I was born blind. Being born blind a man can get along amazingly well when he's moving around a room, or along a crossing. Now take my arm and lead me along. Remember that I am your Uncle Will. We're going down the street to that sign that says . . . hotel. When we get inside, you walk up to the clerk and tell him that we want a room. Here's fifteen dollars. You can let him see that when you pay for the room, because we have no luggage, and we'll have to pay on the spot beforehand. Now, remember, look as sad as you can. Every time you look at me, think of sad music."

We went down to the hotel like that. I was scared, you can't guess how much, at the idea of waltzing into a big hotel with a faker like that along with me. I knew that they pinched you for doing such things. But Aunt Claudia would be worse than prison.

Well, it was easy. We walked into that hotel and

there was everything clean and sassy as you please. A man that looked like a bank president or something was behind the desk, and a couple of old goats were sitting over in great big armchairs upholstered in haircloth. They looked over their papers at Lefty, who was fumbling along, and they said—"Well, well. Poor fellow."—and such things under their breath.

Lefty seemed to get another idea when he was inside. He stopped me, and he said: "Is this the lobby, Samuel?"

I said that it was.

"Find the clerk and tell him that we require a decent room for the night. Tell him that we are without luggage and that you will pay beforehand."

The clerk came right out toward us. He was sort of middle-aged and he looked mighty kind. He asked what could he do for us, and I repeated the spiel. He said to Lefty: "My dear sir, I am quite content to let the matter stand over until your departure."

At that I could see the old goats in the corner wag their heads, agreeing that this was the way to treat a poor blind man. The clerk went on to say that guests often had their luggage delayed. Lefty gave a sad smile and shook his head, and said in a quiet, weary voice—pitched just loud enough to reach to the two other men in the corner—"No, my friend, our luggage is not delayed . . . it is destroyed. Pay the clerk, Samuel. I must go upstairs right away and lie down."

You could see the clerk just busting with curiosity and sympathy. He took my money, but he seemed to hate to touch it. Then he showed us up to the room. It was a great sight to see "Uncle Will" fumbling for the steps a little with his foot. When he got into the room upstairs, he looked around and said: "I trust that dogs are permitted in the rooms?"

Smiler was sneaking along behind Lefty, with his nose stopping just half an inch from Lefty's leg. The clerk said that dogs were allowed. Then Lefty fumbled around with the violin, and finally I took it.

"Gently with it, Samuel," he said. "Gently. It is all our livelihood now. Who knows what would come of you and the dog and me if it were gone?"

The clerk got pale with excitement and pity when he heard that. He tiptoed out of the room as if he were going out from a funeral.

Then Lefty sat down on the bed and shoved the glasses up. He gave me a grin and said: "It looks as though this is a pretty good dodge. I've been blind a lot, but they've always been suspicious before. The blind man and the nephew dependent upon him . . . if I were only a little older or you were a little younger, you could be my son . . . that would fetch us! Kid, why aren't you a little paler? You look about as pathetic as a pumpkin pie."

Chapter Eight
THE GAME

He got up and roamed up and down the room, shaking his head. "If we could work that father and son gag," he kept saying, "we would soon have a bank account."

Then he sat down and wrote out a list of things for me to buy. He had brushed us off pretty good at the edge of the town, but now he put down a big brush on the list and a lot of other things to get at a drugstore.

"Now, son," he said, "when you go down, the clerk will want to collar you and get a lot of information. That poor boob is simply oozing curiosity. He is breaking his heart to be done, but we haven't come down to fish of that size. Not yet. We want the fat boys in the corner . . . the gold-watch-and-chain boys. Those are the ones. If we don't squeeze them, I am a blockhead and a bad prophet. I want you to tell that clerk that you are not allowed to talk. When he asks why, you tell him that we wish to keep our sorrows to ourselves. Understand? Then the two old boys will grab you. They have pumped the clerk by this time, and they know everything that he knows. But they are aching for more. They feel a good deed coming over them. It's making them fairly dizzy, I tell you. Well, let them gradually egg the story out of you. Tell them . . . well, no grown man can lie as well as a boy can lie. Make up your own story and make it good. Lie as you never lied before. Now run along and do yourself proud!"

I went out of the room.

Just as he said, the clerk gave me a fatherly smile and come out from behind the desk. As he walked along with me, he wants to know how my uncle is getting on. I said that Uncle Will was rather poorly.

"Why?" asked the clerk.

"I forgot," I said, "that I'm not to be talking. Uncle Will don't like it, because he says that to tell our troubles is too much like making an appeal to the sympathies of folks. I've got to go along . . . I can't talk."

I got away from him, but I saw him look across at the two old geezers as much as to say: "What did I tell you? This is certainly a worthy case for charity!"

At the druggist's I got a lot of stuff and brought it back, but when I came to the lobby again, there were the two old boys waiting for me. When they saw me, they collared me quick. One of them laid the fat palm of his hand on top of my head and turned up my face a little. I thought of taking a high note and give him the same sort of a sad smile.

He said: "Son, we have seen you and your proud, unfortunate Uncle William. Do you mind telling me his last name?"

I hesitated. "I am not to talk," I said.

"Is there any harm in a name?" he asked. So I pretended to be convinced and I told that the name was William Gobert.

After that he said: "Now, my boy, do not think that any idle curiosity prompts me. But I have a feeling for good men in distress. And I should like to know the story of your uncle's distress."

Here the other fat man broke in. "Young man, this is President Johnson of the Orchard and Alfalfa Bank."

"Tush!" said the bank president, but I could see that he was glad enough to be introduced.

I said: "If I was to talk about what has happened, Uncle Will would never forgive me for going behind his back like this . . . and I'd rather die than hurt his feelings, he's so terrible sensitive and proud."

"Ah!" said President Johnson. "I could see it in his face. Could I not, Harry?"

Harry said that he could.

"But you want to help your uncle, my brave lad," said the president. "And who can tell that I might not be able to assist him?"

I wouldn't be persuaded for a long time, but finally I let it bust out that we had been ruined by fire.

"Fire!" cried the president. "Poor man. Fire." He said this in a whisper to Harry.

Then I let it all bust out in a flood. I told how my mother had died when I was born, and my father had died two years ago. I had gone to live with Uncle Will, who got along pretty well except that he had a bad heart. About two weeks before, Uncle Will's house, where all his money was tied up, was burned down . . . the crops was wiped out in the fields. Everything in general was badly spoiled, so's he couldn't get money—he just owed money everywhere.

"And what did he do then?" asked Mr. Johnson. "Come now, my dear boy, and please do tell us what he did then?"

"He called in all the gents that he owed money to," I said. "He told them that he was a ruined man, as they knew. There didn't nothing remain to him but his land, and he was blind and couldn't handle it. So he was going to sign everything over to them, and they could sell it. After it was sold, if anything was left, they could give it to him. So the creditors got together and sold the land, but they said that there was just enough out of the sale to pay for all of the debts that was owing.

"Uncle Will, he said that though he didn't have much strength, and though his heart was weak and his eyes was blind, he still had an honest heart, a clean hand, and a fiddle. He would go out and make his strength last as far as it could. We started off, and, after we had gone a little ways, the dog, Smiler, comes running after us. Uncle Will says for me to send the dog back, and I pretended to, but I didn't really have the heart to, because I knew that Uncle Will loved the dog better than he did anything else in the world, hardly, besides them creditors had enough when they got hold of all of our land. Don't you think so yourself?"

Mr. Johnson let go of my head and hit his fat hands together so that they popped like a paper bag that is blowed up and then squashed.

"What wolves. What wolves without a heart! His dog, too. Even his dog they would have taken from this . . . heavens, I can't speak of it! Child, from what part of the country . . . ?"

"Right near to . . ." I was about to say Gunther, and then I remembered that I was not to say that, and so I stuck a little. I gaped at them and then I said that I had talked too much . . . that I had told them nearly everything, and, if it came to the ears of Uncle Will, it would break his heart . . . and would they swear never to let him know?

They said that they would swear it, and they pressed their hands on their hearts as they said it. As I went up the stairs, I could hear Mr. Johnson saying: "Harry, I could weep, it broke me up so . . . when I see honest pride . . . and sorrow . . . and courage. . . ."

I could have cried myself, I had got to feeling

so sorry for us. When I got to the room, Lefty wanted to know what had happened. I told him that I had burned a house down and left him broke, and that he had even wanted to give up Smiler to pay the creditors. That tickled Lefty a great deal.

"Son," he said, "you have talent. I can see that. You have talent. When I think of how you might have wasted yourself on the desert air back there at Gunther, I feel like . . . a horticulturalist on stilts. All we have to do now is to be calm and grand and sad. Money is going to rain down in this town, my boy. Money is going to shower all over us. Both my palms are itching."

I told him, then, that he had a bad heart. That tickled him still more. He began to walk up and down the room and exclaim: "Some men would have made out a whole story for you, but not Lefty! I trust a boy's head. All the lies that I could have invented would never have had as much nerve to them. I could never have thought of the stroke of putting the dog in like that. I never could. Nor the heart, neither. Oh, Sammy, you and I are going a long, long ways together! You have talent . . . you have a voice . . . and I'll do the rest."

He was feeling so good that his face shone— almost the way the face of the fat man downstairs had shone. One was with rascality and the other was with goodness, but it would have been pretty hard to tell them apart. Lefty couldn't stay still. He walked over to the window and leaned out, and he said: "Come here. Look at this. Just lean out here and don't speak. Don't say a word."

The minute you stuck your head out of range of the electric lights the night air rose up around you, all cool and sweet, and voices came up off the street, bubbling and soft. Somewhere an automobile started up and went whirring around a corner with two girls in it laughing like bells. It had been a hot day, and now the watering cart had gone around and washed down the streets so that the big lamps would send yellow paths of light a whole solid block long. The town looked like it was standing in water. You almost looked to see the reflections of the buildings.

"Look out there," said Lefty, "and soak that up and just think about it for a while."

It made me feel pretty good to breathe that air. It was so cool because the mountains weren't far away. I could see the frosty heads on a few of them even by the starlight, looking blue and awful cold and calm away off there on the edge of the horizon.

"Look at it," said Lefty, "and just think about it for a minute." There was a hush in his voice like the minister's when he announced a new contribution from somebody to the church. "Look at it," said Lefty, "and remember that this is just one town in ten thousand in this country of ours.

There are ten thousand more just like it, or bigger, better, richer . . . with more spare cash floating around then they know what to do with. Oh, Sammy, when I think of these things, I feel proud to be an American citizen. It does me good just to know that fact. I wouldn't sell that fact for millions. I really wouldn't! A town like this is to me what the oasis of the desert is to the traveler. Believe me, Sammy, this country of ours is full of such towns. We can travel around all our lives and still keep going to places where they never saw our faces before and where we can pull off the same old dodges again and again. It's touching, just to think about it. Confound it, it almost makes you have a tear in the eye, it really and truly does!"

Chapter Nine
LEFTY'S TACTICS

It wasn't all put on with Lefty. He believed a big part of it, I think. When he got heated up with talk like that, he hardly knew what he was doing in a way. The words just floated him away out of himself. He should have been an orator, or something.

After that, he said that it was time for us to go to bed, because tomorrow had the earmarks of a mighty rich day. When Smiler saw me getting into the same bed with his boss, he almost died it worried him so much. No matter what his boss said, the Smiler kept mourning over this situation. He wouldn't be peaceful until Lefty had let him jump up on the bed. There he lay where he could stretch out and watch me so's I didn't wake up in the night and cut Lefty's throat. You would have laughed to see that dog, except that a bull terrier has no sense of humor. He would just as soon have sunk his teeth in me as he would have winked.

In two shakes I was sound asleep; it seemed to me that I was falling deeper and deeper into perfect blackness all night long until something shook me by the hand. I looked up, and there was Smiler, with my hand in his teeth, growling and pulling harder and harder.

"You'd better get up and come to me," said Lefty, grinning, "or he'll tear that hand right off at the wrist."

There was seventy pounds of that dog, or pretty near that much, and he was tough and hard. When he pulled, you knew that something was happening.

I slid out of bed, and he walked me over to the boss, wagging his tail when he dropped my hand, just as if he had brought Lefty a stick, and you can lay to it that Smiler didn't look on me as any more than a stick! It was a nervous job, being led around by Smiler, but it was a good way of waking up in the morning. All the wrinkles were out of my head that quick.

After that, we tumbled through a bath. Then Lefty worked on his face a while. What he had done to himself was a shame. He worked for not more than fifteen minutes with the things that I had brought to him from the druggist's. When he finished, he called me to look at him.

It was a shock, I can tell you. I hardly knew the man! His eyes were all surrounded with deep shadows. His face was mighty pale, and his hair was filled up with gray hairs, with one white patch over the temple. Also, he had brought out all the wrinkles in the center of his forehead. Down beside his mouth there were deep seams that made him look extra sad.

"Do I look like a broken heart, Sammy?" he said.

I admitted that he did. He shook his head and said that for a poor, broken-hearted violinist who had just been burned out of house and home he really should have hair twice as long as what he was wearing.

We went down into the dining room, me holding his hand and him leading along behind me very slow, with his feet fumbling and stumbling just a little—whenever he looked down through the edges of those dark glasses and saw something worth stumbling over.

The clerk and the two fat gentlemen hadn't

wasted any time about starting their talk. Every eye in that dining room swung around and hit us full blast. There were little ohs and ahs from every direction as we went over and took our chairs at a corner table.

I ordered ham and eggs, mush and milk, chocolate, strawberries and cream, toast and marmalade. Then what do you think that grafter that was with me got?

A glass of milk and some crackers! Yes, sir, I give you my word that that was all he took. I could see why he did it, of course. It made a grand contrast—me being the wasteful, idle, pampered nephew and him the sad and self-sacrificing old gent who was refusing me nothing, yet starving his poor old self on my account. You should have seen the black looks that I collected, and you should have seen how they looked at him. Why, there was one woman with a face like an Indian squaw's—or a chief's, maybe. When she saw the picture over at our table, she began to snivel. Finally she had to get up and sneak out of the room with a handkerchief up to her face. That started a lot of the others that had been holding in. I can tell you that the crying there in that dining room was a whole lot more open and wholehearted than any crying at any funeral that ever I seen. It would have done you good to sit in and listen to it.

It was wonderful, most of all, to be on the

inside and hear and see the boss at work. He was a jim-dandy, and don't you make any mistake about it. He pretty soon forgot even to drink his glass of milk and eat those crackers. The darned old faker held out his hand and stuck it in the sun, where everybody could see how bad it was shaking. Then he said in a tragic sort of a deep I-may-be-dying-but-I-won't-let-on sort of voice: "I think that I feel the sun . . . I think that I feel the honest sun, Samuel!"

I said that it was shining right on his hand. Then he stuck out his other hand, too, and turned them over in the light.

"God bless the sun, Samuel," said Lefty. "God bless the sun, dear boy, for you will find that there is more kindness and honesty in it than there is in many human hearts. Ah, yes!"

This voice of his, you understand, was one of them controlled voices that ain't supposed to fetch more than the ear of the person that they're talking to, but you can hear them plain all over a room.

Well, that speech of his sank them in flocks. They couldn't stand it. Every one of the women was finished and had to get up and walk right out of that dining room, which was a shame, because that made them miss the rest of the show. The men didn't miss anything. Lefty had saved up some extra good licks, and he gave them the advantage of them.

All the time he was saying in an aside to me: "Don't eat so fast, kid. We have to lengthen this out. I'll tell you the difference that this show makes to us. It means that most of these boobs are going to go home and write out checks and send them to me. A lot of five- and ten-dollar bills are going to arrive in the next mail. I can feel it coming, Sammy. There is nothing like tears, Sammy, to dissolve the glue and threads that hold the strongest wallet in the world together. So take it easy . . . but seem to be relishing everything a lot. Smack your lips some. And show a lot of pleasure. Because it will do a lot of good for contrast. I'm going to die of hunger, though . . . I can see that."

This is the way he was talking under his breath to me, while he was pouring out bunk for the rest of the crowd. Pretty soon the hotel clerk came in like he was walking right out loud in church. He leaned over the table, and said: "When you are at liberty, Mister Johnson, the president of our oldest bank, would like very much to have the privilege of meeting you, sir."

You could hear people catching their breaths all over the room. At the same time you could see them shuffling the burden off of their own shoulders and leaving it to the banker to do the charity for the whole outfit. Well, you would know that Lefty wouldn't be fool enough to undo everything that he had managed up to that time.

He says in that voice which makes everybody in the room feel like an eavesdropper: "Can you tell me on what account Mister Johnson wishes to see me?"

No, the clerk couldn't, but he had an idea that it would be to the advantage of Mr. . . . what was the name?

"My name is William Gobert," said Lefty, loud enough for those with checking accounts to hear and understand.

"Mister Gobert, I am sure that it would be to your advantage. . . ."

"Ah," said Lefty, "do I understand you, my kind young friend?"

The clerk was at least ten years older than Lefty. Lefty had the folks so groggy by this time that they would swallow anything. He took off his dark glasses and let them see his eyes, looking terrible deep sunk, he had shadowed them up so well. And he had pulled down his eyebrows, so that they looked very shaggy and long.

"I think that I do understand. I feel the kindness of Mister Johnson. But . . . will you express to him the deepest thanks of a poor violinist and tell him that I cannot take charity. I cannot, sir, and I fear that is what he is about to offer me."

By the time this sad, soft whisper had ended, everybody in the room was almost standing up in his place to see how proud and sad and dignified Lefty was—and most of all to look at those horrible blackened eyes. The clerk was finished; he didn't dare keep on talking and spoiling the effect of a grand picture like that. He turned around and tiptoed out of the room, humping all over in a silly way, like he had stolen something.

Lefty leaned his head wearily on his trembling hand. He closed his eyes and sighed. His murmuring lips you would have said were breathing out a few chunks of a prayer. What he was saying was: "Sammy, there are a dozen of them scribbling down my name, and the rest of them are too full of salt and tears to see what to write, but they can learn later. There is going to be at least one twenty-dollar check in this haul. Oh, kid, it was a lucky day when we started teaming! Wait till I water this fair plant of charity by turning loose your voice and my violin on them!"

Chapter Ten
PREPARATIONS

Right after breakfast he went down to the town hall and tried to hire it for that night to give what he said was to be a violin concert, assisted by a boy's voice. The owner looked over the pair of us, and asked if I was the boy. When Lefty said I was, the owner said he reckoned that he could get along without hiring his hall out to us; besides, he said, it was usual to hire his hall out for advance payment.

Lefty had to admit that he didn't have any money for paying in advance. The owner laughed at him. He said that he took no chances on charities like that. Altogether he talked pretty rough. I wondered how mad Lefty would be when he got away. Lefty just said as we got to the sidewalk: "I was afraid that we would have to perform in that hall. But that old codger played our game for us."

I asked him what in the world he meant, and he said: "Do you think that I want to get up there on the stage of that hall and fiddle for these people? Not me! There used to be a time when a man could hire halls and go all over the country very respectably. The good old days have gone, son. They have all gone. There's a whole crew of real artists that are flocking over the country. A lot of Polish and Russian 'skis' are wandering around with their fiddles, giving concerts and educating the public until you can't find any town that hasn't heard one of those foreigners."

I told Lefty that I thought he fiddled so good that hardly nobody could be any better. He only laughed. "Why, some of those Russians could stand on their heads and play better than I can standing on my feet. They've got their start when they're five years old, and they keep right on for ten hours a day until they're a hundred. Well, son, could I compete with a man that has gone through ninety-five years of it? I couldn't!"

Lefty was that way. Always talking up in the air where you could hardly follow him. He said that his playing needed lots of air and probably that my singing voice would need the same thing, that there was nothing like the open to make a rough thing seem smoother.

"Look at what the night does, kid! You can take the worst burned-up desert that was ever made, and a heap of mountains off on one side all jumbled together like a junk pile. Well, you wait until the sun goes down and the old desert is all covered over with fancy blues and violets and such things. It looks like neither water nor dry land, but better than both . . . the junk heap of mountains has turned into something that looks like a castle . . . maybe in ruins, but all the better for that. And the same way with us. Night will smooth us off and make us look pretty polished."

Well, you couldn't beat that fellow. He smoothed everything off so perfect. He had ideas about everything. Mostly they were the ideas of a rascal, I suppose, but they were always interesting.

In a little talk with the hotel proprietor, Lefty let it leak out that the boss of the town hall had refused to hire it out on credit. Well, you never seen anybody so mad as that proprietor was. He said that it was the last time he would ever buy tickets for a show in that town hall, and he would arrange it so that other folks would do the same way. Lefty tried to pretend that he didn't want anything like that.

When we got upstairs, Lefty was tickled, I can tell you. He laughed and carried on and said that the town was ours, that the news would go all over, how the cruel hall owner had refused to give us a chance.

Then he took an extra long time feeding Smiler, brushing him and washing his paws and legs. Lefty said that washing a dog all over—except just his face and his paws—was bad for the dog, that a good brushing was a lot better.

We managed to kill the day until the evening came along. Old Lefty waked me up, but wouldn't let me have a bite, because eating might spoil my voice, and, if they saw us eating so many squares, they would lose some of their pity.

Then we tried over some tunes, very soft, Lefty just touching them in on the violin so light that you could hardly make them out, and me talking the words out so that he would see I knew them. He didn't want anything fancy.

"We'll give them the good old tunes that they've known all their lives . . . the sort of tunes that the tired businessman wants his daughter or his wife to play and sing when he lies around easy after supper. This world that you're living in is made for that same tired businessman, son, and don't you forget it. It's his own private possession. You mustn't turn out anything that is going to give him a shock or a start, because the poor dear is fagged. When he comes home, he wants nothing except the nice light things that you can lay back and listen to without using any brains, or, if he goes out to a theater, he wants to hear a musical comedy. I mean he wants to see it. Because the music at one of those shows makes better seeing than it does hearing. Or else he goes to a moving-picture show, and there he doesn't have to even applaud. His wife sits alongside of him and reads the captions out loud, so that he can almost see that picture with his eyes closed.

"Well, son, that's the sort of a person that we want to please this evening. We want to catch him on his way back from the moving-picture show and give him another close-up with glycerin tears of poverty and art going begging in the streets."

Lefty enjoyed that little speech of his a good deal. You could depend upon that. Lefty would always appreciate himself. Even if he had been on a desert island, I suppose that Lefty could have put on a show and enjoyed it all by himself. If he told a joke, he always laughed at it harder than anybody else would laugh. If he said anything bright, he would lean back, smile a little, and taste the pleasure of his own brightness for a long time.

The evening came along, and Lefty let me have

some banana. That was all. I went to sleep again, and, when he woke me up, it was almost the middle of the night. I got up with a groan and I said why should we go out in the night and wake up folks that was in bed. But Lefty said that the tired businessman was rarely in bed long before midnight, because it took him a long time to get over the tired feeling that the day had give him. Besides, he said, what good would it be to go fiddling right after dinner time, when people were too full to lean out the windows and be sorry for you. Along about midnight people had already spent so much money that they didn't mind spending a lot more.

"What is a quarter," said Lefty, "after a ten dollar party?"

Would you have thought of that?

First he fixed himself up, and put some more shadows around his eyes. He said that he would not wear the dark glasses, because it was no use wearing a label when the whole town already knew that he *was* blind and would have fought anybody who said that he wasn't.

When he was all fixed up, he took Smiler along and we started out. I said that it wouldn't do for Smiler to look like a regular trained begging dog. Lefty asked if I thought that there was only one side to Smiler. I wondered what he meant by this, but I figured it was a wrong time to be asking too many questions. We started out.

Chapter Eleven
ONLY A FAKER

I would have gone to the brightest corner in the middle of town, where the people would pass pretty thick as they began to float along homeward from the theater. Lefty wouldn't do that. He picked out a dark spot near an alley's mouth—so dog-gone dark that there was no street light worth noticing. The moon shone down there. Lefty took off his hat and shook out his hair, which he had fixed extra gray for the occasion. Then he told Smiler to guard his feet. That dog-gone dog lay down right across Lefty's toes just as if he understood.

Lefty put back his head and began to play. The moon shone down on that imitation gray head of his; it splashed all white on Smiler, till that dog looked like he was cut out of shining snow—only mighty dangerous.

Instead of picking sad tunes, Lefty said: "Kid, you and me are out here being forced to play in the street like beggars because we couldn't hire the town hall, as everybody knows. But you and me haven't had any begging experience. We don't even know enough to get onto a bright corner where a crowd is passing. All that we do is to sneak off into an alley mouth, and there, out of the darkness, we start in and play bright and cheery little tunes to make everybody happy. And the tunes we play are so bright and gay that they make a pretty good background for showing off our poverty more than ever. You understand?"

Could you beat that? Nobody could. He was just a regular scamp, that Lefty was. But he knew an awful lot. Well, he led off with something all by himself, played very lively and dancing, sort of. It was an Irish jig tune.

The first thing that you know there was a couple of men coming down the street with a couple of girls. They stopped, and one of the men said: "Good heavens, here they are . . ."

The other one said: "Reduced to begging in the street."

"How frightful . . . poor things!" said the girls. "Go and tell somebody. . . ."

One of the men ran down the street.

You could see that things were going to come our way from that minute. When Lefty finished up that tune the first time, I hit in with the words. It was just right for me. Not too high, but high enough—easy words that didn't mean nothing, about a girl down in the county of Mayo whose name was Molly, and was waiting for you to come down and look into her blue eyes. My throat was feeling pretty good, and my stomach was empty as a drum, so's I could breathe deep and hang onto the notes. Somehow a voice sounds better at night, the same as an auto seems to run better, too. The first note I hit made a shiver run through Lefty. I knew that he was tickled and terribly surprised. I went right on making those notes cut clean all over that town, every one of them ringing like a bell.

It put tears in my eyes, it made me feel so good to sing so loud and so fine.

After that we went right on, old Lefty just stopping for a minute to rub rosin on his bow or something that gave him a chance to hear what they were saying out in the crowd.

At first nobody could see the hat, they were so busy looking at Lefty's grand face and listening to the violin and me. After a while they saw the hat, and some man stepped forward, cleared his throat a little, and very carefully dropped two fifty-cent pieces in, so that the people could tell by the *jingle* that he had given something really pretty good.

The next man rolled up a couple of dollar bills and dropped them in. The first man looked pretty mad and small. After that, the men kept sneaking up one by one and dropping something in. They had to be careful about it because, if they leaned over the hat, old Smiler grinned at them and lifted his lip, showing his four fangs.

"The poor fellow picked the worse place in town," said one.

"Hush, you silly!" said a girl. "Do you think

this poor, blind, sad man knows where the best places for begging are?"

They went on like that, and the money in that hat grew deeper and deeper. I pretended to stumble and stepped into the hat, squashing down the paper money pretty flat. That gave the hat quite an empty look.

After we had been there forty minutes, everybody in town was there, or coming pretty rapid.

Then Lefty put across another emotion for them. He stepped on my toe and started in to play a piece that was all on one string, mostly. Lefty said it was the G string, and that an old German wrote it down a long time ago. It was very grand and solemn. It came at the end of all those jolly tunes very striking, like it was something that Lefty couldn't help playing, like it was something that come right out of his heart and showed you how miserable he had been inside, all the time, while he was making happy music for the rest of the town! Well, sir, it sort of startled me and gave me a choke in the throat. I had to give myself a shake to remember that this wasn't a poor, blind, old chap with a failing heart that had just been burned out of his home. It was only Lefty, a faker.

Nobody else in that crowd, of course, knew what I knew, and the effect of that piece on them was more than you could say. I'm ashamed to think of how those poor people stood around and mopped their eyes and sniffed and swallered. Some of the women was so affected that they just leaned up against one another and moaned. The men stopped thinking. They just reached into their pockets and hauled up all the cash that they hadn't spent on their girls. I saw whole handfuls of dough come up into the light. While Lefty was putting away his violin in the case, taking plenty of time, he said in that whisper of his that would have carried through a five-foot wall: "My heart is giving way, Samuel. We must go home. Take up my hat, and, if there is anything in it, put it in the violin cover. . . ."

There was a green cloth cover that went around the violin case. Old Lefty was pretty wise, because if we had emptied that hat into our pockets, it was so crammed that the people would have known pretty close to what we had. I dumped it into the green cover so quick that it looked like nothing at all. Then Lefty put the hat on. I took his hand and led him away through the crowd. When he came to the gutter, he stepped down to the street with such a bump so that anybody could see that he was stone blind!

That crowd was just buzzing and milling around us. We had to walk slow through just mobs of people. As we went by, they jammed money into our pockets until they bulged. All the men were saying it was an outrage that a great artist like this had to play in the streets. Did anybody ever hear such a grand piece as that last one? No, nobody ever had.

They stuck right with us up to the door of the hotel, and we collected money all the time. With Lefty saying every once in a while in that whispering of his: "Hurry, Samuel. I am failing fast."

Every time he said that, there would be another rush, and wallets would open up and more money would be jammed onto us.

We got into the hotel at last, and Lefty staggered up the stairs with me. A couple of men came along saying they were doctors and that they could be of assistance. Lefty said that all he needed was to lie still and rest.

So they went away and there we were.

We dumped everything on the floor, because the table would hardly have held it without overflowing, and sorted it out—there weren't many nickels and dimes to count. There were more quarters, and still more fifty-cent pieces, and the bulk of the stuff was dollar bills and upward! Yes, there was a whole flock of fives and tens; there was seven twenty dollar bills. You would hardly think that there was that much money in the world! We counted it up. It was twelve hundred and fifty dollars!

Lefty sat cross-legged on the floor looking sort of grim, saying at last: "It doesn't seem possible! It's more like robbing a bank! Here we have all this money thrown in our faces, you might say . . ."

"And it's the first haul," I said. "Maybe this will just warm them up a little. Maybe the next haul will be twice as good!"

Lefty smiled down at me, sort of pitying. He said that we had worked the town pretty well, that it was always best to leave a place while you was still lucky, because you never could tell what would happen. He said that tomorrow we would get out of that town quick and slide away for the mountains to try a dodge up there. Our worries were over; most of this money he would plant in a bank where it could keep on growing just as fast as it wanted to at five percent.

He was a great thinker—Lefty! But it seemed a shame to me to leave that town before we had dragged it dry.

We were sitting there like that when all at once Lefty began to straighten up with a far-away look on his face.

"What's the matter, Lefty?"

He whispered: "Do you hear anything?"

I didn't, but, the first thing that I knew, Lefty had reached in under his coat and slid out a revolver. Right then a little draft of air came over our way and started all the money fluttering and whispering, and I looked over my shoulder.

The door to the closet had just been opened. Then I seen him standing for the first time, looking like a devil, which he was. There, with a gun in his hand, pointed at us, was Jake.

As always, he had the upper hand and there was no chance to fight back at him. But even if there had been a chance, who would have wanted to take it, seeing what he was?

Chapter Twelve

THE HUNCHBACK

There is no real use in describing Jake. Nothing that you can say gives any idea of him. I can say that he was about five feet high, and no more; his head was stuck right in the middle of his shoulders, with his great, long chin sticking out over his chest. He looked sort of like a monkey, his arms dangling down so long that every minute you almost expected him to drop over a little and run along on all fours. Though when he was facing you, you just noticed these things and the width of his shoulders, which was something amazing, still, you could swear that there was something wrong with the part of him that you couldn't see. In another minute, when you had a chance to look, you could see what it was—a great big bunch on his back that hiked the tail of his coat away up.

Calling him a hunchback doesn't give just the right idea, because most hunchbacks seem to have pale faces, caved-in chests, and walk with sort of a hitch. Big Jake's chest stuck out the same as anybody's, or more. Only, on his back there was that great, big lump. And it seemed like he had a lot of strength there, more than you would ever imagine that a man should have.

I've been saying that Lefty was very strong, particular in the shoulders and in his hands. Nobody needed to ask you to say whether he was as strong as Jake, because he wasn't—not half!

Taking him, all in all, it wasn't more than one thing that made him so terrible to look at. It wasn't his hump; it wasn't the fact that his head was stuck on his shoulders without any neck—stuck on so stiff that his face was pitched down toward the earth. It seemed hard for him to look up at you, and, whenever he looked up, it was with a frown. None of those things was so bad. The worst was his arms and his hands. I suppose that one of those hands of his would have made both of Lefty's with something over. There was thick black hair that grew curling all over the back of those hands and down, too, over the first joints of his fingers. Those fingers was so big and so long that, if he wanted to, he could catch hold with one finger as hard and as strong as another man could with his whole hand.

Take for instance that gun he had in his hand. It was the biggest size, but it looked just like a little thing—not like heavy steel, all loaded with six big bullets—in that grip of his.

He gave me a shudder, like he was a toad and a spider rolled into one. And you couldn't look at those bright, black eyes of his for more than a second without beginning to have the horrors so bad that you had to make yourself stop thinking.

Lefty just looked into my face. He didn't turn around at all, just as though I was a mirror that showed him all that he wanted to see. Then he drew in his breath—"Ah-h!"—with a sort of bubbling sound that made wriggles run all through my inwards. "He's got us at last!" said Lefty.

Jake grinned. It was like when you step on a nail and make a quick face before you holler. That was his smile. It came flashing on and made him look twice as bad as ever. Then it flashed right off again, and there was just the ordinary nightmare that was there before.

"Here I am, right enough," said Jake, "and I have to admit that the only reason that I've been quiet so long is that I've been standing here behind the closet door admiring you, Lefty . . . partly by hearing, and partly by looking through the crack and seeing."

I wondered what Lefty would do. Because it didn't come into my head that he could be beaten. I was sure that he would find some way of defeating the hunchback. Then I saw him simply put his revolver away under his coat again, and for the first time I knew that there was something in the world that made him afraid.

He stood up and turned around to Jake. He was quivering all over, he was so scared and so disgusted. Jake saw, and Jake grinned, saying: "You don't seem very happy about having me here, Lefty. A man would think, to see your face, that it sort of hurt you to have a man like me around you. Is that right?"

Lefty could hardly answer him for a minute. Then he said: "All right, Jake. How much is it? What'll you have?"

"What'll I have?" said Jake. "Why, I'll have the first thousand out of that twelve hundred and fifty that you've just been counting aloud, there. And I'll have the goose that laid the golden eggs, too. I'll take the kid along with me."

I would rather have died. Matter of fact, I almost thought that I *would* die when I heard that. The first thing that I looked at was that big, hairy hand of his, and his arm that could've reached halfway across the room to me!

Lefty just sat down on the bed and smiled. He was trying to be easy, but you could see with half an eye that he was shamming. His face was all gray, and his mouth was twitching.

"You don't want a lot," he said. "It wouldn't take a lot to satisfy you, I see. Only a thousand dollars and the kid, too. But I tell you, Jake, that you're not going to get a penny . . . nor the kid."

Jake rubbed his hand over his mouth and grinned again. That grin went through me like fire.

"You would think that even a skunk like you, Lefty, would have better sense than to talk like that. You would think that you would know that it's damned near more than I could do to keep from you. Suppose that I was to just satisfy myself by sending a slug of this here lead through your head, and then scoop up all of the money!" He said it with a glare in those queer, greasy-looking eyes.

Lefty blinked and got a shade whiter still. "That's bluff, Jake," said Lefty. "It doesn't work. This is not that kind of a town. They've got police here . . . and they've got the means of scooping you up before you could ever get away from the hotel."

"Have they?" asked Jake. "Lemme tell you that I come into this room without being seen by anybody, and that I'm gonna be able to get away from the hotel again without being seen by nobody!"

He looked toward the window, as he said that. You could be pretty sure that those long arms of his would easy swing him up and down the side of a building, as easy as a monkey could climb through the limbs of a tree.

"It won't go," said Lefty. "You can have half

the coin, Jake, but the rest of it and the kid stays with me."

A wave of rage went over Jake's face and he said: "Are you gonna talk back to my gun? I'll have half the coin *and* the kid!"

Lefty winced away. He shrank back from the bed and leaned against the wall, breathing hard and looking cornered. I was almost as sick to see the fear in his face as I was sick to see the horror in the other man. Jake seemed to see that he was paralyzing Lefty, like a wasp does with a tarantula, and he came a step nearer. Even his walk was different from the walk of other men. His whole body rolled a little, but he didn't look awkward exactly—just queer and ugly in his motions the way he was in his looks, but all the time fast and smooth and sure.

"It would be pretty soft for you," he said, "to go loafin' around the country soakin' up money that don't belong to you, and workin' the kid for everything he's worth. But the kid is meant for your betters. He's meant for me, old son, and I'm gonna have him. I'm in need of a rest, and the kid is gonna supply me with the hard cash to keep me easy."

He was in the middle of the room now. When he made another step forward, it looked like he would be right within reachin' distance of Lefty. And Lefty's hand jumped inside of his coat.

"Don't you pull out that hand, Lefty," Jake

warned, "or I'll drill you! It's a terrible big temptation to stand up here and not drill you. Now you back out of the room. I don't need any more of your company!"

You could see Lefty waver. There was nothing that he wanted in the world so much as he wanted to get out of that room and away from that devil of a man. He looked to the door, and then he looked back to me, and, just when I was giving up hope, I seen a flash come in his eyes. I knew that he would fight for me.

He said: "Jake, you've got the drop on me, but, if you shoot, you'll be dead before long. They'll get you sure. Right now I'm the poor blind man in this town. I'm the honest beggar. And if you murder me, they'll hunt you and kill you like a dog . . . and you know it. More than that, I'm not going to drop without some chance at you. You'll have to kill me with the first shot, Jake, or else I'll surely kill you. It's been growing in me these years. Someday I'll be the death of you, Jake. I can feel it in my bones. And maybe the time is now."

He was like a man that was drunk. He was blinking and glaring at Jake. All the same, he was getting into a sort of crazy fighting mood. Jake seen it and seemed to be bothered. He squinted at Lefty as though Lefty was a long ways off, and as though he was seeing something strange and dangerous.

"Where's my half, then?" said Jake.

"Split the pot in two, kid," Lefty said.

I dragged my foot through the money and divided it into two parts. Jake leaned down and with about two scoops of his big hand he had one half of the coin into his pockets. Then he backed away toward the window.

"Well, Lefty," he said, "now that I've found your trail I expect to be living easy again for a while." He straddled the window sill, his gun still in his hand. "Because I'm not through with you. Oh, no. And you, kid, you remember me, too. I ain't pretty, am I? And believe me, I look better than I am. But salt this away in your head . . . one day you'll be workin' for me!"

That horrible grin flashed on his face and went out again, and then he swung himself through the window and up out of sight, exactly like a monkey—his big, long arms carrying him, and his scrawny legs sort of dangling.

Chapter Thirteen

PURSUIT

Old Smiler had watched big Jake all that time with his mouth just watering for a word to go after him. After Jake swung out of the window, the dog stood up with his feet on the sill and looked out into the night as though he had a mind to be after that ugly-looking man.

I wondered, too, why Lefty hadn't sent the dog after Jake as soon as he saw him in the room, but it was easy to see that Lefty was more than half paralyzed all the time. He had just made that one big effort—sort of desperate—to get Jake out of the room—and he had won out on it, though it cost him half the loot.

Not quite half, because, while I was dragging my foot through the heap, I had managed to put the little stack of twenties and most of the fives in the smallest half that I divided the pot into. The result was that we had nearly eight hundred dollars, and Jake had about four hundred and fifty.

Lefty had fallen into a chair. He lay there with his head back, breathing hard and looking at the ceiling out of glassy eyes. He was all in. If a baby had come into the room, Lefty wouldn't have been able to raise a hand to help himself. It was awful to see him like that. He hadn't been touched by that monster, but you would think that he had been more than half killed.

Finally he managed to get a flask out of his pocket, and he poured a big drain down his throat. In a minute it began to work. His wits came back to him on the jump.

He said: "Scoop up that money. We're going to leave!"

"Leave . . . now?" I asked, not able to believe him.

"We're going to leave now," said Lefty. "Right

now! While Jumbo is counting the money that he's stolen, and while he thinks that we're still in the hotel. Right now is the time when he'll be napping and taking it easy. And right now is the time that we'll give him the slip."

By the time he finished, we were ready to leave. We opened the door, and Lefty listened at the hall.

"Don't walk too soft," said Lefty. "And . . . lead me along. There may be somebody in the lobby."

So we got down to the street. When we stepped out onto it, it seemed to me that Jake, like a big shadow, was standing there flat against the wall, ready to grab one of us in each big hand. But no Jake was there.

We looked at each other. It scared me worse than ever to see how badly Lefty was frightened.

After that we legged it right across the town until we came to the outskirts—then through the outskirts, where even our lightest steps made a sneaking echo behind us. We got to the shadow of the trees at last. A road was winding away through those trees. Lefty said that we'd hit a good pace and should keep along that road as far as we could until the morning. Because he said that Jake could almost smell out a place where a man was hiding.

I said: "Will you tell me one thing?"

"Yes, I'll tell you that I'm glad that we're away out here. What else?"

"That time that you woke up in the night and dreamed that a man was in the next room . . . ?"

"Yes, that was Jake."

It was all clear to me. They were old enemies. Jake was hounding Lefty across the country. As we walked along, I asked Lefty why it was.

He said: "It's for a reason too crazy to be talked about. What's important is that that devil is after me and wants nothing in the world so much as to get me. Yet back in my head, Sammy, I've an idea that I'm the one that's going to win. Mind you, I'm afraid of that fellow. I don't want anything to do with him. But in the end, I think that I'm going to have his life under my thumb . . . and put that thumb right down."

I didn't say anything, of course. Just the same I couldn't help feeling that Lefty was talking through his hat. It was what he wanted to do that seemed to him like what he was *going* to do.

From the top of the next hill you could look down and see a curve of silver in the hollow of the valley over to the left. That curve went out— and then it began again. It was a river, running along with the view shut off by tall trees between here and there. I thought that I would sort of like to stop there and look, for a while, but Lefty said: "We'll do no stopping at all. I have a queer feeling in my bones that our trouble isn't over for a while yet."

Right pat on top of that an automobile came

whirring around the corner of the road below us, back toward town. Lefty jumped as though he had been shot, and then he dragged me down the hill through the trees for a way.

"It's not *possible* that's Jake," said Lefty. "And yet if it is . . ." He looked wildly around him, as though he would want wings to get away from that trouble. And then—right up there, above us, on the road the automobile stopped. We could hear the noise of the driver's feet when they hit the pavement.

That was enough for us. You can believe that we didn't ask no more questions, but we headed down that slope like the wind. I was taking steps about twelve feet long, with the slope to help me. When my legs crumbled up under me, I rolled head over heels about fifty feet. *That* didn't bother me. I only wished that I could have gone a hundred times faster—because ahead of me there was Lefty running away through the night and leaving me behind—so that that big brute could grab me and squash the life out of me with one swipe of his hand.

I wanted to scream. I could feel that scream jump up and take hold of my throat like a hard hand. I kept it back, because it would be like turning on a light to show Jake the way to me. Besides, it wouldn't make Lefty turn back.

When I was about halfway down the slope, I heard something behind me and looked back.

There was something that was a man, and yet didn't look like a man, coming down the hill with a sprawling stride. I knew that was Jake, running like the wind.

My legs were a little tired and sore from the pounding of running down that steep hill. You better believe that I forgot all about being tired then. I got rubber cushions in my heels and wings in my knees, and I just flew.

There was nothing in front now, to guide me, just the blackness under the trees, and I kept praying to myself: *God, be good to me, and don't let me trip. . . .* It was that prayer that kept me on my feet. In the day I couldn't have taken half a dozen steps, even walking, without stumbling over some of the roots. But nothing mattered to me, and nothing stopped me then. I just winged it along. I could only pray, too, that I would be traveling along behind the path that Lefty might've gone.

It seemed to me that a dozen times I passed a glint of something white at the side, where Lefty and Smiler would be crouched, waiting for me to lead big Jake by them. And then—why, they would simply sneak back up the hill, grab the automobile, and drive away in her!

I thought of those things, but I didn't waste any time stopping. I only ran all the harder and took longer steps every second. Behind me, I could *feel* how Jake was gaining.

"Stop, you brat, or I'll drop you!" gasped out Jake behind me.

I looked back over my shoulder to see him smashing along with his gun in his hand. A slab of moonshine fell through the trees just there and showed me his horrible face. Suddenly I knew that he was after me, just as much as he was after Lefty. He wanted me to do as he said—live with him and work for him, begging in the towns. I was awful sick. I almost wanted him to shoot. Maybe he would have, but there was a crash and Jake went down with a smash. He was up again right away, and once more I had the feeling that a hand was reaching out right behind me. Now there was no gun—he had lost that when he fell.

The slope got more gradual, and the strength went out of my legs at the same minute. There was no longer any sharp drop of the ground to help me along, and there was no strength in my legs to swing me along. I was pounding hard on my heels, and my lungs were all lined with fire, but there was no sign of any feeling in the rest of me. Below the hips my legs were just numb. I could only know that they were working by the banging of my feet.

I knew I was losing ground awful fast. When I looked back, I seen that big Jake was feeling the run, too. Maybe he was hurt by his fall. Or maybe those skinny legs of his could carry him along fast only for a short ways before he got tired. He was most awful tired now, and his face all screwed up into a knot.

There was no doubt about who would win out in the end. There wasn't anything left for me to call on when I was used up—and then I busted out from the edge of the trees and I saw before me—the water! It looked fine to me, I tell you. If only I was to die in it, instead of in those awful hands of big Jake.

More than that was waiting for me. Down yonder a voice called. The next minute I seen my friend Lefty sitting in a canoe right in the shadow of the bank—sitting in that canoe and cutting the rope that tied her to the bush on the water's edge. There was Smiler sitting in the bow and sticking out his tongue and laughing in the moonshine.

I dived for it just as the hand of Jake, reaching for me, stubbed against my shoulder, but missed any finger hold. I went sailing ahead through the air.

I dived right under the boat and came up on the far side. Lefty got me by the nape of the neck and jerked me right into the canoe.

The first thing I saw was Jake standing there on the bank above me, throwing his arms up over his head—yelling, stamping, and cursing like he was crazy, until Lefty took a shot at him. Then he ducked back into the bushes with a roar like a beast.

Chapter Fourteen
AN ESCAPE

We had the current with us. Lefty's legs may have been tired, but his arms were fresh. He made that canoe talk, digging in deep with long strokes of the paddle. He took her right out into the middle of the channel, where the current would foam us along at a good clip. So we went tearing around the next bend and out of sight of Jake.

Just as I was about to thank my stars that we were out of range of him, Lefty turned the canoe to the side of the river where the current was almost dead, and there was nothing but standing water. Right in there, where the bank threw down a shadow as thick as ink, he began to drive the canoe upstream!

He hollered at me to take a paddle and help him. I did what I could, shortening the paddle up so's I could use it, but I wondered what he was about. He didn't say a word, and enough had happened that night to keep me thinking without asking any more questions, so we slid along very easy, making the time, except where the roots and the limbs of trees bothered us. When we were about a mile from the spot where we had seen Jake last, Lefty caught hold of a bush and steadied the canoe for a minute while we rested.

He said that Jake had seen us scoot down the river, and so he would be sure to start in that direction after us. Now every mile we put behind us was better than two, because it would bother Jake a lot, to begin with, and, besides that, it would puzzle him to find out where we *had* gone.

We kept on digging along, doing three miles an hour in the shadow of the bank where the water was the stillest, and we steadied along at this for about two or three hours. Then the water ahead of us slid out into a long, narrow lake. That made our going pretty easy, of course. The best of it was that there was a good strong wind now snapping into us from the rear. That helped us along almost as much as the paddling.

Finally Lefty took our two coats, pinned them together, and stretched them out on the two paddles. Then he fixed those paddles up against the ribs of the canoe. Lefty and me stretched out back of the middle of the canoe. It steered; all Lefty had to do was to trail a hand overboard a mite, that kept us headed right along.

You've no idea till you've tried what a lot a small sail like that will do. It just foamed us through the water. Lefty said that we must be doing about eight or ten miles an hour. It seemed a lot more than that, because it was like sitting down in the blackness of that water and racing.

We began to feel better, now that we had the cool of the night blowing in our faces. Finally, with a feeling of satisfaction, Lefty said: "Well, who would have it any different? Starve one day, live rich the next day . . . lie around with your pals one day . . . try to cut the throat of an enemy the next. And that's the way that it runs all the time . . . Sammy, would you have it changed?"

Well, when you come down to think about it, I don't suppose that I *would* have changed it, though I still felt pretty queer in the knees. I told Lefty that I would as soon get along without any Jake in my world, and he even laughed at that, saying maybe Jake was only the salt that made the meat of a tramp's life better.

It was the beginning of the day, now. We seemed to be sailing into the sunrise. Lefty dropped his cigarette overboard, and we both lay back to enjoy it. It got brighter and brighter. Then we both looked up and said—"Oh!"—at the same minute, for we seen a great, big cloud hanging in the sky, turned to a big lump of flame from head to bottom—yellow-red it was. It seemed to light up the whole world the minute that it caught on fire.

The whole side of the sky began to be ribbed out with gold and red, and where you hadn't noticed any clouds at all, you could see long fingers of them stretched across the curve of the sky. The lake in front of us turned so wonderful that you wouldn't believe it—the little waves being indigo on one side and gold on the other—

and then snakes of red went wriggling over everything, once in a while.

Even the shore seemed to change, and every time that there came a gap in the trees so that you could see a meadow you felt that right there was where you would like to put a tent and stay the rest of your life. Pretty soon we came in sight of a town. Lefty and me just looked at one another, because it looked just like it was the finest town that you ever seen. Then—*bang!* The sun came up.

All that fineness faded off quick as a snap. All you could think of was the emptiness of your stomach. Even Smiler seemed to feel it; he shoved his nose into the hand of his boss as much as to say: "All this is very fine, but it ain't raw meat . . . not half."

Well, we fetched on by that town; a couple of curls of smoke were beginning to twist up from over the roofs, and we skated on down the lake with the wind getting stronger every minute.

We were shivering pretty much about two hours later; the sun was behind a cloud, and the face of the lake was all wrinkled and black with the wind, when we came to another town. I mean we came to a couple of wharves sticking out into the lake and some powerful poor-looking houses behind them.

I wanted to go on for a better place, but Lefty said: "No, right here is where we stop. Those wharves are too big to be needed by only those shacks . . . there must be a little town beyond. You come along. Some time you'll see that the biggest and finest-looking town ain't always the best."

He was right.

Down there by the edge of the water, he washed the shadows off his eyes and the gray out of his hair. We got cleaned up and brushed up as good as we could and climbed up the bank, through the woods, and right into as good a town as you would want. It wasn't slicked up like the last place we was in. It looked more like Gunther—the sort of a town that you could be comfortable in and wouldn't have to wear a coat and a necktie all the time. We went right to a hotel, and we said that we had been canoeing down the river and our canoe had sprung a leak. We had barely got into wading distance of the shore when she went down and she took our luggage with her.

We got a room and settled down for a rest after we had had a breakfast. That was a breakfast and a half, too! There was everything from bacon and eggs down to hot cakes with maple syrup. I put away a couple of stacks of them before I lost that gone sort of feeling.

I had a snooze then. When I woke up, it was afternoon, as I could tell by the way that the sun was sliding into the room and by the warm, lazy feel of the air. You can always tell that way. Right then, Lefty came in. You wouldn't have knowed him!

His clothes had been a little messed up from the work that we had been doing lately. There he was rigged out in a fine, new brown suit about as fine as a body could ask. He had a lot of bundles over his arms and in his hands that he dumped in the room. He sat down by the window, lighted a cigar, and turned it around slow and easy in his mouth while he blew out rings.

"Well, partner," Lefty said, "things are beginning to look up."

It tickled me a good deal to have him talk like that—him being what he was and me just an ornery kid. I didn't say anything. Mostly, when you begin to get warm in the middle of yourself, it is a good thing not to talk, because usually you will say something foolish. The brightest boy I ever knew, he never would do no talking at all except to say—"Gimme. . . ."—whatever it was he wanted. Usually he got it, too, because it looked like he wouldn't ask for a thing he didn't need. But I never had talent for silence like that.

After a while, I got up. Then I could see that Smiler had a new, green patent-leather collar on. He seemed awful proud of it and grateful.

"Well," I said, "you and Smiler certainly look fine!"

"Rustle among those packages," said Lefty. "Maybe you'll find something for yourself there."

The first thing I saw was a cap; it fitted me perfect; it had a leather visor and everything.

Then I found a big cardboard box with a suit in it of gray tweed. And that fitted me perfect. And then there was a couple of flannel shirts, tan-colored, square-toed buckskin shoes, as supple as could be and as strong as iron. There were stockings wove extra double across the knees and the toes. You could look around a long ways before you could find an outfit like that so sensible! You wouldn't be afraid of sitting down on the ground in those clothes. They were loose and fine for climbing trees, but just as good for walking right into church, if you had a necktie on.

I seen my old trousers lying on the floor with the two patches on the seat looking up at me. "Jiminy! Lefty," I said, "I never was togged out like this. But how could you spend so much money on me?"

"Why, you damn' little fool," said Lefty, "ain't it just as much your money as it is mine?"

Chapter Fifteen
HAPPY DAYS

I asked Lefty what would we do in that town. He said nothing except enjoy ourselves. Which we did it fine! Only, what a lot of money it cost! Lefty bought us a good buggy with a tough-looking buckskin horse to pull it. He wasn't very big, that horse, but tough as iron, and he had the way of those mountain roads so thorough that nobody could ever expect him to trip up. There were two suitcases. One held all of our clothes, packed in tight. And the other one held some pots and pans that Lefty got, and then there was places for spices and such things. Besides that, we had potatoes, bread, flour, coffee, tomatoes, bacon, and baking powder all the time along with us. And a few jars of jam to fix us out for a dessert at the end of the meal.

When we got through collecting these things, we found that the clothes and horse and buggy—which was second-handed—and a new pocket knife for me and a lot of other fixings had all cost up around six hundred dollars! It was like throwing money away, spending that much in two days, but everything that Lefty got was mighty good. He was that way. When he got me a knife, he didn't stop asking until he got the best steel that there was and then a handle that just fitted my hand fine. It cost him two dollars and a half— just for a pocket knife! And it took near an hour of his time to choose it, but that didn't matter. He would get nothing but the best for himself or me. It was surprising to watch him. If a clerk said— "This is good enough for a boy."—Lefty would say: "I've noticed that boys give things harder wear than men do."

That was the way with Lefty. He didn't always ask me what to do with the money, but, whatever he spent, he spent just as much for me as he did for himself, which was something extra special, you might say, and a thing that most folks would never bother themselves about doing. It made me feel mighty good about Lefty.

When he got all through, he said: "Counting out everything, and hotel bills and meals, and cigars and cigarettes and all, there is just a bit over two hundred dollars left to us. We've sunk in the rest. And there is the list of what I've spent. I want you to look it over."

I got a little hot in the face and told him that I didn't doubt but what he was honest.

"It isn't that, Sammy," he said. "I want to stay honest. I've started square with you, and it tickles me a good deal to keep on being square. If you start in trusting me too much, maybe when we make a fat haul, someday, I'll take most of the profits and put them away for myself. The best way to do these things is to do them like a business. Here we are, you and me, in partnership. We're wandering musicians, aiming to make the public pay a little more than theater prices to hear our performances, and everything has to be done the same for both of us."

He never changed a mite. Right up to the end he was always just as honest and as fair.

We started across country in that rig, the buckskin stepping along. Our plan was like this: When we came to a town, we would stop somewhere near and get fixed up in our old clothes. Lefty would blacken his eyes, put on the smoked glasses, and make up his hair gray. He would go in with me in the evening when it was dark enough to cover up any rough spots in his make-up. We would work the town as well as we could, while Smiler stayed out and took care of the horse.

Sometimes there was two or three days in between towns. We didn't care how long it took from place to place, except when we eased across a piece of real flat desert with nothing but sand for drinking water. In the main, we kept to the hills or mountains, where we would find good wood and water—the main things for camps.

Lefty got a big .32 rifle for himself. He got me a .22, which I could shoot pretty good. I always had a hankering for guns and such things. Lefty improved me a lot by teaching me to shoot low, and how to allow for wind, and why things at a distance always seemed farther off than really. Sometimes we would go along for three whole days, never doing a stroke of business, just shooting, lying about in camp, Lefty telling yarns, and me listening hard.

I got to like that life awful well. Aunt Claudia would have said it was the natural devil in me. She said there was a natural devil in every man. But I reckon that everybody likes to be lazy if he can. It was particular easy for me to loaf and beg because the right or the wrong of the thing sort of all lay on the shoulders of Lefty, if you know what I mean.

Pretty soon I got to see that there was as much difference between towns as between people. Some towns are open and easy; some towns are hard and mean. Some towns had prime cooking, and some towns lived on boiled pork and boiled potatoes, something terrible to see. Some towns have big trees for shade, and some cut them down for wood; some towns have constables that are earning their salaries, and some have constables that are just hanging around, smiling to get votes for the next election time.

Lefty was a great one to notice the differences right away quick between those villages. He would take a good look, and then he would say: "We're gonna be jolly and happy beggars."

That was for the hard, mean places. Then we would go down and sing Irish jig tunes; I would dance some jigs that Lefty had taught me and wind up with a "buck and wing," my feet going so fast that you wouldn't hardly believe it.

I worked a good deal to get those steps down pat, but it was easy work for Lefty. He never praised you much, because he knew how things had *ought* to be done. Neither did he keep on panning you, but he did everything gradual. One of his favorite sayings was that all the time in the world was not used up yet.

He would sit for half an hour and watch me trying a certain twitch or step in a "buck and wing." Some of them are mighty uncertain and hard to do. He would go through the thing for me, slow, half a hundred times, while I was trying to follow him. I've seen him take off his shoe and sock to show me with his bare foot how the heel and the toe had to work in the making of a rattling good step. He never tried to have me do a lot at once, either.

In the mean towns, we acted very gay, and in the happy, easy-going towns, we always were special sad; Lefty would pull out his face very long and get afflicted with heart trouble. He would say: "You got to give people what they haven't got. In the long run, it is better to give them tragedy. That's what pays. You may raise a crowd with a comedy any time, but a street comedian gets paid with pennies, and a tragedian gets paid with dollars. There's a difference."

It was true, too.

You could depend on a mean town having a constable with a hungry look; he would tell you to run along or you would be picked up for vagrancy. At the best, he would ask you questions and write down all of your answers. That was very embarrassing and kept Lefty inventing new lies wonderful fast.

When I remember how jolly and happy those days were, it doesn't seem like I can go on to tell what happened next. I suppose that you got to come to the end of happiness, no matter how fine it is, and you got to tell about the blue days that followed.

I would like to quit writing right here. Or else, I would like to go on and tell about all the good times that we had, one by one. There were enough of them to fill a book. But the whole thing has to be wrote down.

It was the fall of the year; the night was turning chilly. We had come out of a crossroad town where we had worked pretty hard; our pick-up was only about twenty dollars. Even that was enough to keep us going along pretty smooth. We had come up out of the hollow where the town was. Through a gap in the woods I saw Lefty stop and look up and stand there a long time. I stopped, too, and listened to the way that the ground was making a crinkling noise as it drank up the rest of the last rain. I looked around me, but I could see nothing for Lefty to watch except some geese flying south across the face of the moon.

Right then I guessed that there was trouble lying ahead of us.

Chapter Sixteen
HOME

Since Lefty didn't say anything right then, I didn't ask. We went on to the camp. Smiler came to meet us with Tippety behind him. Tippety was the horse, you know. He and Smiler had become great friends. Being always together, they had got to know each other pretty well, and they were like pals. If you saw Tippety out grazing, you could be pretty sure that Smiler was along somewhere, lying down in the grass. Sometimes Tippety would wander off a long ways from the camp to graze, but all that Lefty had to do was to go and holler for Smiler or whistle. Smiler would yip and pretty soon, here he would come, looking back over his shoulder at Tippety who would be behind him as comfortable as you please. It was a funny thing to see. Pretty, too!

Smiler wagged his tail for Lefty, but he seemed not to see the dog nor the buckskin, either. He just walked into camp, and, while I made a fire for our regular midnight coffee, Lefty dropped his chin on his fist and studied. When he got half a cup of hot coffee inside of him, he said: "I think that we'd better head south."

I said was there any very good towns down that way?

"Too good for you and me," said Lefty, very solemn.

He looked up into the sky again. There was nothing flying against the moon, this time, but out of the sky I heard the cry of the wild geese, the coldest and most mournful sound ever made to come falling through the night.

It muddled me up a lot to have Lefty acting unhappy that way. I didn't say anything, and pretty soon he went to bed. I didn't get much sleep, I was so worried.

When morning came, we packed up and headed Tippety south, making a beeline over the hills and camping next night in the mountains. Right while we were starting the fire, a buck jumped out of the brush and stood too scared and surprised to move for a minute. I had a chance to scoop up the .22, and I fired without hardly aiming. That buck made three big jumps, and then just dropped over dead.

Even that didn't rouse Lefty much. I wanted the skin off that deer, because it was the first that I had ever shot, but Lefty hadn't any heart in the work, and finally I said: "I don't really care much about the hide, and it's getting pretty late. . . ."

You know how you say things when you really don't mean them? But Lefty quit right there and took me at my word.

We had broiled venison steak that night— almost the best thing that there is in the world.

Particular when you pick it right off the tree, as you might say. That supper didn't mean much to Lefty. He would forget to eat after a couple of bites and begin to look at something ahead of him.

The next day we came down out of the mountains. The way that Lefty drove poor Tippety was a shame to see. He was in a hurry; he would near have killed a horse that wasn't as tough as Tippety. That buckskin wouldn't drop. The last mile that he had done that day his knees was still coming up high and his step still had a lot of spring and snap to it.

Finally Lefty brought that horse up on the edge of a valley. It was dished out there before you, very pretty and complete. It looked like a picture. Lefty, quite a-thrill, sat there in the rig, and he dragged off his hat, letting the wind ruffle his hair. His face looked mighty queer.

I said: "Lefty, are you maybe sick?"

He said: "This is home!"

And me having been thinking that he would never be bothered with such an idea as "home"! It was a shock to me—the first shock, with a bigger one coming. You would never have tried to tie Lefty down to any one place. He should have belonged to the whole wide world. Now that I saw him weakening, I begun to have a lot of fears of him.

Even Smiler noticed that something was wrong.

He put his paws up on the back of the seat and whined right in the ear of Lefty.

"That's home," said Lefty. "That's Perigord." He said it soft and low, the way that you would speak of your dead mother, or a couple of dead aunts, maybe.

There were hills, pretty steep on the sides, but not too steep for the cows to be grazing along them, sprinkling little spots of color all over. Outside of those hills, there were mountains right in a circle all around you, going right up to snow all the year 'round. Underneath the hills, that valley spread out smooth and gentle, coming down to the banks of a river that went moseying along, taking its time, looking at everything, spreading itself out for a nap in a string of ponds, and then turning in for a real sleep in a jim-dandy lake that was about half of the length of that valley. Then it started on again, sneaked around the lower corner of the valley, and dived under the hills and the foundations of those mountains, so that it could get away.

All over the floor of that valley there were patches of trees stuck down here and there. Inside of every patch, nearly, you would see the roof of a house—red or yellow, mostly. A pair of white roads streaked along on each side of the river; down by the side of the lake there was a little town standing. It was wonderful how clear you could see it, looking down like that, in spite of the mist rising up out of the valley like steam in a glass.

You could look right through the mist and see the town, as if it was lying behind a handful of blue smoke. You could see the sun reflecting from the steeple of the church; the weathercock on the top of it was just a little diamond of light. You could see the streets, too, and the houses, a good ways apart from one another, with orchards in every big back yard.

Lefty looked more foolish than a man ought to, just on account of a little old town like that. Then he threw up a hand and hid his eyes. "I'll never go back!" said Lefty, almost crying.

He give Tippety a jerk, turned him away, and drove him right on down the road. Pretty soon we had a wheel in the ditch at one side of the road, so that I could tell that he was driving blind. It scared me, too, the way that it does when you see a growed-up man acting like that.

It was pretty lucky that we didn't hit any trees or a rock, because, though Lefty was looking straight ahead of him, he didn't see anything. Tippety came into a little round clearing with a wall of trees all around him and, being tired, stopped.

"Hello," said Lefty, as cheerful as a man that had an arm cut off. "Hello, here we are in a place made to order for us. A pretty good camp, eh?"

I didn't stop to find out if he meant what he

said. I was so glad to see him *trying* to be happy, that I tumbled out of that rig and had the fire started in about a jiffy. I rattled the pans and the pots out from the back of the buggy.

All at once I saw that Lefty was standing there with one of the tugs in his hand, stabbing away to make a knot and tie it up, but not making progress at all. Then he let the tug fall, and he said: "You start things. I'll be back in a minute. I think that I saw a rabbit out yonder that would look pretty good in a stew tonight."

He went off without his rifle, and a man don't go shooting rabbits with a revolver, unless he had lots of ammunition and is an extra special fine shot, which Lefty was not. I saw right away that he was going to go down into the valley, in spite of what he had said.

I sung out as cheerful as I could: "All right, Lefty. But come back quick, because the coffee is gonna be boiled pretty sudden!"

He didn't answer me, only said to Smiler: "Go back! Get away from my heels!"

All the courage and the happiness leaked right out of me. But I kept on bellowing away and singing because I knew that, if I stopped making a noise once, I would be lost. I had a supper just about cooked up when I had to stop because of the way that Smiler was acting. He had come sneaking back into the clearing with his tail between his legs, and he lay down under a tree, put his head down on his paws, and flattened out his ears. Every now and then he gave a shiver like he was sick at the stomach.

I went over to him finally and, though he never did like me to touch him, I couldn't help reaching down and patting him a mite. Well, sir, that dog raised up his head and looked at me with terrible sad eyes, and he actually give my hand a lick or two. Not that I mattered. But being down low like that, a little attention from even me, helped him not to feel quite so sick. Well, I was just as sick as he was. Or sicker. I figured that here was the plumb end of our good times.

Finally I left the coffee to boil and went along with Smiler, who had followed me to the edge of the clearing and whined. I said: "Sure, you come along, too, if you want to. He's a lot more likely to come back for you than he is for me."

Smiler was ahead of me in one jump—not too far though. He just danced along on his toes, like he was held on a leash, and he kept looking back to me to tell me please to get a wiggle on and hurry along, or we would lose him. I let Smiler lead along.

It was turning dusk. The sun was down. The west end of the valley was dark, but there was still some red behind my back, and the lake in the hollow hand of the valley was like an apple, yellow and red, very dim.

We went down the slope and hit the town. The

streets were all dark. We came along past the houses with their windows lit, the sprinklers all swishing on the lawns, a different smell out of every garden and a different smell out of every kitchen. You could tell just what was happening—cabbage—and the best of all was bacon, which is the sweetest thing there is when you are that hungry.

Then Smiler ducked back quick behind me, and I knew that Lefty must be just ahead.

Chapter Seventeen
THE GIRL HE LEFT BEHIND HIM

It was scent telling Smiler that was as far as it was safe for him to go. When I got to the place where the dog had stopped, I couldn't see a thing. There was just a hedge in front of a little house. But when I slid through a hole at the bottom of the hedge, I saw him right away. He was standing up close to a window at the side of a house. I slipped around behind him, very soft, to see what was holding him there. There was a kitchen, and a woman walking around inside of it.

I got just a flash of her sailing by the window with a steaming pan of something in her hands. Lefty folded his hands over his face and dropped his head. I thought it was most likely his mother, or someone that he should have been taking care

126

of instead of bumming around the way that he was doing.

Then I saw that woman come sashaying back across that window again with a heaped-up white bowl of something good to eat, her face red and happy, the back of her white apron all sailing out behind her. Right then all of my sympathy for Lefty jumped away from me; I almost had a contempt for him. It was not a woman at all; it was only a girl, only a pretty girl, with her hair done up into a knot at the back of her head, all flushed up and happy because she was taking into the dining room something that was good to eat.

This was the thing that had brought Lefty a hundred miles across the mountains; this was the thing that had made him run off from Smiler and me and come down into the valley. A girl! I have seen boys act foolish about little girls. But a man acting that way about a growed-up girl was something almost too much for me. I tried to make it out, but I couldn't.

"Jiminy! Lefty, what's the matter? You've pretty near broke the heart of Smiler," I said, going up to him.

He didn't give a start; he was only sort of dazed. He took me by the arm, and he led me over by the hedge, saying: "I don't know what to do, kid. I don't know whether to go in and see her. . . . I don't know whether I'd dare to do that!"

I said: "If she's as mean as that, let's get out of

this here Perigord and get away into the mountains again."

"You don't understand," said Lefty. "She's not mean. Only, she's too good to be true. Too good for any man to stand up and lie to her. The way that I would have to lie if I went in to see her."

"Then don't lie," I answered.

He *did* give a start then. Finally he said: "I'm not sure but that you're right. And yet . . . how could I do it? How could I go in there and tell her what a useless, worthless loafer I am?"

I said: "Here's Smiler. Are you going to speak to him?"

He answered: "The devil with Smiler."

It pretty near finished Lefty, so far as I was concerned. You wouldn't believe that a man like him could talk that way. But he was all upset. It was easy to see that he was in love. From all that I can make out, there ain't anything half so unreasonable and mean and selfish as that. Poor Smiler stayed there in the background wagging his tail in a hopeful way every time he heard the voice of his boss. He never got noticed.

Lefty was thinking things over. At last he said: "We've got to bluff our way through. Look here . . . you're a boy who I've been giving music lessons to. Singing lessons . . . and your rich parents, in San Francisco, have sent you out to me through the mountains to recuperate . . . you understand?"

128

"Why, Lefty," I said, "have I got the lingo that would go with polite folks that have a lot of money?"

"No," he admitted. "That's right."

"And do I look as if I had ever needed any recuperating in my whole life?"

"Don't make things any harder for me than they are," said Lefty. "It's not so easy to make up a lie that will stand telling in front of her." Then he thought for a minute, and he said: "Yes, that will have to do. You have had scarlet fever and been pretty sick. And the doctor wanted you to have a long vacation and have your strength built up. You haven't a very polite lingo, as you say. We'll explain that. Your father is a farmer in the San Joaquin valley. His brother died, left him a lot of money . . . and he went to San Francisco and built himself a fine house there."

"Why do I have to be rich at all?"

"Because your dad has to foot the bill for this vacation. Why else would I be wandering around through the hills with a kid of your age? You understand?"

I said that I did.

"Did you ever hear much about San Francisco?" he said.

I remembered something out of a geography book. "It is out in Mexico," I told Lefty. "They have the bullfights there and just . . . ."

He gave a groan. "California, you young idiot!

And I haven't much time to tell you about it. But in case she should ask you any questions, ever, you remember it is like this." He was so excited that he began to draw a map on the ground with his finger. How could I see that map in the dark? Love makes a man like that, you know, sort of crazy.

"Here's a big bay. Berkeley over here. And Oakland. Boats go across. Big ferry boats. Take people to San Francisco. That town is out here on a peninsula with the Golden Gate at the end of it. Some of the big streets are Market Street and Kearney Street. Y'understand?"

My head was spinning, but I said I did.

He stood up with a big sigh of relief. "All right," he said. "Then we'll go in. Her name is Kate Perigord. One of her ancestors was the frog that found this valley and settled it a long ways back. He gave his name to it. And you've heard me speak of her often, you see?"

We were almost back to the house by that time.

"And what about Smiler?" I asked.

"Come along with me. Here, Smiler. Come here!"

Smiler just turned himself inside out at being taken back into the company of his boss. He wiggled his tail so hard it made his head all shake, he was that glad. He wiggled so hard that, when we stood on the porch, his paws kept moving a little and scratching. And Lefty rang the bell.

"There's the boy with the milk," sang out a girl's voice. "I'll give him fits for being so late, you better believe!"

"It's her," said Lefty, very hoarse. "Kid, be my true friend . . . you stand here and let her see you first, will you?"

Now, wasn't that disgusting? But I never seen a woman yet that ever made me back up, excepting Aunt Claudia, who had the right of whacking me, and used it so good and plenty. Down come this girl with her heels tapping along the hall, and pretty soon the door was snatched open.

"Jimmy Murphy," she sings out, "you little rascal, what made you so late with . . . oh, you're not Jimmy Murphy at all, are you?"

Well, it was pretty easy. Even when she yanked the door open and acted like she wanted to eat me, you could tell that she didn't really mean nothing by it. Her voice kept as soft as anything. And now she was laughing down at me and blushing a little. It seemed a lot more natural for her than the other way of acting. She was what you might call pretty. She had yellow hair, quite a lot of it, and blue eyes, and altogether she looked healthy and fine. I didn't feel near so hostile toward her as I would've felt to any other girl, hardly. I pulled off my cap, and I said: "Are you Miss Perigord?"

She said that she was. And then I stepped back a little.

"A friend of mine is here that wants a lot to see you," I said.

Lefty came up a step with his hat crumpled all up in his hands. He just said: "Kate!"

She leaned a hand against the door and said— "Billy"—in a whisper.

Turning around quick, I called Smiler. For the first time in his life, that dog—dog-goned if he didn't mind me!—came down the steps along with me.

The door closed when I got down to the foot of the steps; I didn't have to turn around to see whether Lefty was inside or not. I just knew. What beat me more than almost anything was for her to call him Billy. I knew a pie-faced butcher's son in Gunther that was called by that name. We had a good fight once, and what I give him was enough to cure him of a name like that. There is only one thing worse—Willie. I never could understand why women got to put a "y" or an "ie" on the end of a name. What would I have thought, say, if Lefty had called the Smiler "Smilie"? You can't beat womenfolks. They are naturally queer and have to take roundabout ways to get at everything!

I sat down on a stone in the garden, and Smiler came right up and pressed against my knee. Now and then he would give a quick look up and give his tail a waggle, like he was saying: "Well, you're still here. I got you still, and you're something, though you ain't very much." Then he would fix himself again, all rigid, and stare at that door, saying as plain as day: "Why the devil don't he come out? What's holding him? Say, Sammy, shall we go in and see if he's in trouble?"

Chapter Eighteen
SMILER TAKES THE FLOOR

The door of the house busted wide open, and the girl ran all the way down the steps. "Heavens!" she exclaimed. "How rude I have been! And where could he have gone?"

I got up and came into the light. She caught my arm and took me into the house.

"I don't know how it was," she said. "The wind must have slammed the door, and so you were shut out. And I was so excited about seeing Billy again. . . ."

Oh, well, what was the use? You could see that she had been crying. There were two streaks down the front of her face. It wasn't the heat of the kitchen stove that had made her red and shining.

She carted me down the hall, saying that she had a room where she would be awful delighted to have us, and then: "Why, Billy, you haven't told me the name of your pupil?"

There was one thing about Lefty's lying that

you had to admit. If it wasn't so exciting, it was mighty quick, at least. He had been saying "how do you do" to that girl and hugging her—and, also, he had been cried over some. Yet he had managed to tell about me, all in between the important spots of what was happening to him. I appreciated that real well.

A wild look in Lefty's eyes told me that he was stumbling over a little thing like a name. No, it wasn't that which was bothering him, but a great big lot of useless emotion—love—that he was packing around loose inside of him. So I cut in quick and easy and said that I was Sam Jackson, and that I was pleased to meet her, which she was the same to me. We went up the stairs. The bathroom was here—and our door was right next, so it would be handy—and would we mind a double bed? No, we wouldn't—and how stuffy the room got with the window down—which she raised, or started to, only Lefty beat her to it. They gave each other terrible sickening smiles while that was going on. . . . Anyhow, we got up to the room safe. And then would we wash our hands and come downstairs, because the boarders were all through with their supper by this time, and there would be a pair of places laid for us?

Then she noticed Smiler. He had turned himself so small that you would hardly see him. All he wanted to do was to disappear complete, if only he could just stay around at the heels of his boss.

134

He had managed to sneak in through the front door and trailed us right along.

"I forgot," said Lefty, real cruel. "I forgot that you don't allow dogs in the house."

"I can put him out in the back yard to keep company with old Bruno," Kate said.

"We have no muzzle for Smiler," I put in quick, seeing Lefty look wild again.

"Oh," said Kate, "is this a fighting dog?" She lifted her eyebrows and pulled herself together just as though she had said: "Poison."

It made me mad—awful mad. Now, what good is a dog for, if it won't fight? I saw red when I saw that look on her face, and I couldn't help busting in: "No, ma'am, he ain't a fighting dog . . . he just inhales the other dog, and that's all there is to it. There wouldn't be much pain for Bruno."

Lefty gave me one terrible look, as if to say: "Now you have stabbed me to the heart!"

"Hm-m-m!" said the girl. "He doesn't look so terrible vicious."

"Ma'am," I said, "a sawed-off shotgun is mighty peaceful-looking, too, unless you stand in front of the muzzle with a pair of eyes looking down at you."

I thought poor Lefty would die. I hardly cared if he did. I was just wild to think of him turning against old Smiler like that for the sake of what? A girl! You wouldn't believe it if you hadn't been right there to see.

"As dangerous as that?" said Kate Perigord. "Well, I just don't believe you. Nice old doggie, you're not so savage, are you?" She stretched out her hand and leaned over. . . .

"*G-r-r!*" growled Smiler, and seventeen green devils jumped right up and shined out of his eyes. All the fur along his back stood up so's you could see the skin under it.

"Smiler!" Lefty yelled.

Good old Smiler gave one quick glance at his boss' face and one quick waggle of his tail. Then he turned around again and faced the girl. He knew she was dangerous. Don't you tell me that he didn't. He had seen her take his Lefty right in her hand, snatch him into the house, and keep him there some mighty long seconds. He liked her about five hundred times less than he had liked Tiger.

"You don't have to speak to him like that, Billy," she said. "I am not afraid of him."

Now, wouldn't that beat you? She was big enough, you know, but sort of soft like a baby around the mouth and the chin. Taking her all in all, she looked like the kind that would cry easy and laugh easy. But here she was not backing up a step from that man-eating dog.

She said: "I have never hurt that dog. And he won't hurt me. There's no reason why he should."

You see how she reasoned? Like a baby! She hadn't hurt poor Smiler, when all she had done was take away his boss, which was more to him than both lungs and his fighting teeth.

"Good old boy!" said Kate Perigord. "I am not afraid of you. I think you're just a sweet old thing. . . ."

It was disgusting to hear that talk; it was something else to see the devil in that dog's eyes.

"Kate," said Lefty, "don't . . . for heaven's sake! I tell you . . . the brute is really dangerous . . . but if you insist . . . I'll sort of introduce you. . . ."

She staggered me again—like a swift right hook coming when you're expecting a straight left. She said: "Just leave it to me, Billy. *I'm* not worried by your silly dog. I've never been bitten yet. And I won't be bitten now by a dog that I've never harmed. Good old Smiler . . . that's a sweet puppy . . . will you shake hands with a new friend and get a . . ."

"Grr-r-r-ah-h!" growled Smiler, backing into Lefty's legs.

He stepped out of that quick, though. Perhaps he was lifted at the end of Lefty's toe. I give you my word that just for growling a little at that girl, Lefty kicked that dog right across the room, throwing him into the opposite corner.

It happened that I was standing in that corner. Smiler gave me one look and one waggle as he crushed up against my legs, whining—saying as plain as day: "Stick with me, Sammy. The boss is plumb crazy. Stick with me and help to see

137

me through. But I won't see that snake around him. . . ."

I was so wild that I couldn't even yip for a minute. Just as I was about to turn loose and blast that Lefty away from a lot of poor ideas, and maybe hurt that girl's ears with a kind of vocabulary that she never heard before—well, right then I was stopped by somebody else taking the wind out of my sails.

It was the girl!

She said, all trembling because she was so mad: "Billy Chelton, I've never seen such a brutal thing in my life! And I'll never see such a thing again. You . . . you ought to be horsewhipped . . . if I ever were a man . . . kicking a poor little puppy senseless. . . ."

There was seventy pounds of that puppy standing between my legs, with a weather eye out for Lefty, just shaking with eagerness to put a tooth in the girl that was standing up for him. . . . It was just flabbergasting!

"Oh, Kate," said Lefty, "I love that dog better than my own flesh. How can you talk like that about him? Only, I really thought that the white devil might hurt you. . . ."

"Stuff!" said Kate. "It is brutal treatment which has ruined the disposition of that poor little dog!"

Then, it seemed to me that I got a great big light busting all over my mind; I saw why that girl loved that scamp, Lefty. She was one of them that can't love anything but a lost cause. And Lefty was a lost cause, you see. This mean dog was a lost cause. And the meaner and stranger and wilder things was, the more she would love them.

Chapter Nineteen
A GREAT IMAGINATION

When an idea like that comes bulging its way into your head without being invited, it sort of takes your wind. I only followed in a general way what happened after that. Kate got more merciful to Lefty when he called the dog over to him. Smiler came over and had seventeen conniption fits. When Smiler wanted to make friends and tell his boss how sorry he was that he had done anything wrong, he would go through all of his tricks. He would walk on his front legs and then on his hind legs, lie down like dead, turn a somersault over in the air, and always wind up by sitting up and begging. He did all those things, one right after another, very quick.

Lefty just gave him a grin and said: "Good boy, Smiler!" That was the signal that everything was forgiven. Smiler dropped down on his haunches, began to sweep the floor with his tail and worship Lefty with his eyes.

Kate saw that she had followed the wrong lead. It was pretty nice, I had to admit, to see the way she said that she was sorry that she had said so many things, some of them not being deserved.

We all went down to the supper table, with the Smiler quite considerably in the house and in the party. I should say that he was. He was extremely polite to Miss Perigord, having had his lesson. Smiler would stand around out of her way and not even notice that she was in the same room with him. The more distant he got, the more friendly *she* got. She would drop down on a knee while she was passing back and forth from the dining room to the kitchen. She would call him pet names, which made him roll his eyes over at Lefty mighty sick. She would offer him cake, or even meat, but Smiler wouldn't notice her any more than if she wasn't there at all.

"I *can't* understand it," said Kate. "I've never had a dog treat me like that before, and I won't stop until I've found out what there is about me that he doesn't like. Oh, I know what it is! He doesn't like white. And white is a strain on the eyes, isn't it? I'll see."

You couldn't stop her. She tore out of the room.

Lefty went off eating, and he got up and began to pace up and down the room. He said: "Now, you're a bright kid, Sammy, but I want you to tell me, man to man, did you ever see a girl like her before?"

I could only grunt.

"Tell me the truth! Can you see anything wrong

in her? I just ask you that . . . could you *change* anything about her? No, you could not. Her hair and her eyes match just exact. And her height is perfect, for me, and she's twenty-two, which is the perfect age for a girl . . . young, but not kiddish . . . full of sweetness. What a heart of gold she has! Tell me, Sammy, could you imagine her improved?"

What could you say? Or what could you do except to pity a man that had it as bad as all that?

Back comes the girl in another minute. She had put on something in green and yellow gingham very easy to look at, and crinkly. "Now see if he still doesn't like me!" said Kate.

As hard as the girl looked at Smiler, Smiler looked over to his boss, and his boss looked at Kate. It was like a circle. Smiler wouldn't let himself see that girl for half of a second. He had been kicked on her account once, and he wasn't taking any chances!

Finally I told her that it was no good feeling so bad; nobody in the world could do anything with that dog excepting Lefty himself and that I had wasted more hours than you could shake a stick at, but that it didn't make any difference. She felt a little better after that. We settled down then and finished supper.

It was an extra fine supper. After cooking at campfires, a little home cooking tastes almost too good to be true. As a cook, Kate was something extra. You see, she ran a regular boarding house there and supported herself pretty good. She did all the cooking herself and just had one girl servant to do all the cleaning and such. She was extremely cheerful about it, telling us what a fine gang of boarders she had, making her work nothing more than a lark, because they was all so nice. If she could afford it, she would want to keep them all for nothing, just for the pleasure of their company.

There was a schoolteacher who knew about everything that was to be knowed, and, though she was only about forty years old, she was teaching the eighth grade, so you could see how clever she was. There was a female doctor who was the grand prize, who stayed there because Kate did little extra things for her such as running errands any time of night or day, carrying up her breakfast tray to her bed, and waiting on her. There was an old building contractor who had retired from business; he was just lying around, taking things easy; he could tell the most wonderful yarns about what he had done. There was a bricklayer who was a fine fellow, Kate said, outside of getting drunk every Saturday and spending all his money, owing her about three weeks' rent. There were six others, about the same kind.

It was a sight to see her telling how grand all her boarders was. Every once in a while Lefty, who was listening very serious, would wrinkle up the side of his face that was towards me and wink. I could hardly keep a straight face.

After a while, I went on up to bed, and Lefty and Kate stayed downstairs. Right in the middle of getting into bed I remembered that poor old Tippety was up there in the hills with half of his harness on. I slid out and dressed and sneaked out of the window. I got to Tippety in about an hour.

You would have laughed to see him. He had that harness all wrapped around his legs. It had tangled him up and tripped him, and he had fallen down. Almost any other horse would have set to work to kick right out of that harness, but Tippety was no fool. He just lay there and he had eaten away all the grass that was near him by the time I come up.

He give me a whinny as much as to say that he hadn't seen anything better than me for a long time. I got his legs unwrapped, after a while, and he got up and gave a run around and kicked up his heels. He was a fine little horse, tough as iron and nice as pie! When he had run the kinks out of his legs, he came back to me and stood there and let me harness him up. I drove him back down the valley to the town. I took him into the first livery stable and left him mighty snug, stamping in his stall and trying to stand on his nose in the feed box, he was so anxious to get that barley all down in one swallow.

I wanted Lefty to know what I had done, so I hurried back, feeling pretty proud of myself. Thinking he would be about ready to go to bed by this time, I went around to the back of the house to climb up over the kitchen porch. Just as I turned around the edge of the hedge, I saw them sitting in a hammock stretched between a couple of apple trees with the moon throwing a black dappling of shadow all over them. It came over me that they would think that I was spying on them, and I would rather have died than to have them think anything like that. So I dropped right there onto the ground and flattened out there.

Kate was saying: "That must have been wonderful, Billy dear."

"Oh, no," said Lefty. "But the gate receipts were rather pleasant."

"I suppose that the papers were filled with the story the next day, about how well you played!"

"I paid no attention to that. These little provincial reviews, Kate. . . ."

"Oh, but people in big towns are just the same as people in little towns."

"Don't you think so. When we're married, our first long stop will be Paris, and there I'll show you the difference."

"Paris!" cried Kate.

"As soon as the kid is really well and I've sent him home."

"He doesn't seem sickly, does he?"

"No, he doesn't. But that's the way with lung trouble. Very often there's a sort of hectic flush. . . ."

I couldn't wait any longer there. I began to worm my way back behind the hedge—mighty hot. I was so ashamed of the whoppers that Lefty was telling that poor girl. I would never have believed it! Telling lies to some is real fun, because it's a sort of a sporting proposition, but lying to her was all the world just like taking candy away from a baby.

As fast as I could shinny up the column on the front porch, I got back into the room. When Lefty came in, I breathed deep and regular like I was asleep. I didn't dare to wake up, because, if I had, I would have told him to his face just what a low sneak and crook that he was.

Chapter Twenty
"UNCLE HARRY"

I begun to feel a bit different about him right away, though, because, when he seen that I was asleep, he went around undressing in the dark and stepping very soft, which always make more noise than walking right out loud, because of the floor squeaking.

In the dark, things kept getting into his way: first he would bump into Smiler and cuss him in a whisper, and then he would ram into a chair and it would squeak terrible loud. I would hear him standing still and holding his breath for fear that noise might've wakened me. Finally he banged his toe into the leg of the bed. I could tell that it was his toe, because I could hear him draw in his breath real sharp, and then he went hopping around on the other bare foot. Smiler followed, whining, and Lefty whispered: "If you make a noise and wake the kid, I'll kill you, you fool."

I couldn't help laughing then. I swallowed the noise, but my shaking started the bed to squeaking a little. Pretty soon the light snapped on, and, before I could close my eyes, Lefty seen me laughing. I tried to get out of his way, but he was quicker than lightning and got me by the neck.

"You are the sort of stuff," said Lefty, "that the hoofs of the devil are made out of. That's how tough you are!"

That was all he said and all that he did. He was like that—gentle when you expected that he would be rough.

The next morning after breakfast, Lefty went down to the stable to see Tippety, and I stayed behind. Kate brought in a big pan of peas from the garden, and I helped her shell them. She said: "You're from San Francisco, then?"

I said that I was.

"And where do you live in San Francisco?" asked Kate.

There were two streets that Lefty had named. I picked the first one.

"Market Street," I said.

"Oh," said Kate.

San Francisco had hills. I could remember that Lefty had said that.

"Yes, we live out on the hills," I said. "And from our garden it is pretty slick to look out at night and see the ferry boats all lighted up and going across the bay."

"I hope that you have a nice big garden," said Kate. "Because sometimes there isn't much room for such things in a city."

"Oh, yes," I said. "We have about two acres, all set out in roses and such. And a lot of trees, too, in front. So's you can't see the house from the street."

Kate looked up from the shelling of the peas and there was something behind her eyes.

"Are you smiling?" I asked, beginning to feel a little sick.

"I suppose that you've never seen San Francisco?" she said.

The bottom was cut away from under me. I only wanted some place to drop into.

"Have you?" I asked her.

She smiled at me to take out the sting, then she said: "Yes, I went out there last spring."

I could only gasp.

She went on: "Market Street hasn't hills,

Sammy, and there aren't big residences along it."

I couldn't have got out a word for a million dollars. I was never in my life more willing to die. But she wasn't the kind to leave a man feeling like that, and she went right on: "Don't be embarrassed about it, Sammy. I suppose . . . I suppose that poor Billy put you up to it?"

Moistening my lips, I managed to say that Billy hadn't anything to do with it. She shook her head, held up a finger at me, and smiled very sad and kind.

"You needn't protect him," said Kate. "You needn't protect him from me. Only . . . I wonder what in the world he is doing, traveling across the country with a boy like you. Is it something bad? But don't try to answer me if it hurts you to talk about these things."

It was sort of the unexpectedness that hit me all in a heap. It was the quick turn around the corner that knocked me flat. You would have thought that all she ever did in her life was to be cheated by folks, and work for them, and be talked over big by maiden-lady schoolteachers and female doctors and things. Then you found out that she did have a brain and that she did see through things—all the clearer because she didn't pretend to be wise.

"But," said Kate, "shouldn't you be home and at school? And have you any parents to worry about you while you're wandering around the world?"

She said it very affectionately, not smiling and pleased with herself for having run down to the earth that lie that I had been telling her, but wonderfully simple and wonderfully kind, as if she loved me. Not on account of myself—but like Smiler, interested in me because I belonged to Lefty.

I said at last: "I can't lie to you any more. But I just don't want to talk about things, because it don't seem fair to Lefty."

She didn't press me a bit. She just nodded. Then seeing me fidgeting, she gathered back all the peas that I was trying to shell—and mashing, instead. She said: "I suppose that you'll want to go tell Billy what has happened. When you tell him, Sammy, will you please tell him, too, not to run away? Because I don't care if he has fibbed a little. I've given over caring about that."

There were tears in her eyes when she said it. All I wanted to do was to kill Lefty, kill all the men in the world, and then to jump into the river last of them all. Because it was easy to see that you could probably hunt all over the world, but you would never again be able to find anybody one half so good and so kind and so true as Kate Perigord.

I did what she said. I found Lefty in a little back room behind the stable, playing cards with two men. When he saw me, I gave him the wink, and he came out to me and broke up the game.

"What's happened?" he asked. And then he turned me around to the light and studied me.

"She found out, then," said Lefty.

I told him what had happened as quick as I could, because it wasn't nothing that I wanted to linger over. He was struck all of a heap.

"I can never hold up my head before her again," Lefty said. "I can never face her again!"

I told him what she had said in the finish, particularly how she had looked, and I said: "Why, Lefty, there ain't any reason why you should be ashamed. Because she knows you right down to the ground, better than I could ever know you. Everything that is bad in you, she sees or at least guesses. It don't make her like you any less, does it? If I was you, I would tell her everything that I had ever done that was bad, and after you had confessed it, you would feel much better!"

He stood there with his hand dangling, very helpless. Then he said, the idea beginning to hit him hard: "Maybe you're right. Yes, you are, and I'm going right now to find her." He took half a dozen steps very bold and big. Then he stopped and called: "You come along with me, Sammy, less this idea should sort of melt out of me and leave me dry again for the first wind to pick up and blow away."

I walked up the street with him, and, as we turned the first corner—*crash!* There was Mr. Johnson, the president of the Orchard & Alfalfa

Bank right in front of us, taking off his glasses and peering very hard at me and at Lefty.

"God bless my soul!" he said. "Has the blind man learned how to see? William Gobert, are you a cheating rascal, after all?"

"*William* Gobert?" said Lefty, as quick as a wink. "No, sir. I am Harry Gobert, poor William's brother. Did you know Will?"

"*Humph!*" said Mr. Johnson. "I suppose that you pass the boy from hand to hand?"

"I do not like this tone, sir," Lefty said, extremely dignified—which he could do it grand.

I said: "Uncle Harry, this is Mister Johnson . . . that man that I told you about, that wanted to be so kind to poor Uncle Will down in . . ."

Lefty seemed to come to himself with a jump. "Indeed!" he said. "Mister Johnson, I have to thank you for your kindness to my unfortunate brother." And he put out his hand.

Mr. Johnson put his behind his back. "Young man," he said, "I've always been a good deal of a fool . . . as we all are like to be on this earth . . . but I hate to be fooled twice by the same man. May I ask where your brother William, the blind man, is at present?"

"In Arizona," Lefty answered, "in Arizona, where the air is dry and so fine for bad lungs. We managed to rake up enough money to send him there. . . ."

"Lungs?" queried Mr. Johnson. "It was a weak

151

heart, the last time I saw him . . . before he made that night exit."

He had jumped right on top of the slip that Lefty had made.

"His heart has always been weak," said Lefty, "but the consumption is a new matter. That is what is dragging him down so fast. And as for the night exit of which you speak . . . the poor fellow was ashamed to face the townsfolk who had filled his pockets so generously the night before."

That was pretty good. As an off-hand, made-to-order lie it wasn't a bad lie at all. But this Mr. Johnson was not an old goat today. He was the bank president, and his eyes was looking right through Lefty, then taking a spell off and prying me apart.

"Everything that you say may be true, young man," he said, "but there is something in your voice that fits in with every wrinkle of my memory of this blind brother of yours. What you say may be perfectly honest and true. If it is, I have not done trying to be of some help to the poor blind man. But I am going to make inquiries at once. If you are lying to me, I shall move heaven and earth to make you sweat for it. Good afternoon!"

And he turned around and went down the street with a nice, quick, springy step like a man who was headed some place, and who knew just where.

Chapter Twenty-One
THE ROAD AGAIN

When he had turned the corner, I said to Lefty: "Well?"

"Back to the stable, kid, as fast as you can trot with me," said Lefty. We headed back that way. "Because," he went on, as we hurried, "what we have to travel in is a buggy with a trotting horse. If they take a notion to light out after us, they have riding horses in this town, and they have some damned fast-looking ones, too."

You couldn't get around logic like that. Those Western towns were real fire, when they got started. They were very easy and lazy, mostly, about hunting down crooks, but when once they got on a tear after you, it was a good idea to make a fast start. They would think nothing of giving you a roll in tar and feathers. If it was anything serious, they stopped all wasting of time by just arranging a little rope around your neck and hoisting you up to swing in the wind and dry out there.

We were both pretty serious, you can believe me!

"If I get out of this town," said Lefty, "with a whole skin, we won't stop in another this side of a hundred and fifty miles." He meant it, too.

In the livery stable, we slapped that Tippety into the harness, tumbled into the rig, spanked him out of the stable, down the back alley, and up past the house of Kate. When I saw that Lefty intended to go right on past, I could only turn and stare at him.

"Lefty," I said, "it ain't possible that you mean to go right on by and not even say good bye to her?"

I could see that he was hard hit, but he didn't say a word. He just whistled a sharp note that he used for calling Smiler. There was a crash of glass, and Smiler sailed right out of a second-story window. That fool dog would have jumped right over a cliff if he had heard the whistle of his boss. He landed in a shrub with a crash, and in another minute he was sitting up in the rig beside us with a couple of cuts on the head and another on the shoulder where the glass had sliced him, but just as happy as a picture to be back there with us on the road, again.

I watched that house for what I was afraid would happen. Sure enough, I was right. Around the corner of the house came Kate Perigord. She didn't stand and stare. She just gave us one look, turned right around, bowed her head, and walked away. So that I knew she didn't need to be told what was happening. There was hardly anybody in the world so understanding as her.

Maybe Lefty knew that she was watching. He didn't say anything and he didn't let on. He stuck out his jaw, and he drove along down that road with the reins just tight enough for him to push on them, as you might say. Tippety clipped along as pretty as a picture, showing off how gay he was. Old Lefty wasn't thinking about anything in the world except that girl that was behind him.

The minute that we was out of the town of Perigord, Lefty doubled right back up the valley, his old trick of doing the unexpected thing. They would expect him, if they give him a chase, to be spinning *down* the valley. But he was away in the other direction, switching off from the main valley road, and cutting into little side paths and twisting alleys. He worked his way toward the mountains, keeping to courses where an automobile wouldn't have dared to follow without busting its springs.

Tippety knocked along as cheerful as ever, but even his spirits was run out by the time we got up the grade. He stopped to blow right close to the place where we had first stopped the night before and seen the valley for the first time all spread out underneath us. We didn't look back now, it was too plumb sad.

Lefty said: "This is the end of everything. You can cheat and dodge around for a long time, but then, when you do become honest, you find out that you still have to cheat and to dodge . . . or else to die. The habit that you make of living is a lot stronger than the heart in you. And because

I've played the fool and cheated a rube town by being a blind man with painted-up eyes, I'll never see Kate again. Never!"

Tippety, having finished blowing, started on again. He was like that. You never had to whip him. As long as he was feeling right, he would go along just as fast as the road would let him go. When he got tired, he would slow up and give himself a blow. He was a great little horse, always turning his head and cocking it a little sideways so as he could watch us while he went nodding along.

Tippety couldn't cheer me. All the heart in me had run down into my boots and wouldn't come up again. Lefty didn't talk any more, and even after we had had our lunch and he begun to chat about something, you could see that he was just forcing himself. We made a point of never meeting each other's eyes; we knew, inside, that things could never be the same and that most of the happiness, somehow, had leaked out of life. Just the same, it seemed to me that I liked Lefty better than ever, though I seen how bad and how weak he was in lots of ways. Partly I pitied him and partly I just liked him awful well, and it seemed to me that I could see right down to the bottom of him. In spite of how old he was and how many things he could do and how brave and how strong he was, he was really more of a boy than me. I don't expect that you can understand me when I say this, because it is a very hard thing to feel and a harder thing to say. Just the same, it is a fact.

That was the most mournful day that we ever had. It was worse than anything that I had ever gone through at Aunt Claudia's house, even the Sundays. Yes, I knew right then that all the rest of my life, even if I was to live to be a hundred, I would never get the thought of Kate out of my head, and the ache all out of my heart.

We came, along in the evening, to a little side road branching off from the main trail that we were following. There was grass growing all over that side road, not the grass of a month or two, but the grass of a year or two. Lefty said that most likely that road would lead off to the wreck or the ruins of a house, and that we would see what it was. I said that, if we went in there, people hunting us would think that house one of the most likely places to look. Lefty said: "You put in your oar too much. Just remember that you're a boy and that I'm a man. I can't be bothered arguing. You do what I tell you to do and shut up the talk!"

I never had had talk like that out of Lefty before. I didn't say anything back, because I knew what was wrong. It wasn't Lefty that wanted to say such things, but it was the sorrow that was in Lefty.

We came in through the old road and saw the

house; it was a regular old ripper, I can tell you, about sixty years old. It was big, had two stories, and a part of the roof had fallen in. The first thing that happened when we went inside through the door that had fallen down, Lefty's foot went right through the floor. That was how rotten the wood was, if you understand what I mean. Anyway, there was plenty of rotten old wood to make a fire out of. I ripped it away and brought along great big armfuls of it. It burned up like paper. There we cooked our supper; I washed up the tins afterwards. It was the first time that Lefty hadn't offered to help me; he just sat there and didn't even smoke, he was so low and so sick.

After a while it begun to rain, and we dragged our things under the trees because we didn't want to spend the night in that ratty old house. But it wasn't any use, because that wasn't any common rain. It was a real mountain rain, which is different a lot from low-ground rains. The wind began to squeal and snort and roar, and, the first thing you know, the lightning was rip-ripping across the sky. Finally the wind was driving the rain right through that tree we was under and soaking us to the skin underneath—no easy, lazy rain, but one that came swashing down. Take one step in it and you were as wet as a drowned rat.

We got our stuff together and made for the old house. All the windows downstairs were out, and all the places oozing and dripping with water. We tried our chance of climbing up the stairs. They held pretty good, only one of the steps giving way.

Upstairs, it was better, because the roof of that old house had a pretty good overhang to it, and it sheltered those upper windows a good deal. We brought all our junk up there, rolled out our blankets, and turned in. Poor little Tippety came to the door downstairs and gave us a call to please let him come in, too. You would laugh to have heard him! Even Lefty and me, wet and mean as we felt, we had to laugh.

There ain't anything so tiring as sorrow. I just lay awake for a minute or two, listening to the skittering of the bugs and the other things that rain had driven into the house, and then I was sound asleep.

I thought it was the stillness that woke me up, at last, on account of the rain having stopped and only a dripping going on in the night. There was light in the room, too, account of the moon shining very clear. Pretty soon I saw that I wasn't the only one that was awake. Lefty was raised up on one elbow and listening. He turned his head over toward me, put his hand on me, and gave me a grip but didn't say a word.

It wasn't the silence only that had waked me up. It was the feel of danger coming that had aroused me. And now I heard a *creak* somewheres in that old house—and my heart turned over about a hundred times in a second!

Chapter Twenty-Two
THE RETURN OF THE MONSTER

I could only watch Lefty and wait for orders from him. He had drawn a revolver, and now he was up on his knees, looking around him. Pretty soon he begun to wriggle over toward the door. In another minute, I could hear a little *scratch* and *squeak,* like a man whose foot had slipped a mite on a step and come down too heavy.

I got hold of my .22. It wasn't much of a gun; it wouldn't knock a man down, like the slug of a .45, but it would punch a hole in them just as good. The only thing was to pick the right place for the drilling of the hole. It was loaded. I saw to that. I freshened up my grip on it, and I prayed that, if Lefty missed, I wouldn't. Only, I hoped that it wouldn't be Mr. Johnson, the bank president.

Just then I saw the spot of moonshine on the floor wiped out. I looked around, wondering how any cloud could have been blown across it so fast. And there in the window I saw the big, bunchy shoulders of Jake and the glitter of the gun that he pointed at Lefty. Smiler was as quick as me; he let out a snarl and dived for that window—just a white streak of dog! It wasn't at the dog, though, that Jake fired. When he shot, Lefty dropped on

160

his face without a sound. Smiler leaped at that window, and the gun blared right in his face. And Smiler was gone!

Jake sang out: "It's all right, boys! Come on! I've finished the job!"

Feet begun stamping in the hall. And there was I left all alone so quick, with Lefty and the Smiler down in one wallop.

But first thing you know, Smiler got up, staggering. I let out a yell and jerked up the .22 to take my aim, and I got that aim good, and my hand was fine and steady. I told myself that here was where I sent a bullet drilling right through his head, because I was that sure of myself that I didn't even bother about really trying for his body. I was just curling my finger on the trigger when something came looming big in front of the sights and blocking out the moonlight. Then I was knocked galley west.

What he threw I never knew. All I did know was that I went skidding up against the wall, and, when I got up, telling myself that I didn't dare to be knocked out, Lefty was already on his feet. He had got up while I was taking aim. When my yell took Jake's eye that was Lefty's chance.

He had lost his gun when he was dropped, and he just jumped in at that monster with his bare hands—the grandest thing that you ever saw. Jake fired, but I knew that he had missed, because, as he came in, Lefty had dodged like a man doing a fast step in a buck and wing. The next minute I could feel the jar of his fist against the long jaw of the hunchback.

He was hurt so bad that the revolver *clanged* on the floor, and he put up his big hands in front of him to defend himself. He was stunned and blind and helpless with that punch, and those great big arms just hung loose. Jake slumped down on one knee, with his horrible mouth open.

Where was Smiler? His head had cleared right at this minute, but he seemed to know that his boss was handling that one man good enough. Smiler headed for the two new ones that came through the door—and charged. Smiler would have got one of them—and that would have finished everything—but his feet slipped on the wet floor, and the next minute one of them men kicked him head over heels the whole length of that room.

There was nothing but me, then, to guard Lefty's back. I might have done it, if I had used my wits and the gun right. Instead, I went sort of crazy, going in and swinging that rifle like it was a club. It cracked one of them on the head. He went down—but he went down on top of me and squashed me flat.

Lying there, trying to struggle out, I saw the other man grab Lefty around the body. Lefty tried to struggle free. I saw Jake rise up from his knee with the stunned look gone from him, and ten devils danced in his eyes again. His gun was gone, but he had a knife. I saw the flicker of it. Lefty did, too, and grabbed the knife arm of Jake. . . . There seemed to be no use—we were both lost. I didn't want to look, to see Lefty murdered like that, with no chance. Only my eyes were glued to that picture. I couldn't take them away.

Then Jake struck home. I heard Lefty groan, then his body slumped through the hands of the man that had held him all this while—the sneaking rat of a man that had held Lefty from behind. Jake wasn't done yet. He kneeled down there on the floor, grabbed Lefty by the hair, and stabbed him again—I fainted then.

When I came to, I was sort of hanging over Jake's arm. The other two were harnessing up Tippety, and they tumbled me into it with Jake. Behind us, they threw in Smiler, with his four legs tied and a rope drawed tight around his muzzle.

Then the others got onto two horses and led the third horse that belonged to Jake. We started on down the road. They didn't even stop to make sure that they had stole everything that belonged to Lefty and to me, because Jake kept telling them to hurry along, looking back over his shoulder, because, he kept saying, that they was not the only ones that was searching for Lefty and me that night.

What had happened was that they had heard—happening to be in the valley—about the posse that was going to hunt through the mountains for the fake blind man that played the violin. Jake had managed to figure everything out, and then beat the posse to the goal they was hunting for. Nobody could have been more pleased than Jake was with that night of work. He kept laughing and rolling around in the seat while he was driving Tippety along like mad.

Once the roll of the rig, turning around a corner sharp, threw me against him. He caught me by the throat, quick and very hard. I could feel that hand of his, bigger than human, wrapping clean around my windpipe. He said: "Don't you worry, son. Your time is coming. But I'm saving you, and I'm saving the dog." And he laughed again.

It wasn't like being afraid to die only. It was a lot worse than that. It was like being afraid to die, and like being most terrible sick, too, at the way of dying. When he said that, I saw that he could hate not only Lefty, but me, too—and even the Smiler, because the two of us, you might say, had belonged to Lefty.

They drove right on until they got over the ridge and onto a trail where no rain had fallen and everything was dry. In the gray of the morning, they pulled up and allowed that they would camp.

The other two done all the work. Jake was the boss. He said: "Turn the dog loose. I want to see how bad a dog he is."

They untied Smiler, and Jake stood off with a

gun in one hand and a club in the other. When Smiler leaped in, he beat the dog over the head and knocked him down. He did that three times, and the last time he knocked him cold.

"Cut the throat of that brute, Pug," said Jake, "so's we can be sure that he won't come to and bother us none. I wished that I had done the same by his boss."

The shorter one of the two took out a long-bladed knife and stooped over Smiler. Something exploded inside of my head and let off a lot of red fireworks. When I came to, there was Pug picking himself up off the ground where I had shoved him, and Smiler lying still as death on the ground.

"Shall I break the kid in two?" whined Pug, just shaking with rage.

"Wait a minute," said Jake. "Kid, come here!"

I made myself go up to him.

He said: "Are you religious?" I said that I didn't know. He asked me if I had gone to church a lot and that sort of thing, and I said that I had—Aunt Claudia having always taken me with no questions asked. Then he said: "Now, look here. If I got to watch you all the time, I can do it. But I had rather trust something to you, if you got a conscience. I ask you . . . would you swear to me, by God, that you would work for me faithful . . . if I leave that dog live?"

I said that I would. I didn't think about no consequences. Even if I had thought, I guess that it would have made no difference, for if Smiler had been took away now that Lefty was gone, I don't know what I would have done.

He said to hold up my hand, which I did. I swore that I wouldn't try to get away from him, that I would work for him faithful, and all he had to do was to promise not to hurt the dog none and leave him all to me.

"Shake on that, kid," he said.

I looked down, and I saw the smear of red across that hand. I couldn't have touched it to save my life.

"Ain't it good enough for you to shake?" Jake yelled all at once, and hit me a clip across the face with the back of his hand that knocked me flat.

Chapter Twenty-Three
THE TRIO

When I came to, I propped myself up and looked around and wondered how it come that I was allowed to be alive. Jake was in a rage, walking up and down with that long, rolling step of his. I knew that he wanted to throttle me. You could have told that by the wriggling of his big fingers.

If there had been a pretty good haul of money, I think that he *would* have finished me off, but, when he and his pair stole what they could grab from us, they were in a mighty hurry. They figured that the men up from the valley would be coming along at any minute and might arrive in time to nab the whole three of them. That was the real reason that they held off and didn't make so good a search as they might have done. There we were with near nine hundred dollars, yet they didn't get their hands on a quarter of it.

What saved my life, as I found out afterward for sure, was their wanting to use me and my singing to collect enough money for the whole three of them to live easy. That was what made Jake keep from killing me right there.

So long as I had to live with the three of them, you can see that I had made a fine flying start out of it. I had shoved Pug down while he was about to finish off poor Smiler, and I had clipped Boston along the head—which he was the third one of the gang—and I had made Jake know that I hated him more than poison.

The only thing left for me in the whole world, as you might say, was Smiler. I got busy over him right away: washed off his cuts, took some tape that I had in my pocket and plastered the edges of the cuts together. He didn't like to have me fussing over him, partly because he was crazy with excitement because he knew that something or other had happened to Lefty, partly because he wanted to get at Jake, and partly because he never liked to be touched at all except by one hand in the world. However, the touch of the water must have felt fine. Pretty soon he just stretched out and lay there. He was a considerable animal, Smiler was. When he was contented and mighty happy, he would close his eyes and lie there and not say anything. When what you done hurt him so bad that it near killed him, he didn't whine or jerk or try to move away. Not him, because he knowed that I was trying to do him some good. He would just open his eyes and look up at me curiously, trying to make out why it was that I hurt him so much. You couldn't beat that dog.

Just as I got finished with him, Pug barked out at me that it was about time for me to leave that fool dog and go rustle some wood. So I had to go along—and Smiler went along with me and hung around while I collected the wood. It was pretty near the greatest thing that you could imagine, having that dog come along with me that way. I wanted to laugh and shout, if it hadn't been for them other things that was weighing down on me.

Smiler right then forgot that there were such people in the world as the rest of them. No, sir, they didn't exist, so far as he was concerned. That beating didn't break his spirit any; he saw that he wasn't apt to do much good by tackling them, and so he would pay no attention to them at all. He stuck close by me, and he watched me and stayed with me, all the time.

At first I was tickled and happy and flattered, but then I saw that he wasn't really fond of me.

He never did any of his tricks to please me, unless I would tell him to do them. He wasn't wagging his tail every minute that I was around, and he never sat down and worshipped me the way that he was always worshipping Lefty. No, he took on with me because I was just something left over out of Lefty's life.

Right now it is about time that I should tell you about the gents that I was with. You know about Jake already, and you're going to know a lot more later on.

The others weren't so important, and they knowed it. They tagged along after Jake to live on the big things that he done.

The one that they called Pug had got his name because once he had been a "pug," and a pretty good one, too. The way Boston put it, Pug had once been good enough to get licked by all the best middleweights in the country.

"Not that he never done no winning," said Boston, "but he moved in good circles, as you might say, and he *never* was licked by no dub. Which is a big consolation."

Pug was made short and thick, and his face was sort of flat, looking more like it had been stamped on a lot than merely punched good and hard. He had a whispering sort of voice, and he had a confiding way in him, as though he was always telling you a secret. Why, he couldn't even tell me to go get some more wood without leaning away over and putting his hand in front of his mouth and winking at me and talking out of the side of his mouth. Just as if he was saying: "Come on, kid. You understand. It's a secret between you and me. Too bad that it has to be done, but as long as it does, maybe that you had better do it right away now." That was the way he talked.

He walked pigeon-toed and swung his shoulders. He always wore a cap on the back of his head and over to one side. He wore an old red and blue sweater, one of the pull-on kind, that was terrible dirty.

Boston was different. You would see by a look that Pug had some pretty good stuff in him. He had been a fighter, and there was still a lot of fight in him. Boston was just a sneak. He was no good; he was so low and so bad that he didn't shock you with his lowness—he just amused you. He didn't shock himself, either—he just amused himself. Quite a lot. This man, Boston, didn't have any other name. Take him altogether, it was hard to see what he was good for. He couldn't work; he couldn't fight. You look back there where I was telling about the battle where Lefty went down and you'll see where I tell how I laid out Boston. No growed-up man had ought to be laid out by a boy like I was. But Boston wasn't ashamed of that. He held no real malice against me at all, no more than he held against everybody.

He just hated everybody a little. You couldn't imagine that he had ever been glad because anybody else was happy, or that he ever had been sad because anybody else had been put into trouble. No, sir, he wasn't the kind that bothered his head about other folks and their ways and their wants. I suppose that Boston had never had a friend in his whole life.

He was made long and lean and light; his wrists were small. His arms had no muscle in them. His hands and his fingers was extreme slender and not made for carrying anything heavy. He would sit for hours and for hours, doing nothing all that time but turning a ring on his finger, a great big seal ring that was too large for him. All the time he would be thinking, and his flat gray eyes would be jumping sideways and up and down.

Boston was along because he was a thinker, more even than Lefty was, more even than Kate was. More than anybody. He would think, and he would think, and he would never be wrong. All of his thinking, though, would never get him to be fond of anybody or ever wanting to do anything for anybody. You understand what I mean? Jake kept him along because Boston flattered him so much, always talking soft around him, and admiring him, always saying how strong Jake was in a quiet, convinced sort of a way.

Only, when he was talking with you by yourself, he would tell you what a fine fellow you were. He would tell me how wonderful I could sing, and how big and strong I was sure to grow up. He would tell you all these things with a very grave face and serious, nodding to himself, as though he had spent a lot of time brooding over that stuff. But when he spoke about the other two to you, he would smile and shrug his shoulders, and there was a spark of fire in his eye, because the only thing that he could really enjoy was stabbing somebody else, when his back was turned. Oh, how he loved that!

Well, it was always interesting to listen to Boston talk, and it was always interesting, too, to watch him. He was just different from everybody else. It was like seeing all that is bad in the world—laziness, cowardice, selfishness, cruelty, and greediness all wrapped together. You knew perfectly that as bad as he talked about the others to you, he talked just that much worse about you to them. You knew that he didn't mean any of the fine compliments that he paid to you, but, just the same, you always couldn't help listening. Because he had a way about him, more even than the way that Lefty had—different, of course.

Well, these three bad men, they made me the cook right away. From that time I had to work pretty hard, because it is a lot more to have three bosses than it is to have one, even if the three were good, and the one was bad.

We plugged away across the mountains for

three days. Then they decided that we would have to try to work the next town.

This is how they did it. They got up into the trees close to the town. Two of them waited there, and Jake unlimbered a pair of crutches and said I would go along with him. Smiler walked right at my heels.

When we came down the street, it was just disgusting. Jake took off his hat and hopped along. Every now and then he would stop, rest himself on one crutch, stick out his hat, and smile at the people that went by. It was queer to see how they would all shy away from that horrible smile of Jake's. But after they had gone on by, they would come back and throw something into his hat, but always without looking into his face again, because one look at that face hurt enough to last for a day or two.

Jake didn't have to use any make-up beyond the crutches. He just looked so terrible that you really didn't see how he could breathe even, without giving himself pain. Though it wasn't a great lot of money that he made this way, he picked up a few dimes and quarters and such, and you could see that he wouldn't have to starve, no matter where he went.

Chapter Twenty-Four
JAKE'S SHOW

It was very hard to watch. He told me to take off my hat and hold it out, too. I couldn't, even though the look in his eyes promised me a good beating when he got me away from that town. He seemed to think that I would try to get away, so he said when there was nobody right in sight: "If you try to run, kid, I'll up and after you. When I get you, I'll give you one squeeze and then break you in two. Now, you hang right onto that idea like a bright boy, because it is worth remembering, and don't you make no mistake!"

I figured that he meant it. There was no doubt but that murder was what he was best fitted for by nature and by liking.

It was a good part of the country that we was in, more hills than mountains. There were ranches and cows grazing on those hills by the tens of thousands. There was mines stuck here and there, and into that town of Crossman the big freighting outfits kept coming and then working back to the mines. It wasn't a big town, and it was all built out of shacks, but the men and the women in it were prime. They held their heads right up in the air like they didn't owe money to anybody. They had the look of work around their faces and in the hang of their arms. You look at the shoulders, too, of a gent that does regular labor, and you will be able to see how they've been pulled and strained a little by the wear and the tear of it. One man out of every two, you wouldn't've minded going into camp with, which is about all that you could say of any of the men.

These fellows hated the sight of Jake, as you could see. Just the same they hauled out their money and left him something. Jake was pretty pleased with himself when he had a small scattering of change in his hat. He said: "Well, kid, I dunno that you and Lefty ever improved on that very special. Did you? This is a pretty good part of the country to work. Well, I'm gonna sit down here, and you tune up your voice and sing, I don't care what, and I'll accompany you!"

"Are you gonna sing, too?" I asked him, because he had a voice like a big toad's.

"I got a musical instrument," he replied, "and here it is."

He took out a mouth organ—a dirty-looking mouth organ, and picked out from it some threads and straws that was lodged there. After that, he sat down cross-legged and fetched that organ a whack across his mouth. Dog-gone me if it didn't make a regular scale as true and pretty as you please.

I gave him another look. It seemed like I must have been mistaken about him, but he just looked up at me, giving me a grin that sent the old shudder home in me. It was like standing by and listening to a monkey play!

"Lead off, kid," he said.

There was nothing that I wanted to do less, but I had sworn to him, and I couldn't back out as late as this. I put my back against the wall, sort of closed my eyes, and hit into the first tune that come into my mind. That tune was the one about the Irish girl in the County of Mayo that was waiting for you, and the rest of that rot.

When I started out singing on that, all at once I got to remembering about poor Kate Perigord and Lefty—and what would have been passing through Kate's mind if she knew? Aye, and by this time most likely she did know, because they must have found Lefty's body and brought it back to Perigord. Well, there was one thing sure. The grave of Lefty never would lack flowers. She would see to that. And inside of her mind how would she feel? Well, as time went on, I knew that Lefty would keep getting greater and greater in the eyes of Kate just because she was one of those that always wanted to see the best that was in everybody. So she would see it in our Lefty.

With all of this busting inside of me, I kept on singing, I don't know how, but with the mouth organ coming in very easy and straight all of the time, it helped me along so that I wouldn't get off the track of the tune at all. Then I felt that a crowd was gathering. I opened my eyes and saw them for myself. There were about fifty folks gathered before I hit the chorus the second time, and that fifty was growing fast. Well, when you stand up there before a crowd like that, it acts sort of funny on you. I couldn't help warming up a little.

Now I would like nothing better than to have you all think that I was extremely true to old Lefty, and that I was grieving pretty bad for him. But how can I make you think that if I step out and tell you the truth—which was that, after I had been singing for a moment or two, I forgot all about Lefty; all that I was thinking about in the whole world was the faces of the men in front of me and wanting to tickle them with that song.

When I slammed through that chorus the second time, I busted out into a buck and wing dance. It was a nice, hard, smooth section of boardwalk that had been done just new, and it was as level and as fine as any stage that you would want to try your steps on. Which I started soft shoeing a part of that dance, and then, after I had danced through a few soft-shoe steps, with my arms swinging free in the gestures that old Lefty had taught me, I lighted in and I gave them a ripping double shuffle that rattled on that sidewalk like a drum being beat.

When I stopped and stood there, panting and laughing at them, they give me a cheer and called me a good kid. That was what I wanted, and that was what I did it for—not at all for the money that they began to rattle into the hat of that swine, big Jake.

You bet that he got his day's haul right there. He was so surprised and so tickled to see how money could be got in that way that he hardly knowed what to do. He gave me another tune, and I went through that. I danced the verse, and I came easy soft-shoeing through the chorus and singing it out. Those gents they just busted themselves laughing and hitting each other on the backs and admiring me very open and fine. They didn't look at what they threw in that hat. That wasn't their way at all; they just dived into their pockets, grabbed what they found there, and chucked it.

Well, I danced about six songs and sang them out. They wouldn't let me go, even when I got tired. That crowd got thicker and thicker, and finally I was so tired that I got old Smiler out and started him off on the tricks that he had done lots of times with me when Lefty was along with us. Smiler liked it, too, it was so much like old times. It would have done you good to see him. Oh, him and me had practiced more times than you could shake a stick at, hours at a time. We had a regular performance that we used to go through, which was something like this: First, old Smiler would come out, growling and seeming to be terrible mad, shaking his head and showing his teeth extreme ferocious. The only way that he would seem to be able to get along would be to stand up and walk on his hind legs, and, of course, I could keep out of his way very easy when he was doing that. Then he would change off and start walking along on his front legs, which is extra hard for a dog to do, but still he proceeded to not want nothing in the world so much as to sink those teeth of his into me.

When he couldn't catch me by walking on his front legs, then he would haul off and come at me throwing somersaults, which he done remarkable well. When he still couldn't locate me that way, he would start after me doing *back* somersaults. They were wonderful to watch him make, because, right up to the time that he landed, it always did look as though he was going to be hit right on his head. After that, he lit in after me, came a-whacking, dived into the air, and looked like he was going to rip my throat right open. Right at the last minute he would do a flip and so he would miss me entirely. After he had lit out after me and missed, he would come back again, until I was dodging a regular shower of dogs that seemed to be coming from all directions. He would be slipping through my arm on one side, diving over my shoulder, skidding between my legs, and always just missing me with those terrible teeth of his.

It was fine exercise for Smiler. Lefty always used to say it was what kept that dog so fit and ready for a fight; it kept him so very nimble that another dog, fighting him, was mostly biting the air until Smiler would use his chance and rip in with a nose or a throat hold.

Those gents in the town of Crossman thought that was extra fine. They shouted and yelled and hollered and whooped and stamped; some of them got very hilarious, sort of, and begun letting off guns in the air.

Finally old Smiler wound up by sailing through the air and landing right on my shoulder. I staggered around under him, because there was seventy pounds of that dog. It made a pretty good close to our show, and I would be ashamed to say how full that hat was of money.

Old Jake, when I give him the wink, dragged himself up and started to climb onto his crutches. Those gents stepped in and give him a hand under each shoulder and held his crutches for him.

"Who is the kid?" sings out one oldish chap with long mustaches.

"He is my son, gents," said Jake.

It gives me a shiver just to think of being that.

"He is, your foot!" said the gent with the red mustaches. "Is a trout the son of a shark? He is not!"

"Shut up, Red!" said somebody else. "Ain't the show good enough for you?"

"I like half the show real well," answered Red, "but I got ideas of my own about the other half!"

I was in hope that Jake would let them see some of the devil in his face, but he was too smart for that. He just hung his head and started off down the street.

The gents hollered to Red: "Why don't you pick on someone with two legs, Red?"

Chapter Twenty-Five
ALONG COMES "JEFF"

When we got out from the crowd, Jake swung down a side alley and away toward the trees till I saw a gent coming along behind us. I told Jake that somebody was trailing us. Jake was a little bothered at that. He stopped and waited for the other man to come up.

He was a tall fellow with a fighting face, very broad across the cheek bones, and with the dark skin and nose of an Indian. I think that there was dark blood in him, too. He couldn't have looked the part so good without there being some of that. He came right up to Jake and said: "Hello, Jake! I see that this game is going pretty well with you!"

Jake gave him a hard look, but said nothing.

"Leave off the crutches and stand on both feet," said the stranger. "I'm a friend. You remember Jeff, back in Denver that time when the two shacks jumped you at the yard and tried to show you . . ."

It seemed to hit Jake all at once. His face

181

lighted up a little, and he stuck out his paw. "Why, Jeff," he said, "I got a rotten eye for faces, and I nearly forgot all about the good turn that you done for me that night."

"Oh, it wasn't much of a turn," said Jeff, "because you had the pair of 'em broke up before I could do much. But right here in Crossman, I got an idea that you and me might be able to do a job that would beat that one all hollow."

"Kid," said Jake, standing up and taking the crutches under one arm, "you skin on ahead. Don't go too fast and lemme keep you in sight all the time, because if you was to start playing tag with me, I wouldn't trouble to run after you. I'd just tag you so's you'd be it, and you'd be out, too." He slapped his hand to the spot where his revolver was hid.

I didn't have any idea of trying to get away. I had found out once before how fast he could run, and I didn't want to try out his legs again, revolver or no revolver. I walked on ahead, wondering what rascality that Jeff had brought along to suggest to Jake. I had to watch to keep from losing them. They walked along very slow, Jeff doing most of the talking, Jake just nodding now and then.

When I come to the camp, I found Pug and Boston sound asleep under the trees, taking it mighty easy and soft. I settled down and waited until Jake sang out to me to rustle up some wood for a fire and start up something to eat.

I saw that I was in for a regular life of slavery with Jake and his gang, but I didn't so much mind that, just then. So long as I had to be with them, I wanted to be busy all the time, so's I wouldn't have time to be thinking about things. I suppose that is about the best way all the time, no matter how you would figure it. I rustled up a fire, then I took my .22. Boston, who woke up, went along with me to see me hunt. He wasn't in the way. He didn't make any more noise than a snake sliding along beside me.

Well, I got a couple of mountain grouse pretty quick, and then, when I was starting back, I saw the long ears of a fool rabbit that was squatted out there behind a clump of grass. I hauled off and let him have it good and plenty.

That Boston was full of compliments. He said that he never saw more easy shooting than I did. He said: "I seen right away, when I first got a look at you, Sammy, that you was an extraordinary kid. And when you grow up, you're going to be a man that a whole lot of folks will want to mark. Now, don't you mind Jake and Pug. Because this ain't gonna last long. You never would think that I was gonna stay around with a pair of ruffians like them, would you? No, sir. I'm with them only because I have to be, for a little while. When I get the chance, I'm going to slip away, and, when I do, I'm going to take you along with me . . . not to use you to make a living, the way that scoundrel Jake does, but to take you back to your home, if you want to go there."

He talked a lot more than that. I put this down just to give you an idea of the sort of a gent that he was. When I got back to camp, he sat down near me, hugged his knees, and remarked a lot on how smart I was in getting the feathers off of those birds, how slick I cleaned the rabbit, how fast I cut up the meat, and how well I managed to keep that fire going. You would notice, when he was talking like that, that as much as he was praising you, he was never doing any of the work himself. No, he was just a sort of an audience, admiring what other men did—so long as it was for him. I guess that he never raised a hand in all his days to help himself to anything, unless he got his back against the wall.

Jeff stayed on for supper. He sat apart and mumbled in a low tone to Jake. Finally Jake says to Pug and Boston that they were to go on in to the town and mix around there with the crowd and put themselves up for the night in order to hear what folks were talking about, in case there was any suspicion about the big, crippled beggar and the boy that sang and danced.

"Here," said Jake, after they asked for money. "You dig in and help yourselves. I never saw a pair like you, that never had nothing. I'm tired of supporting you." He reached for his wallet that was so full of the money that he had got in town. Boston and Pug shoved their hands in and took out a little.

"Jake," asked Pug, "did you raise all of that with just one try?"

"It was a performance," said Jake, grinning, "and it wasn't any begging. Those bums just paid on the street for a show that was too good for them. Here, take some more . . . take a handful apiece. Drinks is most likely pretty expensive in that town right now."

I watched them then and wondered why Jake put up with the pair of them. Pug, of course, was a good fighter and he was pretty faithful, I suppose, but he hadn't any brains. And Boston that *did* have the brains was so much of a hypocrite and sneak that you couldn't trust anything he said. I never knew for sure, but I think maybe it was because even Jake, mean and hard as he was, had to have some sort of company. He knew that he was such a bad one that folks hated him so easy and so natural that the only way that he could have them around him was to pay them plenty. So he kept these two trailing along after him like a pair of coyotes that follow along after a cattle-killing grizzly, getting themselves all fattened up on the meat that he can't put away.

After dinner, Jeff got up without thanking anybody for the grub. He beat it back toward town, and Jake sat around by the fire and smoked his pipe, grinning at his thoughts broader and broader.

You could lay your money on it that the scheme of Jeff's was crooked, and that it was also big, because Jake had that sort of a guilty look. Well, I watched him, feeling pretty shivery, you can bet. I didn't speak up that evening but crawled off into a corner of the camp with Smiler.

It wasn't like the old camps with Lefty. There wasn't the good talk, the laughing, and the fools tricks Lefty and Smiler were always playing on each other, more like a couple of boys than a man and a dog. There wasn't any of the fine stories that Lefty could tell, about the time when he pretended to be a gondolier in Venice—or about the time when he played his violin for the Russian robbers near Odessa—nor about a thousand other things, because Lefty, of course, he had been everywhere, and everything had happened to him. More than Smiler and me missed the talk and the jolliness—much more than we missed that, we missed Lefty himself.

When I lay down in my blankets and stretched out that night, old Smiler lay down beside me. For a long time he licked his wounds, and then he lay stretched out there with his head raised high, his eyes almost closed, facing the fire. You would have swore that he was squinting, so's to make the big Jake disappear and let him imagine old Lefty was sitting there once more, whittling something funny out of a stick of wood.

• • •

I woke up in the morning before the rest of the gang. I could have sneaked away pretty easy, but there was no real use, because that Jake had been smart enough to follow Lefty. He had been fast enough to catch up with him twice, almost three times, in just the little time that I had known them two. So what would he do with me, that didn't have half Lefty's brains nor half his ways of doing things? Besides, I had sworn my oath, and an oath is sort of binding on you, particular when you can't very well *help* doing what you have sworn that you would do.

I settled all of these things in my mind pretty fast, then I just took up my rifle and went off by myself to shoot a breakfast for all of us. Smiler went along at my side. Whenever we came to a little knoll, he would run up to the top of the knoll where he would stand wagging his tail and looking all around. You would never have guessed what was going on inside of his mind, but I guessed it fast enough, because the same sort of an idea used to come whirling through my brain, too, when I would come up to the top of a hill. I just couldn't help giving a quick look around to see if Lefty was there somewheres in sight, not that I really expected to find him, you understand, but because the ghost of him used to be floating in front of my eyes. I wanted him again so powerful bad.

Chapter Twenty-Six
A TIGHT SQUEEZE

I got three more mountain grouse for breakfast. Then the tramp told me to pack up, because we were going into Crossman, and we might be staying there for several days. I packed up, and we drove into town. He knew right where he wanted to go—to a shack in the middle of town, right next to a bank. He told me to go to the door of the house and, if the owner was there, ask if it was true that he wanted to rent that place.

A ratty-looking old fellow came to the door and said that he would rent the house, and all that he wanted for it was eighteen dollars a month.

It was pretty high. There was only three rooms to it, and none of them was prime. The furniture—well, it was just nothing but bundles of sticks, not good sticks, at that. Jake let out a holler that was worth listening to, but, before he got very far, the owner started to close the door. That changed Jake; he offered to pay a week in advance, which wouldn't do, because the owner would have a month advance, or nothing. Jake said that the whole house wouldn't cost eighteen dollars to build over again. Anyway, he paid the money down, groaning a good deal. He asked when he could move in, and the owner said that his own satchel was already packed, and that we could have the place right quick if we wanted it.

So that was how we got the house in Crossman, and I took Tippety back and staked him out in the back yard, which was quite a piece of land, all covered with sun-cured grass. There were a couple of little sheds back there, too. I had just looked into them when I hear Jake roaring from the house.

He made me write out a piece of paper: **Rooms To Let!** I wondered which rooms, but he said for me not to bother asking questions, because he was able to think for himself and for me, too. I put out that sign, and quick as a wink here comes a rap on the door and Pug walked in, saying: "You are a pretty lucky sign painter, kid. Here is a roomer right away, and I got an idea that another is coming pretty soon."

He had hardly got inside of the house and was laughing with Jake in the back room when there come another rap. That was old Boston standing out there, leaning against the wall of the house. He came in and smiled at me, saying behind his hand: "What a frightful shack! But don't you worry. We won't be here long." That was the way with Boston. He was always telling you inside information, when mostly he knew just nothing. Even Jake had sense enough not to tell any secrets to Boston.

I was pretty busy the rest of that day, getting

things in order. When the evening came, Jake wanted to go right out and try a song and dance on the town again. I persuaded him that, if we were going to stay here any time, it would be better not to wear our welcome out right away.

So he stayed in. Then he sent me off to bed, which was in a corner of the attic. I was so tired that I went right off to sleep. The next morning when I came downstairs, I smelled something like freshly dug-up dirt. There ain't any hiding of that smell, because it is pretty strong. Any boy could spot it almost a mile away, I guess. I smelled that smell, and, after I got a chance, I took a look down in the cellar. There I saw pretty good what was happening.

They had started digging a hole that was six feet deep and three feet across. The loose dirt that they dug out, they took and threw around under the house, filling up the basement with it. They had dug that hole about fifteen feet in one night, and the cellar was about a third filled with dirt that they had brought out. Then they had fixed up their tunnel with boards so's it wouldn't fall in, by any chance.

I took a good look where that tunnel was pointing. Then I came up and looked across the surface of the ground, and I saw that ditch was pointed straight at the bank! Yes, sir, already they were a third of the way across the distance between the two places. Of course, I knew right away what they intended to do. They would dig up under the foundations of the bank and they would rob it. Then they would all be rich, because, of course, everybody knows that a bank has got almost all the money that there is. Inside of it.

I sat down and had a think. Should I go and let people know about what those scalawags were starting to do. Then I decided that it would be best not to say anything—not right now. I figured that if they got all the money that they wanted that they wouldn't have any more use for me and Smiler and that they would turn us loose. But suppose that I was to stop them by telling on them—then what would happen to me? I might ask the constable to protect me, but what could he do against a man like Jake, who would be busting then to get me? He had got old Lefty. Could I possibly keep him from getting me?

Well, after I had thought it all over, I decided that I wouldn't say anything, for a while, anyway, because there were still a couple of days before that they would come to the wall of the bank. So I waited until the next morning. Then I went down and had another look and found that they had dug the hole in about another fifteen feet, which was two-thirds of the distance to the bank. When I saw that, I was pretty worried, because it looked to me that if I wanted to keep honest folks from getting robbed, I had better start out and warn them right away. I was thinking about that and worrying when I thought I heard something over me. I looked up to see the trap door being lowered, and I had a glimpse of the face of Boston who was doing it. Boston that had always pretended so hard that he was my friend.

I says to myself that I am fixed now, and I got hold of a pick that I sees laying over on one side, deciding that I would try to kill one of them when they came down for me.

A minute more and that trap door was smashed open, and I heard Jake roaring for me to come up. Well, I'm ashamed to say what I did. I would like to have you know that I think that I'm as brave as most boys, but there ain't any doubt about it—I ain't a hero! I dropped that pick when I heard Jake's voice—and I just did what he told me to do. I came up out of that cellar until he got a chance to grab me with his long arm.

He brought me into the kitchen where the other two were standing around, looking pretty glum. They had just awakened, but there was no sleep in their eyes. Jake give me a shake and threw me down on the floor so hard that I thought that all of my bones would be busted.

"Now," said Jake, "shall we finish the little rat off? Because I got an idea that we ain't gonna never have no good luck out of him. Or shall we let him beg for a minute before I squash him?"

He leaned over, and I seen those big hands of his working. It made me sick—more'n if they had been two big spiders, they made me sick.

"Well," put in Boston, "I dunno that I hanker to start in cooking and washing up dirty dishes."

"Besides," said Pug, "there is a lot of money in the hide of that little skunk yet."

Both of the ideas had a good deal of weight with those rascals, because they didn't either of them want to do the work that I was doing. They hadn't lived so high for a long time, and they hadn't had so much cash money, neither, since I had come along to slave for them. They used to spend a lot of time lying around and cussing when they thought of the money I must have made for Lefty.

Jake was strong for killing me, right there. It was a bad thing to lie and watch his terrible face as that idea came over him, because he got a sort of an idiotic, horrible-looking glare in his eyes, like he was pretty near going crazy with joy at the thought of having a chance to kill something.

"Well," said Boston, "let the kid talk up for a minute and say why he was down there in the cellar."

I saw that it was one good lie, or a horrible death. I said: "Why, there ain't nothing to it! I seen a ferret skin after a rat or a mouse . . . or something . . . and run right in under the trap door and scoot for the basement. So I yanked the door open and started in after it. I guess that the rat found his hole and that the ferret had dived in after him. And then the door was closed on me."

"Who closed the door?" asked Boston, very soft.

"Hey!" said Jake, snarling. "You take your blame for some of this . . . because you might as well let the kid know that it was you that seen him there and caught him."

"Certainly," said Boston, "I'm not avoiding that fact." He shrugged his shoulders and raised his brows and gave me a look as much as to say: "You understand why I did it, of course. But I can't explain before these brutes."

Oh, he was smooth, that Boston was.

"Well," said Jake, "what do you say, Pug?"

Pug was working hard over the idea. He said at last: "Look, here, I followed a ferret once to try to see the little devil make his kill, you know. And I *seen* it. And the way that rat fought was a caution, when it got cornered, and the way that ferret fought, that was *two* cautions. When the rat dropped dead, I beat the ferret off, and the little red-eyed devil tackled *me* . . . and I had to put my heel on it. I picked up that rat, and I saw . . ."

His telling of the story that didn't have anything to do with me helped to take some of the attention off me. Both Jake and Boston were terrible interested in what he had to say, and they wished mighty bad that they had been able to see that fight. Finally Jake said: "Well, maybe the kid would've gone down to see a thing like that . . . and not just to spy on us."

Chapter Twenty-Seven
THE BREAD WINNER

I had an idea then that maybe I would win through.

Boston said: "Do we want to start living on hope again right away?"

"Is the money that is inside of the safe in a bank . . . is that what you call just hope?" asked Pug.

"I believe in luck like that when the money is right inside of my pocket," replied Boston. "And if that don't go through, then where are we except where we was before . . . bumming our way across the country and half starving a good part of the time. The kid is a good thing for us, ain't he?"

The other two both agreed that this was right. "Besides," said Boston, "you ain't asked him what he thought that tunnel down there meant."

"That's right," said Jake. "He's only a kid. Sammy, what d'you think that hole that you seen in the cellar is for?"

That put my shoulders up against the wall again. I could've choked that Boston for suggesting such a question, and it seemed to me that I saw him lick his lips like a hungry cat while he watched my face as I was making ready to answer Jake.

I didn't know what to answer for a minute, then I told myself that maybe it was better to come right out with the truth, because if they saw through a lie, there was no doubt about them killing me that minute.

I said: "Why, the minute I saw it, I figured that it was a tunnel to rob the bank."

Jake give a grunt, and his nostrils flared out—very queer to see. He said: "You hear him, boys? But I guess that he was wrong. It was only a grave that we was digging!" He began to laugh, which made me sicker than ever to hear him.

Pug cut in with: "Well, kid, what made you think that it was to be used to rob the bank?"

I said: "Why, I thought that anybody that had good sense wouldn't be so foolish as to throw away a chance like that."

There was a change in the air right quick. Pug stepped back with a grin and nodded to Jake.

"This kid is all right," said Jake. "He's one of us, even though he don't *act* like one of us. But then, he ain't quite wore off the fancy notions that he got from Lefty just yet." So I saw that there was another chance for me, and Jake nodded his head. "There ain't any of us jumping at conclusions," he said. "I guess maybe that he don't mean us no harm and . . . you get out of here and start breakfast, you little rat."

When I came to the back door, I jumped through it and ran as hard as my legs could carry me. I stopped and gave things a think. No, I saw that it wasn't at all likely that just a kid like me could get away from a gent like big Jake. So I turned around, came back, and started the breakfast fire. Then I prepared and gave them a plenty big meal.

They had been working a lot of the night. Now they lay around all day, and in the evening I had to go out with Jake and try to make another raise out of the crowd.

It worked pretty good. The men all remembered us. When they saw us coming, they gave a yell and made a ring around us. When I finished up the first song with a dance, one of the men said that I needed a better surface than that to dance on. He said they ought to take me in and give me a chance on the bar. So they picked me up and big Jake, too, carried us in, and sat up Jake at one end of the bar to make the music and they stood me up on the bar to sing and dance.

That bar had started when Crossman started, kept on growing all the time. There were rival saloons, now that the mines were opening up pretty strong, but Double Luck saloon had grown more than all of the rest. There was about a mile of bar.

I did my turn on that bar, with those gents standing around, yelling, hollering, and having a fine time. They chucked everything that they could reach into Jake's hat. Then they called for the dog, and Smiler went through *his* act with me.

That brought them down more than if they had never seen it before. One gent, just down from the mines and all covered with dust, got up and said that everybody in that saloon—there must have been about two hundred men there—was to drink with him and on him. At fifty cents a throw, that was a considerable treat, enough to make the boys give him a cheer. He said he didn't care about the money, but that, if he was able to digest it, he would dissolve the gold and drink that to see if it would put a gilt edge on a whiskey drink. He said: "But the first glass that is filled will be the kid's. Give Sammy a glass there, bartender. And fill it up to the top. The kid has danced for us, and now he is gonna drink for us."

There was a glass stuck in my hand and a bottle raised—when *wham!* went a gun. That bottle just turned into crumbling glass and flying whiskey in the hand of the bartender. He let out a yell, jumped back, and began to dance around, yelling that his eyes was put out. They weren't, but they felt about that bad because a lot of whiskey had got into them.

"The kid *ain't* gonna drink," said a voice I had heard before. There was the gent with the red hair and the red mustaches.

Well, that made the man who was buying the drink so mad that you wouldn't believe it. He said to the red-whiskered gent that he would take him outside, and that he would break him into little pieces to see if he could find the place where such a fool idea could start in to circulate through his system.

Somebody up and said in the sort of a whisper that means something: "Look here, Charlie, don't you be a fool. That is Red McTay."

I had never heard of Red McTay before. That was one trouble with the mountains and mountain men. A gent up there was like a grizzly or a wolf—he had a regular range and that range he very rarely got off of unless he was crowded. A gent could work up a reputation that was a regular snorter in one range, and in the next range he wouldn't be knowed at all, or he would be just a name, you might say.

But it was plain that the man they called Charlie had heard of Red McTay; it was plain that he had heard plenty about him. He sobered up, got a little pale, and looked around pretty foolish.

This Red McTay was not like a lot of other fighting men. He seemed pretty decent, saying: "I'm not in here to look for trouble, partner. I want you to have your little drunk and all the fun that you want. But I happen to own this saloon, and no kid has had a drink in it yet, and no kid is gonna have a drink in it so long as I'm alive and wearing a gun that ain't been worked overtime." Red went on: "Charlie, don't bear me no hard feelings. But I couldn't let a thing like this happen. And I know if you had had one drink less under your belt, you wouldn't have wanted the boy to put away that red-eye." Then he stepped up to the bar and said to the bartender: "You skunk, you're fired! Get out of this saloon and out of this town . . . and get mighty fast!"

The bartender didn't see any use in asking questions. He just up and started and got, while Red got behind the counter and peddled out the drinks faster than you would believe.

That round went down, and then I did another dancing turn. When I got through, Red McTay took me and Jake into a little back room of the saloon, saying to Jake: "This kid that you have picked up means pretty good business to my place here. I suggest that it would be a good thing, partner, if you and him agreed to come down here regular and turn on your act. Or I could do better than that. That mouth organ of yours does as a novelty for a while, but I've got a real piano in this joint, and I have a real piano player. You can stay home and rest up those legs of yours . . . if they really need any rest . . . and you send down the kid here to collect every evening!"

"That is extremely soft for you," replied Jake. "I throw all the trade your way . . . and you let me do it and pass the hat. But what would I get on the side? I might go over to some of the small saloons and raise the crowd for them, just as easy."

"You couldn't," said McTay, "for two reasons. One is that they ain't as well known. The other is that they ain't got the room, and they ain't got the decent liquor. However, I can make it more worth your while here, and I'll give you a flat rate of ten dollars for every evening that the kid comes and sings and dances here."

Jake didn't have to think that over none. He just made Red agree that *he* was to get the pay and not me, and that, after the hat was passed and everything collected, it was to be sent to him and not just given to me. All of that was agreed to. After that, Jake and me went home.

You would think that he would have been a little grateful for what he had got out of me this time and the prospect of the easy money that was still to come, but he wasn't. He started in: "Well, you see that there is a little difference between me and Lefty, that rat! He let you sing around on the streets, but I get you a swell indoor job where everything is easy for you, and where you got a whole bar for dancing on by yourself, and where you will have a real piano player for to accompany you . . . but that Lefty . . . he was such a skunk that he . . ."

I couldn't stand it. I said: "Leave off slamming Lefty, will you?"

He had got me just inside the house, and he slammed the door, hard, and said: "What might you be meaning by that, you young rat?"

Well, I shouldn't have said it, but I hated Jake so, and I was so sad about Lefty that I couldn't very well help busting out: "Because you ain't worth a trimming off of his fingernail!"

He just drew in his breath and took me in one hand by the hair. With the other hand he bashed into my face and knocked me silly.

Chapter Twenty-Eight
THE NEW ACT

When I saw that fist hanging in the air over me, I figured that I was no better than dead, but after a while I came to with Boston sponging my face. There was a big cut under one eye, and my face was swollen up a good deal.

Boston helped me to sit up. He said: "Poor kid. It don't seem possible that a man the size of Jake could hit a kid the size of you, but there ain't no doubt that he's just a brute."

I said nothing, for I couldn't help remembering about how he had closed me into the cellar and then called the others. Of course, he knew right away what I was thinking about.

Well, he had an explanation for that, even. He said that he had seen me down there in the cellar, and that he had closed the door for fear that one of the others might see me there, but that, when he come back from the cellar, Jake seen something in his face and had cornered him, making him confess what he had seen.

"Otherwise," said Boston, "he would have wrung my neck and thought nothing about it, because you know his style."

Maybe Boston thought that I was pretty simple. I pretended that I believed him, because there is no use in having people that you live with know that you can see through them easy.

I went to bed after talking to Smiler a little and feeding him his meat.

After I had been asleep for a while, I heard the men cussing and ramping downstairs. I listened for a while, and I heard them run into stone. They had dug the tunnel a little, both ways, but it looked like a solid wall of rock. Then they tried to dig down under, but the rock seemed to stretch just as far down, too.

They didn't know what to do. They groaned and swore that somebody had put bad luck on them, and Jake said that it was me, because he said that I was Lefty's luck and that you could steal a man's purse, but you couldn't steal his luck.

Well, I was feeling too glad about them losing out in the tunnel to worry about what they thought of me, so I went to sleep again.

Those rascals didn't sleep, though. The next morning they were still groaning and saying that it was just like having thousands of dollars sliding through their fingers.

All that day and the next they sat around, worrying. The next day after that, in the afternoon, Jeff dropped in to ask how things were coming along. They told him that they were snagged, and he seemed a good deal upset by what they said. I gathered that this Jeff was the night watchman over at the bank. After that, I didn't have to ask any questions; I knew what was what. He was the one who had started everything the minute he saw Jake in town. He had a hope that maybe he could help Jake to clean out the bank, and he had suggested renting this shack and digging in from there.

Now that there seemed to be no very good chance of breaking into the bank and cleaning up a lot of money that way, Jake and the rest got to thinking that I was more important, and started taking good care of me. They put bandages on the cut under the eye, and they fixed me up so that in two days I could go back to the Double Luck saloon of Red McTay and sing there. In the meantime, they mostly sat around and squabbled about who was to do the cooking while I was on the shelf. All the time they were talking and wondering about what they would do to tackle the bank in some other way. Jeff came every day with some new suggestion. However, nothing was done. In the end, the talk always wound up just the way it had started, with nothing accomplished.

I went down to the saloon the next evening. Red

McTay met me there and had a talk with me in his little back office. He took me in there and he sat me down on his desk, right in front of him, and then he leaned back in his chair and blew cigarette smoke at the ceiling and he said: "Well, kid, I suppose that you ran into a door in the dark, didn't you?"

I asked what did he mean.

He said: "I suppose Jake didn't hit you. I suppose that you just cut yourself by running into the door."

I saw that he was trying to get something out of me, but I would stick to the yarn that I had planned out with Jake. I said: "No, but I fell down the cellar stairs."

"You weren't knocked down the stairs, I suppose?" remarked Red.

I said that I wasn't.

"Lemme know how you fell into the hands of that big gorilla," said McTay. "Did your old man sell you to him, or did he kidnap you?"

"No, Jake is my father," I said.

"He is my uncle, then," said Red McTay, and he brushed out his mustaches so that they stuck right out stiff to the side, like the horns of a bull. "Now, look here, kid," he said, "do you call your own dad by his first name?"

"When his back is turned," I said.

McTay said: "Look me in the eye and tell me that he is your father."

Well, I couldn't have done that a little while before. But since Lefty had been taken from me, I didn't seem to have very much spirit. What was happening didn't make very much difference. So I could look right into those bright eyes of McTay as easy as nothing.

He leaned back and shook his head. "Poor kid! I suppose he's got you so paralyzed that you don't dare to even make a break to get free. You wouldn't trust me, now?"

I only smiled at him. I knew that he was a pretty brave man, but I knew that Lefty was brave, too, and I saw what had happened to him. No, I wasn't trusting any man to get me away from that Jake. I don't know, now, what I was waiting for. But sometimes I figured that it would be a lot easier to die right quick and be rid of everything.

When Red saw me smile at him, he got up and shrugged his shoulders. "You're too old for me," he said. "You can give me aces and spades, and you'll still win. You go in and try over your songs with Jack, the piano player. He's right in the back room and . . . hey! what's that?"

We heard some dogs baying in the street, very deep and mournful, then we went to the window and saw a man go by with two great big dogs on leashes. They were tugging and straining at the leashes, slavering at the mouth almost, they were trying so hard to get at a man running along the street ahead of them and pretending to try to get away. The man who held those two dogs was just able to manage them.

It was the faces of those dogs that interested me most, because they didn't look like Smiler. Their faces were all covered with folds of loose flesh, their lips hung down, and their ears were very long. They looked extremely wise and sad, you know.

McTay said: "Bloodhounds, and cracking good ones, if they're up to their looks. And this here is the very town that may be having a use for them dogs almost any of these here days."

Well, I went back to see Jack who was a little pink-eyed fellow, always having a cigarette hanging out of one corner of his mouth. He kept it there, wobbling up and down, even when he talked. He always was in his shirt sleeves, and his shirts had big, bright stripes in them. He wore little elastic bands around his upper arms, to keep the sleeves right up to any place on his wrist that he wanted them to be, and this Jack was finished off with bow ties knotted just perfect.

He didn't think much of me, and I didn't think much of him. Yet, when we started rehearsing, we warmed up a good deal. He was slick at the piano, and he seemed to like what I did with my voice and with my feet. He knew a good deal about dancing himself. He said that I had a good start, and that, if I kept on practicing, I might get somewheres with that art of mine. So he showed me a trick or two, then we had supper together, and he talked all about how he had been on the vaudeville stage in the little-big-time, he called it. He had always done pretty good, but he had never been able to get talented partners to work along with him. So here he was out in the sticks, where nobody appreciated his art and his talents.

Our act went over fine. I had Smiler there, and he did his little act and enjoyed it. I enjoyed the singing and dancing; afterward, I fed Smiler his raw meat in front of all of them. When they tried to feed him, too, he just wouldn't eat for them, any more than he would eat for me the first time. They all said that he was a wonderful dog. Because it works the same way with dogs and with people, I guess. The ones that you can handle and run dead easy, no matter how useful they may be, don't seem half so wonderful as those that wander around and act wild, who nobody can control.

I finished up that job that night a little tired, but pretty well worked out and hungry and fit. I pranced out of that place with all of the boys hollering for me. McTay told them I needed a rest, and that this wasn't the last time I was coming down that way.

On the street, when I got a little ways from the saloon, I stopped and leaned up against a tree. Smiler, he came, sat down on my feet, and whined. That was his way of asking me to go and find Lefty for him.

It was a clear, cold, mountain night. The air you breathed ran down into your lungs as cool as water and very sweet. I leaned there against the tree, and I couldn't help wondering how it was that the stars was so bright and so happy, and why it was that I hadn't never noticed it before—when a gent came along and stopped beside me.

Chapter Twenty-Nine
THE MAN IN THE NIGHT

He asked: "May I have a moment of your time?"

I replied: "That's all you can get out of me, stranger. Nothing but time. And right now, I got little of that. So mosey along, will you?"

He stood back a little from me, and I thought he was taking his distance to make a swipe at me, so I said: "Partner, lemme give you some free advice that is a lot better than anything that you'll ever find in a guidebook . . . which is . . . leave me be and don't start no rough stuff, or this little dog of mine, that has started purring, will just naturally chaw your windpipe right in two."

"Ah?" said the gent in the darkness. "You keep a guard with you, youngster, I see?"

"Sure," I said, "that is just what I do. But look here, if you're down on your luck, here's a quarter. It's all I got. It'll get you the shady side of a meal in this town. Or it'll get you one drink. Which is more your speed, I suppose."

He didn't say anything for a minute. Then: "Thank you."

I was already pretty near forgetting him, resting against that tree. I said: "For what?"

"For the money," he answered.

"All right," I said. "Now run along and leave me be. The dog is enough company for me."

"And yet," he said, "I think that you could spare me something else."

It riled me a little, I got to admit. It ain't everywhere that you find a growed-up man that will bum off a kid like I was. So I said to this man in the night: "You ain't born to starve for the lack of asking, I see. Now, what might your line be?"

"Why," said the gent, "you seem to have guessed it quite accurately. I am only a beggar, my friend."

You could see that he was one of them that get along with a soft voice and plenty of use of it.

"Well," I said, "I am a beggar, too."

"Do you call it that?" he asked. "But it seemed to me that you were working very hard and honestly for what you got, and that you deserved it."

"I don't remember any face in there to fit up with your voice," I said. "Where might you have been standing?"

"I was outside of the window."

"Outside!" I exclaimed. "Why, you poor boob, that was a free show. If it had been an honest show, it wouldn't have been free. But you could have been in there for nothing. What's more, lemme tell you that the singing and particularly the dancing warms them up a good deal, and you could have bummed a good many quarters off of them at the wind-up of a song or of a dance. It makes them feel free-handed."

He answered: "No, they wouldn't have given anything to me . . . not willingly."

"They know you, do they?"

"Yes," he said, "they know me." He let out a sigh, stood there a moment, saying nothing.

All at once, I feels sort of pulled to him and sorry for him.

"Look here," I said to him. "I have been talking sort of rough. But if you're down on your luck . . . I could raise some money for you, pretty quick. Are all the boys in Crossman down on you?"

"All, or nearly all," he said.

"Then why do you stay here?" I couldn't help asking.

"There is no place for me to go. I may as well make my effort here as in any other place. I may as well go to work here, you know. If I can't succeed in this rough little town, I'll never succeed anywhere."

That made me loosen up and give him some good advice. I said: "You look here. This town looks simple. But it ain't so simple as it looks. These gents with the hard hands, their *skulls* ain't so hard and thick. And mostly they got no use for a gent that won't work. I dunno what your line may be. Maybe you're a pretty talented blind man . . . or maybe you're no slouch of a cripple . . . or maybe you got a spiel about a lung disease and a family back home waiting for you . . . I dunno what your line may be, but just because you fail to work Crossman, ain't a sign that you can't work other places. Why, back in the little town where I come from, it was dead easy for a bum to get along. You couldn't batter three doors before you would get a regular sit-down meal with a napkin and everything. Why don't you try some of the dressed-up towns? They're really very much better."

He didn't say nothing to this, either, but I could see that he was thinking it over. It struck me kind of sad, him being a growed-up man, to be standing there like that with his hands hanging at his side, getting advice from a kid like me.

He said at last in that soft voice of his: "Yes, it is worth a try. I might knock at the kitchen doors . . . I might do that."

That let in a light on me.

"Oh, you been trying the *front* doors, have you? Well, unless you're an a-number-one man, you ain't gonna be able to do that and get by."

"Yes," he said, very sad, "you are right. I am

not talented enough to go to the front doors and beg there . . . that is why they will give me nothing."

I got sort of confidential with him. I never hardly felt so sorry for anything as I was for him—next to being so sorry for Smiler, because he missed Lefty so bad. But I thought I could help this gent along, so I said: "I'll tell you something. You got a good voice, which it is a great help. You got a good, soft voice, and you can work it pretty smooth. Your line had ought to be the women. You keep away from the rough men and you try the ladies."

He threw up his hands and he give a sort of groan and said: "Ah, I've tried the thing before, and I know that you're right, boy. I know that you're right, but I don't want to work with the women. I'm tired of it. I'm sick of it. And that's why I've come up here into the wilderness. I want to work with men . . . real men . . . and I don't care who they are, so long as they are men, men, men!" He meant every word of that.

I said that I was sorry, and that he had better come back with me and let me get him a stake from Red McTay. I knew that Red was awful generous.

He said: "It's not the money that I want, my son. It's not the money."

That put me against it, and I said: "Well, you're too many for me. What *do* you want?"

213

"Oh, I only want the scraps of the lives of men . . . the time that they throw away . . . the odd minutes. I would give all my soul if I could persuade one real man to open his heart to me. So that in the end I could give."

I couldn't help laughing.

He asked: "Why do you laugh at me, child?"

"I don't mean to hurt your feelings," I said, "but it sort of stepped on my funny bone when I hear about you wanting to give things to people. May I ask, maybe, what you got that you can give?"

"That is it!" he said. "What have I that can be given away? What have I that is worthy to be picked up and saved by another man? I don't know . . . I don't know!"

"I see," I said, "you've been pretty rich, I suppose?"

"I thought that I was very rich. I thought that I was almost one of the richest of men."

"And then you went bust?"

"Yes."

"All in a day?"

"All in a moment!"

"Somebody double-crossed you, then?" I asked, because it is always sort of sad to see a rich gent that is down and out.

"No one deceived me," he said. "It was all my own self-deception. I was a fool! A fool! My gold was nothing . . . lighter than feathers!"

I could see that he was sick with himself, so I

didn't say anything back to him to let him settle down, if he would. Then he said: "But you are right. I must not try the front doors. I must be humbler still. And I must go to the kitchen doors and beg there."

"Not that you would get much coin . . . ," I had to put in.

"Money? Money? No, that is not what I want. But only the time, which is more precious than money."

"I never seen time," I said, "that couldn't be bought."

"Ah, but there is in nearly every man's life. He does not know it until it is too late. When he lies dying, then he knows that there is time that cannot be bought and paid for. When that moment comes, then men will listen to me, but it is too late."

"Too late for what?"

"Too late to make an exchange of what they have here on this earth for the great peace, child."

"Look here, bo," I said, "this is sort of big talk. What do you know about great peace, and all that sort of tripe?"

"Little or nothing, perhaps," he said, and began beating his hands together, "but something, I trust, has been revealed to me. I think there has been granted to me some power to help men to a knowledge of that which follows after death."

That hit me where I lived, of course. All at once

it busted out of me and I said: "Now, you put it to me straight, if you got any dope on that, what chance has a poor bum . . . a regular poor old tramp . . . got of getting to heaven?"

"I don't know," he said. "I would have to see the man. Was there honesty in him?"

"No," I said, "he was a cheat."

"Was he at least true and faithful to those who loved him?"

"No," I said. "He left the finest woman in the world."

"The judgment will fall hard upon him, then," says the man in the darkness.

I was afraid to go on for a minute, because there was a sort of a thing in the voice of this here man that gave me a chill—as if he really *did* know. I changed the subject and said: "Well, this is queer, you and me talking like this, but from what I can make out, you ain't got no bundle. You ain't no bundle stiff. You're a regular tramp royal."

He said nothing; his head had fallen; he was thinking hard. It brought back the thought of him I was missing so terrible bad.

All at once I hollered out: "Partner, surely there is one chance for him! There is a ghost of a chance for him!"

"Did he at least," said the man in the dark, "give the labor of strong hands to help his fellow men?"

"No, he was just a hobo," I had to admit.

"Then he is lost," said the man in the night.

I shouted out at him: "You lie! You lie! He's gonna go to heaven. If he ain't in heaven, I don't want to go there. I wouldn't go there. I would slam right out of the door of heaven. And you . . . you don't know anything about it anyhow!"

He said: "Ah, son, you are right, and your friend is saved . . . if he has done enough on this earth to win the love of even one person, even of a child. Yes, and love would take the dog at your feet and carry it into heaven. But for those who have not found love or made it, they will eat bitter bread alone on this earth and when they die. . . ."

Here his voice busted off a little, and he stopped. And then it seemed to me that I would have gone on listening to him forever. I was about to ask him a lot more of questions, because what he had said was so wonderful, but, all at once, he seemed to forget me. He walked right back from me until the light from the nearest window hit him.

And what d'you think I saw? Why, I saw a gray head—it was nearly white—and the black and white collar put on backwards of a minister! It gave me a terrible chill.

Chapter Thirty
ENTER JUD

We went on living like this in Crossman for a long time. There was nothing for those three back at the house to do. They just lay around and blossomed out in the money that I was making for them. They had plenty of good clothes, and the house always filled up with food that was the best money could buy for them. In the days I did all the cooking. In the nights I used to go down to the saloon and do a turn there with Jack.

His pay had been double since he started working with me, so he took to the job very kind, though still hankering to get back to the little-big-time, as he called it. He was always working out new stunts with me, new steps for my dances and new songs for me to sing. He taught me some old plantation songs, and one night dressed me up as a nigger boy in ragged clothes, no stockings on, and barefooted. I had on a man's shirt, all worn out at the elbows.

That night, when the boys began to holler for me, Jack announced that Sammy wasn't there that night, being sick, but that he had a little nigger boy that would want to sing for them. So he brought me out. It was a cold night, and in those rags I stood shivering in the corner. All the gents stood around sort of hostile, saying: "Hey, Jack, what kind of a joke is this, anyway?"

"Aw, give the kid a chance, will you?" Jack said, and he sat down, starting to whack the piano. I tuned into one of those songs.

Now, you would think that all of those gents, hearing me sing night after night, would sure have recognized my voice. But it was disguised some with the dialect of the darkies, and I made my voice pretty throaty, too. Also I was colored up pretty good by Jack, and he had it down so pat that he even made it paler on the palms of my hands.

They didn't know me! No, sir. I got up there and I sang those songs, and they stood around, getting more and more enthusiastic. Finally one of them said: "Why, this kid can sing *better* than little old Sammy can!"

The rest of them stood around and laughed at him, real superior, saying: "Now, that shows what an ignorant guy you are. You don't hardly know nothing! Sammy has got some real art in him. Besides, he can dance!"

"Maybe the black kid can dance, too," said the man. "Here's a ten spot, kid, if you will dance for us!"

I started and did a verse of another song, then I danced through the chorus, just speaking the words. You know, there is a lot of things that you can do with your feet bare that you can't do when there is shoes on them—a shuffle sounds funny, but pretty good with bare feet doing it. Before I got through, those gents yelled and hollered and raved around, saying that I *was* better than Sammy was. They wanted me to sing a lot more, but Jack wouldn't let me, and I sneaked away.

That started a lot of talk. Oh, they were a dumb gang; they never once suspected me of being Sammy, and the nigger boy, Jud, all in one. The next night they hollered for Jud, then some of them hollered for Sammy. Pretty soon Jack said that he would bring out Sammy for them, though I was still feeling a little sick.

So I came on that night, and I sang some of the *silly* songs for them—about how you love some girl, or about a girl who is dead and done for—I mean like "Annie Laurie" and like "Ben Bolt." I did those songs with a quiver in my voice, and those miners stood around just too worked up to say anything at all. A lot of them came up and shook hands with me, saying that I did them more good than a church ever could. It is remarkable what a lot of bunk there is in the corners of music—how much sham and fake, you know.

I went on being Sammy for some nights, and there was a regular roar for Jud. Jack said I would have to be Jud again, so we tried it once more, and Jack said that it wasn't any joking matter now, because not one of them miners ever suspected that Jud and Sammy was the same. It wouldn't be safe to let them guess, because they might take it out on him. I suppose he was right.

They had got quite worked up about the two "kids." Half of the town, they swore that Sammy was the best singer and dancer of the two, and some of them swore that Jud could just sing and dance circles around Sammy.

The next night, there was three or four real blacks in that crowd; they let out a mighty holler when they seen my black face coming. The sight of them scared Jack and me a lot. Jack said: "Now keep a tight grip, for my sake. Because, if they find out what you-all are, they'll tar and feather me, sure, for making such fools out of them . . . and if you say one word in the hearing of them niggers, they'll know that you're not real. So don't do nothing but sing."

I did just that, and, when they saw that I was so scared, at first, they all hollered out and told me not to be afraid because they was all my friends.

That wasn't what I was afraid of. I was scared that they would see I was a faker, and partly I was afraid that they would begin asking: "How comes it that kid, that got a whole barrel full of money just the other day ain't got any now, at all? And how comes it that he ain't been able to buy himself any clothes?"

Those ideas never seem to come in to their heads, and they just didn't think at all, nor do figuring, you see?

I cut loose and sang and danced the best that I

knew how. The most tickled ones in the whole crowd were the black fellows themselves! Yes, it beat all to see how proud and glad they were to see that their race had turned out a boy that could stand a crowd of white folks on their heads like that.

Well, it went off fine. Then one of the gents that thought Sammy was still the best singer of the two got up, and he said that there was only one way to settle it. That was to have Sammy and Jud sing together on the same night.

They made a great ruction about that, and finally they made so much noise that Red McTay—of course, he was in on it—came along and said that they should have what they wanted, just two nights away!

Jack and I were mighty scared. But McTay took us back into his room and said that it would be easy. He said that he would have everything ready, and that first I would get out there as a white boy—in my own skin, you know. After I had worked for about half an hour, I would go back and get all blacked up, then I would come back and do Jud for them. Nobody would be allowed to come near me, and it would work fine.

That was the way that it was planned. Everything was got ready. In that little back room, they laid out the rags for Jud, and they fixed up the blacking, and they got all handy.

In the meantime, for two days gents had been

dropping into Crossman and coming around to find out about the song contest. There was a good deal of excitement. Some of the boys got together and laid out money with each other. They appointed a couple of gent judges, and they all said that they would stick together and stay with the decision that the judges made. When that evening came, there was a reason for Jack and me to be excited, reason for Red McTay, too, because for days the money had been flowing like water across his bar.

Well, sir, when I came out there in my own skin, I saw half the crowd looked hostile and half of them looked tense. When I turned loose and sang and danced, half of the crowd gave me a real cheer, and the more I sang and danced, that much more they sat around, looking easy and contented and laughing at the other half. The boys betting on Jud got more and more gloomy.

When I finished, half of the boys were yelling and the other half didn't let out a peep. I sneaked to the back room. Jack and McTay blacked me up fine and quick. In twenty minutes I went back into the saloon and, believe me, I was scared. Those that had bet on Sammy looked pretty sure of themselves; those that had bet on Jud, especially those two black fellows themselves, of which there must have been twenty—they just looked like drawn razors. I told myself for sure that on an important night like this they were sure to see through me. I started in and was doing pretty good. Those two were beginning to smile, when all at once I stuck a sliver into my foot— and sat down with a yell.

Well, there was a roar and a groan and they started for me to help me up—all of them who had bet on me looked bluer than indigo ever looked. I saw what would happen. I knew the minute they got to fooling around the blood, they would see that my skin was white. So I got up and yanked that sliver out. I waved to them and made myself grin, though it hurt like sixty, and I went right on dancing, leaving little red spots behind me.

Well, sir, it made a great hit with all of them. They applauded so hard they nearly busted. Then Red McTay tied up my foot, and I turned loose and danced and sang a bit more, winding up with a silly song about how swell it was living in my native Africa, how fine my wife and I were getting along when the cruel white man came along and ripped me away from my native log hut, making a slave out of me, giving me beefsteak instead of bananas to eat, giving my free feet shoes to wear, and that sort of rot.

When I got through, there were tears in the eyes of nearly everybody. There was no doubt about the decision. Sammy was a back number, and little Jud was the king. The ones that had bet on Sammy didn't even peep.

The funniest thing was the two blacks, because the way they let on and ripped around, it would have done you good. The first thing that you know, a couple of them landed a-hold on me and stood me up on the bar. They had a drink, and they jammed, each of them, a month's wages down into my pockets—which they had made—and a lot more by what they had bet on me and won. They were so heated up that finally all of them busted out and they started singing, grand and harmonious.

There I was in the midst of what was supposed to be my kind, but they didn't see anything wrong about me. I guess they couldn't see nothing wrong with me. If somebody had said I wasn't a little black boy at all, they would have carved him into bits right then and there.

Finally they turned me loose. I got away and got the blackness off me. McTay told me he was putting away fifty dollars for me whenever I wanted it. And Jack was so scared and tickled that he hardly knew what to do.

Altogether, it was a boss show and a very funny evening, but I wouldn't like to go through another like it.

The queerest thing was that, even after all that ocean of money had rolled into the pockets of Jud, those blockheads didn't seem surprised when I would come out and sing in rags a few nights later.

After that, Sammy didn't make much money. He was just sort of tolerated; it was Jud that everybody wanted to hear.

Well, now I got to stop telling about this foolishness and tell you about what happened that was a lot more of importance.

Chapter Thirty-One
SUCCESS

It was Pug who turned the trick when the rest of them would have been ready to throw up their hands and give up. I suppose Pug was used to taking punishment in the ring and so he had got into the habit so that he was even able to take it *out* of the ring. When the rest of them were sitting around, folding their hands while they were thinking and talking about what had best be done, Pug used to go down with a crowbar and a pick; he would pound and chip away at that wall of stone that they had run into. Finally one night right after I had got the black washed off my face and gone home, I came in to see Pug just coming up from the cellar, all covered with dust. Jake gave him a sour look and asked how it felt, after being a gopher, to come up and be a man again?

Pug rolled a cigarette, sat back, and grinned, saying nothing. But his little pig eyes were full of light.

Pretty soon Boston up and said: "Look at his hands." Meaning Pug's.

When he pointed it out, we all saw they were certainly a sight. Ordinarily those hands was pretty hard and calloused up, because Pug wasn't afraid of work, but now there were plenty of blisters on them. His hands was a sight, for sure.

Jake laughed and said: "Look at that! There's a gent who loves work so mighty well that he just couldn't stop and lay off it, you see. He had to pitch in and smash up his hands drilling away at a rock that didn't have no end to it. Look at that! He just got himself about wore out . . . on nothing."

He lay back and he laughed and laughed. The idea of ever working—unless it was to do a mischief to somebody—had probably never come into Jake's head in his whole life.

Boston laughed a little, too. He always laughed at the same things that amused Jake.

Pug said at last: "Who says that there wasn't any end to that rock wall?"

Only that, but what he said wasn't so important as the light that was in the back of those little pig eyes of his. Jake gave him one long look, and then he jumped up without saying a word and he started for the cellar.

"What is it, Pug? You ain't done something, have you?" asked Boston.

Pug grinned and wouldn't answer until pretty

soon Jake come up: "Pug has wore a hole through the rock. Clean through!"

We all ran down to look. When the lantern was raised, there was the hole, sure enough. Pug had banged away at that wall of rock at the end of the passage, and finally he had punched a crowbar through. You could see the big chunks bitten out of the rock all around that hole where Pug had grabbed up the crowbar and worked like mad to find out if it hadn't been a mistake. Pug, when we saw the hole, began to laugh and shake, and laugh some more, because he was feeling pretty good, you can depend upon it, and he was pretty nearly wore out.

Boston and Jake started to work then, and I went back up to my room in the attic with Smiler. I could hardly sleep, hearing the little thudding of the crowbar down there under the ground. It almost seemed to me that I could feel a little jar. I wondered why it was that the people passing in the street didn't notice it, too, and come in there to investigate. They didn't. And by the time that the morning had come, that rock had been split right in two. It was only a great big slab of stone that come sticking up there almost to the surface of the ground. A stratum, I suppose that you would call it. That's what they called it in the newspaper afterward.

There was no more work for me at the saloon after that. Jake didn't want to risk having me around other folks for a while, for fear lest I might let something drop and so spoil all of their work right after they had wasted about five weeks of work and of hope.

I stayed at the shack, and, when Red McTay came to inquire about me, Jake told him very ugly that I was sick. When McTay asked how long would I be sick, Jake said that I would be sick just so long as he pleased. Which was about the truth, too, and McTay had to swallow that and go away.

It was day and night work now. I had to keep the coffee pot on the fire all the time, because one or other of them was always coming up to have a swig and a dash of whiskey, and then go back. Mostly it was Boston, though, who had to come up and get refreshment. I couldn't help noticing that, though he seemed to be working almost as hard as either of them, his hands never got calloused.

It was Jake who shone now. Now that he had the hope of something right ahead of him, he had the strength of five men in each of those big, ugly hands of his. I went down there and watched him work.

Pug was a good, strong, hard-working man. He could use that crowbar pretty good and chip off the rock pretty fast. When Jake started, it was all different. He had an extra big bar that he worked with—almost twice the size of the other—yet he handled it with a stroke as easy as you could

229

imagine. He would fly into a sort of passion of joy at his own strength, and he would drive that bar whole inches right into the solid face of the rock and break off great, big chunks. I saw him rip off his coat and his shirt and his undershirt and tear into the work until his face and his whole body turned red and then redder. Still he kept on giving that rock sixty.

When he had worked a couple of hours, he would come up and throw himself on the floor and toss out his arms and lie there sprawling, awful big and awful ugly to see, with his big chest working up and down like a bellows. He would close his eyes and snore till the house shook for half an hour. Then he would roll over, grab a bottle of whiskey, turn about a pint down his throat, and then he would eat a couple of pounds of beef that I had fried for him and toss off a couple of big tin cups of coffee as strong as lye. After that, he was ready to work again.

I noticed, too, that his hands never seemed to get sore. They just chafed up and got a little white and rough-looking; he seemed to be made of entirely different kind of stuff from other men.

Now they carried their trench along right up to the wall of the bank, working only in the middle of the night, when they was pretty close. When they got to the foundation wall, they had another tough job, but Jake, nearly single-handed, wore it through in a single shift. I saw his crowbar, afterward; the cutting edge was as broad as the side of your finger, that good steel having been beaten and smashed against the rock for so long. Nobody else could have used it for anything, but, when Jake wrapped those fingers of his around it, he could plunge it right through solid rock. I don't think any man ever lived who had the strength that he had. He was blind and drunk with it. There was no bottom to it. It was like a well that he could bail out of more and more. The more that was taken, the more ran into the well for him to pull up to the top.

He worked like seven men, and, while he was doing that, he really ate like seven men. I have seen him, my own self, eat a whole chicken, half a pound of bacon, a lot of bread, and drink a quart of strong coffee and finish off with a big bar of chocolate. That was just a lunch for Jake, and, after he had been sweating down there in the trench, he would be hungry again in a couple of more hours, maybe.

The next morning, after they got through the foundation wall, Jake said: "I hope they don't stamp none on the floor of the bank, today, because if they do, they are gonna hear a hollow sound, as sure as you live."

They didn't stamp, I suppose, because the next night they all got ready. The three horses were saddled and put in the shed behind the house; old Tippety was harnessed up to his buggy, and I was told to come along with them and keep close, not that they wanted me to see what they had done, but because they wanted to have me where they could watch me all the time.

So Smiler and I were there and saw everything.

They took an auger and bored up a hole through the floor. Then they sawed out from that hole until they had got a big square opening that a man could get through easy. Then they came up. Pug went first, and Jake threw me up after him— Smiler just jumped.

We were in a place all surrounded with tall iron bars, and in the end of that room was a great big safe.

Everybody stepped back, and Boston peeled off his coat and began to work. He had some soft, yellow laundry soap and a little flask of soup. With that he was gonna open that safe.

You could see, now, why it was that they put up with the laziness and the shiftlessness and the lying of Boston. It was because that they needed his brains. *He* changed, too. He got less ratty-looking around his eyes. He stood up straighter; there was a smile on his mouth that made him look almost handsome. He moved so deliberate that he seemed to be going very slow. Jake got terribly impatient. Boston kept right on, making every lick count as good as two, not saying a word except very polite and fine English, like: "Will you be good enough to pass me that flask,

Sammy? And mind that you don't drop it, because it would snuff us out into thin air like nothing at all. Thank you very much."

That was Boston and the way he acted, now that the pinch came. Pug was pretty good, too. But Jake—well, I was surprised!

Chapter Thirty-Two
ROBBERY

You never could have said that Jake wasn't brave. In his way, he was as brave as could be. But his way wasn't the way that was needed just then. Boston would have taken water from a Chinaman, any day, when it came to fighting. Here, when the danger wasn't a gun pointed at him, but was just imaginary and what might happen, he was a regular hero. His color was fine, and he was cheerful, and he worked away, humming. This was just the thing that he needed to make a real man of him, you might say.

Pug was sort of tense, but very steady. He meant well, and he wouldn't run. You could tell that. Only this sort of danger just numbed his brain a little.

The worst was big Jake—he was paralyzed. Every minute he was thinking he heard noises. When he heard them, he turned as white as a sheet. His eyes was wandering all the time, and

233

he couldn't keep still. First he was at the front window, and he came sneaking back to say: "There is somebody watching us from across the street."

Pug was staggered for fair, and I felt mighty sick. Boston just said: "How can they be watching us? You simply saw a light on the glass of a window. Go back and see if I'm not right."

When Jake went hurrying away, Boston said: "Papa is a little nervous tonight . . . for two pins, he would chuck the whole deal. He is seeing himself in stripes about now."

Boston laughed, but you can bet Pug and I didn't so much as smile. Not us!

In another minute, back came Jake, whiter than ever. He was just shaking with the strain, and he said: "You may have been right about the window, Boston, but I saw two shadows sneak around the corner, and I know that they were men. That dirty Jeff has double-crossed us, and there's about twenty men hanging around this bank, laughing up their sleeves, ready to nab us when they hear us blow the safe. Boys, they're laughing at us. And I say that it's time to throw up this job."

Boston, as cool as ever, gave Pug and me a look. He smiled a little and said: "You boys run along, if you want. I'll keep your shares . . . till you call for them, if you want."

"Is she about ready?" asked Jake.

"Yes."

"Will it make much noise?"

"Yes. Quite a bit."

"But they'll hear us, boys . . . and we're goners . . . they'll block up the end of the tunnel . . . they've got it blocked already . . . or they'll cave it in on the top of our heads. You can be pretty sure of that. There are some smart men in this town. And they're watching me. They know that I haven't rented a house next to this here bank just for nothing."

"Get back, all of you, and lie down!" ordered Boston.

We did it. There was a sound like a big gun fired under a blanket, and then a crash. When we looked through the swirl of mist, there was the door of the safe lying on the floor, blowed clean off from its big hinges. That nitroglycerin had turned the trick.

"Quick!" said Jake. "Now grab the stuff and run . . . I'll . . . I'll go first and clear the way for the rest of you. . . ."

Well, what do you think that Boston did? He just sat down there and he rolled a cigarette as calm as you please. He looked over at where the three of us stood trembling, and he said: "A fine lot of yeggs you fellows are."

Jake cried: "Boston has double-crossed us! Well, you'll be a dead man before . . ."

In his crazy head, he was sure that this idea

was the right one, and in another minute he would have done for poor Boston sure. Even then Boston was cool. He said: "Jake, steady down. You know what they have on me, if they catch me. And you know what they have on Pug. It's twenty years for Pug . . . and for me,"—he give a funny, horrible quick jerk of his body and stretched his lips wide and tight—"Salt Creek! Keep your nerves up, Jake, because this party is only beginning. What can we get at to grab now?"

You see, he was right, because the inside of that safe was all lined with little faces of drawers, each one of them locked, and each one of them fitted in very neat. Still, there was a way to get at them, and Boston tackled them with a small chisel and a three-pound hammer. He would start one of them a little, and then he would take a can opener and fetch that drawer out. The minute he had it out, he would pass it behind him, and the other two would go through the contents as quick as a wink. You would hear them say—"Negotiable stuff!" or "Nothing at all!"—as Boston fetched out drawer after drawer.

Boston didn't seem to be interested in what they said or in what was in the drawers. He was happy in wrecking that safe and in beating the steel and in getting those drawers out so that somebody else could read all of the secrets that was in them. That was his peculiar way of getting pleasure out of life. I suppose that there were hardly twelve times in his whole life when he was really all contented, and those times were always when he was wrecking a safe, somewhere or other.

Right in one minute I could see why Jake and Pug had put up with him so long. I could see why they would have put up with him a lot longer, still. He was worth it and a lot more.

Now there was a noise at the door, and Jake jumped about ten feet and dragged out a gun. Then he crawled up on the door, with Pug behind him. I heard a whisper—and then that door opened!

It wasn't an enemy. If it had been, he would have died very *pronto*. It was only Jeff—and he stuck in his head and said: "You guys are taking all night. Get a move on you, will you? I'm breakin' my heart out here . . . and I think that some of the boys are beginning to move."

"Was there much noise?" asked Jake, all trembling.

"Like a house falling," said Jeff. "And I can hear every lick of that hammer, as plain as day!"

"We'll make our start now," Jake said, just turning green. "We've got something. It's better than nothing."

"So long, boys!" said Boston. "You can have what you got, and I won't put in my claim for it. Not for a minute. I'll be contented with what I get after you're gone."

Well, they couldn't stand the idea of running off and leaving Boston behind them to gather up the primest part of the loot. They hung around, and he went on opening drawer after drawer until Jake was like a crazy man.

They were getting into the cream of the stuff now, and more greenbacks were coming out than you could imagine. Still there seemed to be more to come. Jake would curse and moan and beg Boston to come away, then he would make a bubbling noise in his throat and gloat over something that Boston had just handed back to him.

That Boston was clear grit to the bottom of him—and, when he had opened the last drawer, he spread it out himself. There were four sheafs of bills with five thousand dollars printed on the wrapper of each bundle. You wouldn't think that there was really that much money in all the world.

Pug had been keeping pretty close tab. He had that sort of a head on his shoulders, going pegging along all of the time and making pretty good headway. He said: "We got about fifty-two thousand dollars in cash. And we got about that much more in stuff that we'll have to give a fifty percent commission on if we want to get rid of it. Boys, the four of us ought to clean up about twenty thousand iron men apiece!"

Can you think of that?

You remember the widow back there in

Gunther? The one, I mean, that Aunt Claudia used to bust herself to get to the notice of? Well, it was said that she had twenty-five thousand dollars in the bank, but mostly folks thought that it couldn't be so much, it was such a terrible pile of money. And here were four rapscallions that was to get that much apiece! It didn't seem very much like justice, as maybe you'll admit.

Boston said over his shoulder: "Jeff gets his share, I suppose?"

"Why, ain't he been promised?" said Jake.

"He's been promised enough," said Boston. "I don't want to beat him out of nothing. Only . . . twenty thousand . . . for what he's done . . . it's a good deal."

"Too much," said Pug.

"I think that you're right, Boston," said Jake. "But now let's get out of here . . . I think that I hear . . ."

We didn't want to hear what he thought. We dropped down into the tunnel.

Once outside the bank, Jake seemed to clear up and lose a good deal of his scare. He grabbed me by the shoulders and said: "Now, Pug . . . Boston, what about the kid?"

I heard Pug growl. "Aw, leave the kid be. He hasn't done any harm."

Boston didn't say a word, but I thought I saw the shadows of a gesture that he made.

"I dunno," said Jake. "I hate to take him along,

because, if a pinch comes, he'll be a terrible nuisance. I sure wouldn't leave him behind if I thought that there was any danger that . . ."

"Ain't there plenty of room for him in the buggy behind that Tippety horse?" asked Pug.

I could have blessed him for thinking of that.

"That's so," said Jake. "I guess that he would fit in there pretty good. Who's to drive the horse?"

"Jeff."

"Where's he now?"

"He'll be out at the end of the tunnel in the house."

It seemed a heavy job to be sitting there in that lonely house, waiting for the robbers to come back.

"You offer Jeff a flat ten thousand dollars," said Boston to Jake. "That's enough for him and too much for him."

We hurried on down the tunnel toward the house.

Chapter Thirty-Three
TRAILED

We came down to the end of the passage, and, as we came up into the house, we could hear some people going by in the street. Then there was a rapping at our front door.

Boston and I started for the rear; Pug stood and

hesitated. Jake was the man now. He went right to that front door, opened it, and said as pleasant as he could: "Well, gents, what's up at this time of night?"

"I see you're dressed," said a man out there in the street. "Maybe you've heard something in the bank?"

"Not a thing," replied Jake. "What's up?"

"We don't know. Griffiths, here, thinks that he heard a crash in the bank a little while ago. We can't find the night watchman there, just now. The scoundrel seems to be off drunk somewhere."

That was Jeff that they meant, of course. If Jeff had stayed on his post, there wouldn't have been any doubt that the trouble that followed would have been dodged. But Jeff's nerve failed him.

Jake told these fellows that he was up because he had a toothache that wouldn't let him sleep, but that, if there had been any noise in the bank, he would have been sure to hear it. The men went on, but we could hear them talking. Finally they decided that they had better get the president of the bank and have him take a look to make sure that there had been no trouble there.

That was all that we wanted to see. We got into the back yard—there was the horses all saddled, and Tippety standing under a tree, harnessed up to the buggy. Jeff had done that part of his work. If he had only gone back to stand guard at the bank till the last minute, the danger would never have come.

Well, they gave Jeff a mighty rough reception and a lot of growls when they met him, but he give them back as good as they sent.

He said to Jake: "Here's right where we whack up, now. I'll take my share, thank you."

"You'll take a busted head!" said Jake, very ugly.

"You can't bluff me out," Jeff answered. "I know that they're stirring around, looking, right now, and, if they hear a gun go, they'll come swarming. I'll have my share."

Jake cursed something grand to hear, but he told Boston to hand over ten thousand dollars to Jeff. Boston did that. Jeff lighted a match, looked, laughed, and said: "I'll take mine in cash."

They had given him some bonds, or something like that. Jeff was too wise for that, and he held them there, no matter how much they cussed and raved, until they had given him the ten thousand in cash. "All right, boys," he said. "I have your number, and I know that this is likely about a third or a quarter of my real half. But now I'm in the boat with you, and I have to follow orders for a while. I'll have a chance to remember you later on."

I could see that Jeff was really fighting stuff. There was Indian in him, and no doubt of it. Warpath Indian, I mean!

Jake said: "You boys pelt along. Boston, you ride first, because you got a pretty good eye for trouble and a pretty good lying head on you. Jeff, you drive next in the rig with the kid."

Jake would be in the rear, behind the rig, with Pug. We were to head up the road to the first forking, then, for fear lest people should wonder at a rig and three riders going along together, the buggy was to take the right branch and keep along it down to the river, and the riders were to take the left branch and then turn up the river road and meet us there. Then we would all turn down and go across the river at the bridge.

That was easy and simple, and in another minute I was in the rig. Jeff had the reins, and the dog was behind us. Jeff didn't like that.

He said: "You can see that dog like a lantern, here, in the night. Throw him out!"

I said: "If folks see a dog along, they ain't gonna ask no questions. Bank robbers don't go around with pet dogs, do they? Besides, if it comes to a push, most of the boys in Crossman know me pretty good."

That had a lot of weight with Jeff, and he said that I had sense. He drove Tippety down the road and took the right fork. Tippety was full of the dickens. He hadn't done a stroke of work for weeks and weeks, and he was as sleek and full of the devil as a river in spring when the snow water comes boiling down. He kept shifting around, prancing, throwing his head, and shying at nothing, until Jeff begun to rage around and say that the horse was no good.

"Lemme have a try with the reins," I said.

"Why, kid," said Jeff, "he'd pull you right out of the seat."

"You try me."

His arms were beginning to ache already—Tippety had such a hard mouth—so he gave me a try. The minute Tippety heard my voice, he straightened out, stopped his prancing, and went along as smooth as running water. Jeff was very tickled.

We got to the fork of the road, and we heard the heels of the three riders go scooting down the left branch of the road.

"They've left us now," I said.

"I hope they have," he said, "but I doubt it. They don't want to chuck you up, kid. You've been too much cash in their pockets." We came slanting down to the river, pretty soon, and Jeff said: "Now, I know this creek, and they ain't likely to. I know that the bottom, right here, is pretty broad, but the bottom is hard sand, and the water ain't running more than hub deep. I say that we had ought to try to cross right here and take the road through the willows, on the far side. I know that road, and they don't, and it ain't likely that they would find us there."

That sounded reasonable, and it sounded very

good to me. Because I didn't want to see any of those three ever again. So I said that I'd try the water with Tippety. He came down to the bank, and I didn't urge him. He just looked around as though he wanted to make sure that was where I intended him to go, then he pricked up his ears and went in as dainty as a cat. There was no fear of anything in Tippety, he was so brave.

Pretty soon he was trudging along through the water that come boiling and foaming up around the buggy, but he didn't make any trouble about this sort of work. Once we dropped into a hole. The current caught the buggy and sagged her downstream so hard that Tippety nearly went under. But he scrambled like a dog to find his footing, and then he got it and brought us through safe to the far shore.

A minute more, and we were up the shallows, through the long reeds, and on that road through the willows that Jeff had told us about. We just drove a little piece down that road. The surface was soft sand. It deadened the beat of the hoofs, and there was no noise made by it except the whishing of the sand as it swished off from the wheels.

Then Smiler jumped up with a start, and Jeff asked if the dog saw something. I said that was hardly likely, but that maybe he heard something, so we stopped.

The minute that we stopped, we could hear it

pretty good. It was the mournful sound of dogs baying away, off in the distance. It sounded like it came from right ahead of us. But I knew that was wrong.

"What the devil is that?" asked Jeff. "Is it wolves ahead of us?"

I said: "It sounds like wolves, but it ain't. I've heard them voices before, and they came out of Crossman. It's a big pair of bloodhounds, and they've started those dogs on our trail, Jeff!"

Jeff said: "Well, I hope that they have, because when they come to the forking, they'll be sure to follow the strongest scent, and that means that they'll go along after the three of them and not bother us at all."

That sounded like pretty good logic, too. Just the same I couldn't help worrying a good deal, because, though it's not so hard to fool people, it don't seem so easy when they got the wits of a dog along to help them. I remembered the picture of those big bloodhounds a-straining away at the leash. It troubled me. They looked able to match up with a lion, each of them!

We drifted along very snug in the buggy; I didn't push little Tippety none, because I figured that this soft sand would tire him out quick, and it was better to save his speed for some hard place in the road. That seemed like good sense to both of us. Just the same it would have turned out better if we hadn't gone so slow in through there.

We hadn't plugged along for another mile when there was a soft beating in the road behind us. I looked back, and the first thing that I seen was a big, clumsy shadow of a man in the saddle on a horse. Behind him there was two more. I told Jeff that we was lost. He got out his gun. I thought at first that he would start shooting at once, but he waited until they come up close. Then he sang out: "Boys, you keep your distance!"

"Jeff," Jake said, "we don't want no trouble with you. That was a pretty dirty trick that you played, trying to run away from us like that, but we'll forgive you and remember nothing. All that we want, right now, is to have your help through this mess, because they've turned loose the dogs after us. And you surely know this country pretty good."

Jeff said: "Look here, you can follow me, if you want to, but don't come too close, I warn you. Because I ain't gonna stand for nothing. I don't trust none of you, and I want for you to know it now!"

That was talking up, as anybody would have to admit. So we went along like that, with Jeff and me leading the way and the riders behind, them yelling at us to forge ahead faster. Jeff told me that we was doing pretty good, and not to wear Tippety out—which I did just what he said.

Then we came to a fork in the road and Jeff had me stop.

Chapter Thirty-Four
CONFLICT

As Jake and the rest began to roar and cuss, having seen us stop, they pointed out that the dogs behind us had been gaining all the time. They wanted to know when we would start in to travel along.

Jeff said: "You cuss all you want to, but I'll ask your opinion what had we better do? Here on the left there is a road that winds along toward the upper bridge, and here on the right there is a road that leads toward the lower bridge. This left road is winding and it's roundabout, and it's soft, thick going all the way. This road to the right is a good hard surface and it's straight."

"Then for Pete's sake," exclaimed Jake, "what's the reason for all of the delay? Take the good road! I want to travel!"

"That's easy to say," answered Jeff. "Only, if you take the right-hand road, you got to stick with it straight as a string for a good five miles, and you can't take a horse off of that road any of the distance, because there is a terrible marsh on each side of it."

"And what's gonna stop us in between?" asked Jake.

"I dunno. I'm just telling you that, if we're

stopped, we got to leave our horses behind us. And you know what that means in this country."

Jake said he didn't give a hang, that he wanted some action, and that we would have that action, or just bust. So we took the good road. It was fine to have that steady going under the hoofs of Tippety, to see him prancing along. You believe me that after we had spun along over three miles of that road, there was no yelling for more speed from Jake and his gang, because they had to keep their nags into a good, hard gallop all the way, Tippety was clipping along so fast. He was a natural trotter with a good, stretchy action and springs under every hoof. When he came up off the ground, he stretched out and sailed for a part of a second before he landed again. His hoofs spatted against the road like sledgehammers working.

We covered those three miles, and all the time the music of the bloodhounds was getting fainter and fainter behind us until finally it was away off on the edge of the sky, so dim that you couldn't tell where it was. Sometimes it seemed in front of you, sometimes it seemed behind you, and sometimes it was away over on the side. Another half mile of that going and that would be dropped behind us. Then good bye to the men of Crossman. I thought about that, wondering what the boys back there would think of me going off with a gang of crooks. Would they know that I had been *forced* to go?

I was anxious to get through with that five-mile stretch of road, because now we could see the swamps very clear on each side of us. The reflection of the stars in the water showed us how black and oily it was.

We had seen plenty of that sort of thing, when Jeff grabbed the reins sudden and jerked Tippety to a halt. He said: "Something moved there, ahead of us. . . ."

Jake and the rest whirled to a halt behind us. Just then a voice sang out of the darkness: "Who's that?"

"Friends!" cried Jeff.

"Whose friends?"

"From Crossman."

"Come on, friends, and give us a look at you. Crossman is what we want!"

"Break through them," said Jake. "Give them a rush."

He spoke pretty soft, for him, but his voice had a roll to it that just naturally carried a long distance. Somebody yelled right out of the darkness at our feet, it seemed to me: "Watch the rope, boys! They're gonna rush us . . . and these are our men!"

With that, a big double-barreled shotgun spouted out a couple of columns of fire right ahead of us, and we heard the rattle of the handfuls of shot on the road. There was enough gunpowder and lead used up there to have blowed us to smithereens, all of us. The man who used it had been too nervous, and the result was that nothing carried to us. I suppose the one that fired was knocked flat on his back, because we could hear him groaning and saying that his shoulder was broke. That was all we heard, though, except a rush and a roar of noise—horses snorting, men yelling and cussing, and guns going off.

Rush them? They were rushing us, and looked like they would be making a pretty thorough clean job of it, too. There must have been fifteen or twenty men. But they weren't rushing a lot of pet lambs that would let themselves be eaten up.

Jeff said: "You turn the rig around, kid, and don't dump it over while you're doing it, because I'll try to keep back these fellows!" He turned around in the seat, tipped up a pair of guns, and began to fire them, dropping the muzzles of each of them, alternately, and not hurried. He made every bullet an aimed shot, and it was fine, cool work. Oh, it was a hot corner! I felt something like a wasp sting me on the cheek and a little, hot prickle of blood came down my face. There were bullets singing all around me.

They would have taken us, too. Jeff couldn't do enough. Boston was already down the road. Pug was shooting, but shooting wild. Jake turned the trick for us. He didn't care what happened to Jeff and to me and Smiler, of course. What made him mad was that anybody should dare to charge

251

down on him. He began to rage and bellow, telling them that he would show them. He sat right there in the saddle with a rifle at his shoulder, and the work he did was a fearful thing to see.

Every time that rifle clanged, pretty nearly a man fell out of his saddle. Two of them came swooping just as I got that rig cramped around and turned at last. Before they could fire into us, *whang!* went that rifle of Jake's. And there were only a couple of riderless horses riding down the road ahead of us. Of course, by that time, we had had more than enough. We went down that road at a wild pace. They had enough, too. There wasn't any sign of a chase of us, except a lot of shouting and groaning.

For that matter, they didn't need to worry. There was no call for them to hurry, because as soon as we steadied down a little, we could hear the bloodhounds making music right ahead of us, very clear. There was no doubt about it now. The men from Crossman had come onto the road to the lower bridge. Now it was the marsh or nothing for us.

How we hated it! How we hated it! That black, dirty water was almost worse than death. We stood there bunched along the edge of the road with me at the head of Tippety, rubbing his nose because I guessed that I would pretty soon have to say good bye to him.

They were talking things over to find out if there was any other way. Jeff said that there was not, and that, if they hadn't been so sure of themselves, he would have taken them along the left-hand road. Even if they hadn't made such good time, they would always have had the trees on each side to break away into in case of a pinch.

"Why didn't you tell us?" asked Jake. "Why didn't you say that those dirty swine back there in Crossman would telephone ahead to that other town to have our road blocked this way?"

"How could I tell that?" answered Jeff. "Am I a mind reader?"

"The devil with you!" said Jake. "I've half a mind . . ."

"Now you keep away from me, Jake. I'm taking nothing from you tonight!"

"You ain't, hey?"

"No, I ain't!"

"Why, you big sneak . . ."

There was a gun in Jeff's hand, you see, but he made a mistake. He didn't count on the extra long arms of Jake. He jerked up that gun in plenty of time, but the fist of Jake was six inches closer than Jeff had imagined. He went down as if a train had gone over him. When he dropped, Jake gave a sort of a scream. He threw himself on that body, grabbed Jeff by the throat, and beat his head on the road. Boston, Pug, and I just crowded together and couldn't lift a hand.

Jake got up, saying: "And if there's any more lip and back talk around here, I'm gonna do the same to another one of you . . . not naming no names!" He had had his taste of blood, and he was mad with the liking of it.

All at once the dead man on the ground spoke up. "Sammy!" he said.

I gave a start and jumped to him. "Jeff," I said, "what do you want? Are you all right?"

"I'm all right," he answered. "I'm dead, Sammy, but I want you to know that Lefty is . . ."

"You skunk!" Jake shouted, and he shot into Jeff twice.

"What did he tell you?" Jake asked me.

"Nothing," I replied.

I was half sick, and yet I was half happy. It had been a mighty horrible thing to see Jeff die like that just after he and I had been sitting side-by-side in the buggy. Yet there was something in what he had said that gave me my first hope. He had said: "Lefty is . . ."

That was what he had said. And could he have put in the "is" unless he meant that Lefty was alive?

Chapter Thirty-Five
THE MARSH

I didn't have much time to think. We were headed for the marshes as soon as they had robbed Jeff of the money that had been his share. Jake threw him into the water.

In another minute there was a groan of disgust from everybody, because we had got into the water up to our knees and the rank odor of it was in our faces. We all said that was too bad. Then we tried the marsh on the other side of the road. We found out quick enough that it was just as bad as the other one. We had to go on, whether we wanted to or not, because the wailing of the dogs behind us made us cut all our thinking pretty short.

Jake stopped there in the water. His weight pushed him down until he didn't seem much taller than me, but monstrous big and inhuman-looking. He said: "Curse those dogs! They can't follow us through this water, at least. That's one comfort."

"Can't they find a scent on the top of standing water?" asked Boston.

Jake cussed him something terrible, saying for him to shut up and not start making trouble, or it would be a lot the worse for him. That was the way that Jake was that night—just breathing murder. Right in himself he seemed a lot more terrible than all the men behind us—and all the guns—and all the dogs.

I wondered if any of those men who had been shot down had died. I hoped and prayed they hadn't. Then I wondered why it was that half a dozen of them had been dropped when not one of us had been more than grazed. I suppose the reason was that they had rushed at us and done their shooting while their horses was on the run. The wobbling and the bobbing of a running horse is enough to upset the shooting of the best marksman in the world, as anybody knows. Anyway, it was queer.

Jake said: "I dunno how it is, but we're lucky tonight . . . or else we're being saved up for something a lot worse than anything that could have happened to us so far. Now come along. We'll leave the dogs behind us." After a while, he asked: "How does that bull terrier manage to get along so easy?"

I said: "That's because he's a lot more active than the bloodhounds. They can't jump around the way that he can, because he's a regular trick dog."

Which was true. All the training of old Smiler that had been done was handy for him that night, because he would jump from stump to stump, very active. When he slipped into the water, he would swim along, or else I would give him a lift, though it was mighty tiring to me to do that. Mostly he didn't need any lifting, because, before we went into that marsh, I had said one word. I had said: "Lefty!" That was enough. He figured, then, that we was headed to find old Lefty again. It turned Smiler into a happy dog; he had more energy and strength than you could shake a stick at.

We got to a little stretch of dry land, but it didn't last a hundred yards. When we came to the water on the other side, the day was beginning. On the edge of the water we stopped. It had seemed bad enough to go through that marsh while it was in the black of the darkness, but it seemed ten times worse to think of getting into all of that filth now that we could see it pretty good.

For a long time we stood there looking at the dirty water and at each other, shivering with the cold and very hungry, because nobody had thought to bring along any of the food that was in the buggy.

We were a messy-looking lot, too, you can lay to that. Not one of us but had green slime stringing off him right up to his neck. Jake had been clean under the water a dozen times; it was all stuck into his hair, making him look twice the devil he had looked before—if possible.

Jake said as we started again: "Look here . . . there is birds, and there is animals that can live in this swamp . . . and then why can't we live here? And live off them, if we have to?"

Maybe there was something in that, but we didn't have to answer him back because every one of us thought that it was a lot better to die in any way you could name than it was to live in a place like that swamp.

We struggled along that way for hours. Pretty soon Boston sagged at the knees and sat down on a log. I threw myself down on the wet moss beside him, pretty tired. Jake and Pug stood apart, talking things over. There wasn't any doubt about what they were figuring on. It was to murder me, and Boston, too, then go on by themselves.

Right then, to bring things to a head, we heard the baying of those dogs behind us, terribly close! They had worked it pretty clever with those dogs. We hadn't heard them for hours. It was so restful to the nerves not to be hearing those big voices swelling into your ears. They had made pretty sure that, so long as they were in the marsh, and so long as they patrolled the borders of it, they didn't have to hurry. Everything, nearly, depended upon those two dogs in catching us quickly.

They had picked up the dogs, rested them, and let them have a good feed and sleep. After that, when they were all freshened up again, they took them into the swamp, rubbing them down with oil, so's the cold of the water wouldn't take the strength out of them too quick.

Of course, when we heard the voices of those dogs, we knew that it was our marching orders. We looked at one another, and then Boston shook his head, saying in a very feeble voice that he couldn't manage it.

Jake looked black as the devil. He said: "I suppose that you want us to waste our strength and to drag you along?"

Boston said: "Jake, just leave me and let them catch me here, because I had a lot rather die here, or be given the chair, than to have to work through another hundred yards of them marshes. . . ."

"Then your share of the money ain't gonna do you no good," said Jake. "You just pass that over, will you?"

The dogs, they boomed closer than ever.

"You want to rob me, too?" said Boston. "After I cracked the safe for the lot of you, now you want to rob me? Is that fair and square?"

"Why, what good will the coin be doing for you?" broke in Pug. "Why not pass it over? But let's get started, Jake. What about taking the kid along, too?"

"Aye, the kid," said Jake. "I dunno why we've been fool enough to cart him along this far . . . and why we don't . . ."

"Look here," said Boston all at once. "Those men behind us are Crossman folks, ain't they?"

"What of that?" asked Jake.

"Well, they were all mighty fond of the kid, as you may happen to remember. If they find his dead body, you can lay to it that, when they get the pair of you, they'll . . ." He stopped.

"Well, what?" asked Jake, sneering.

"They'll rub you down with oil, the pair of you, and then they'll tie you up, and then they'll touch a match to you. They'll stand by and see you burn. I think that's how they'll work with you."

You could see a wave of disgust and fear go over the brute face of Jake. It took language and ideas like that to make any impression on him, because he was just that low. You had to use a horsewhip on him in the place of an exclamation point.

"Well," said Jake, "there is your answer. I don't want to be hard on you and the kid. But lemme see you call off them dogs, and then we'll make it our business to leave your share of the dough with you. Besides all of that, we'll give you a part of our shares. We'll help you to get along, no matter how tired you are." He pointed straight ahead of him, and we could see what he meant.

We had got up to the head of a little hill that stuck out of the marsh a ways. Down there in the hollow, wading through the water, coming straight up on our scent, were the two bloodhounds! Behind them, not far, was the men.

Boston looked to me, and he was still loving life, though he was very sick and tired. He said: "Kid, what can we do? Two heads are better than one."

Of course, that was why he had argued for me a while back. It wasn't that he cared at all what became of me. It was only that he thought that, when the time came, I might be a help to him. . . .

Yet what could we do to those two dogs?

Then Smiler give a whine, and I saw him stretched out straight as a string from head to tail, his eyes half closed and a sleepy, happy look in them. It was his way when he saw a fight coming toward him on four legs.

We had a final ace to play.

It was Smiler against both of those big, killing brutes!

Chapter Thirty-Six
SMILER'S BATTLE

I didn't tell them what I thought. I had got hold of Smiler and began to clean him off; I rubbed him so's to warm him up a little. No dog can do himself proud when he is chilled like that. The others were getting ready to make a showdown right there as to what was to be done to me. I said: "Give Smiler a chance to get at those dogs, and, if he can't stop them, then you can do what you please to Boston and me."

"Fight?" asked Jake, his big mouth grinning at the mere thought of it. "Why, do you want one of them to eat him? Well, for Lefty's sake, I'm willing to wait it out and see the little white dog get his. Turn him loose."

I said to Smiler: "Now, boy, it's for me. And make it good. Go out there and take that big pair of bums." There was no need to shout to Smiler, and I didn't need to point. He wasn't that kind of a dog. He knew what you said as well as a man would.

He lighted out for the pair of them, not too fast. He didn't want to use himself up wading through all of that slush and muck. He got almost to them before the leading dog seen him coming and changed his baying on the trail to a high-pitched yipping. Then he dived for old Smiler.

And Smiler dived for him! He never had any doubt about himself, Smiler didn't. Whenever he heard a noise, he would stand up and go for it, and, when he found it, he would turn around to you as much as to say: "Shall I kill that noise?" He was made for fighting; he loved it!

When he got close to that bloodhound, they dived for each other and disappeared under the water. When they came up, Smiler was on top. Smiler would see his way clear for a throat hold. That was what he had now. In another minute, just as the second bloodhound came tearing at him, Smiler got back from the first one and jumped off onto a fallen log that was floating near there. From that he jumped to another, and out of the woods behind him came half a dozen men with guns.

They saw one of their dogs floating in the water, and they saw their second one taking after Smiler, so they knew what was happening. They began to yell advice to each other. Some of them started to run forward to get at the two dogs, and some of them called to the bloodhound to turn him back. Others told those ahead to get out of the way so that they could have a clear field to shoot at the little white dog. Smiler's seventy pounds *looked* small against the big, loose body of that bloodhound.

We thought, even I, that Smiler had been scared off by the coming of the men because he was running away from that second hound. That showed we didn't know him. He only wanted to get onto some firm land. When he came to a patch of it, he slowed up and let that bloodhound catch him. It was like catching a flash of lightning. That bloodhound came at Smiler with a yard of mouth opened up and furnished with some very fine teeth. Smiler wasn't ready to fall into that trap. He ducked off to one side, and, as he did, one of the men from Crossman thought he saw a chance to shoot at Smiler without hitting the other dog. He tried a snap shot, but he only cut the ground beside Smiler. The bloodhound tried again. Again he missed and looked like a fool, blundering past.

"Why don't your fool dog take the big boy by

the leg?" asked Jake, as we lay there in the bushes and watched.

"He don't want any long hold like that," I told them. "I sent him in there to do a quick job. He'll do it. You wait and see."

He started right then. As the bloodhound rushed, missed, and swung around, snarling very terrible, Smiler up and grabbed him across the nose and froze to him. The bloodhound started roaring and turning somersaults to get loose. He *did* get loose, too, because Smiler shifted like lightning from his nose to the throat hold, his old favorite.

We watched him shake the life out of that big dog. Before he finished, the men of Crossman were almost on top of the dogs. I told Jake that, if we wanted to have Smiler with us, we would have to drive back those fellows, because they would surely kill him.

"I'd walk ten miles for the sake of that dog," said Jake. "Bless his hide, there ain't no others like him. And he's saved *our* skins, you better believe. Duck, you suckers!" He yelled that last right out loud and turned loose with his rifle.

Even Jake wasn't crazy enough to shoot to kill when he didn't have to, or there would have been several dead men laid to his account right then and there. He splashed bullets into the water around those Crossman fellows, and they turned and dived for cover.

By the time they got there and were able to start in bombarding that hill where he was lying, Smiler was back with us. Then we sneaked off quick through the willows. Pretty soon we were a good long distance off from that noise of firing. They didn't seem to guess that we had cut and run, for, when we were more than a mile off, we could still hear them blazing away.

Jake couldn't get enough of that dog and would have patted him, if the Smiler had let him. There was no doubt about it. Smiler had saved our lives, or given us a chance for them, because there was no other way of shaking those bloodhounds off the scent.

Jake was eloquent after a while. "Look how the five of us have teamed it!" he said. "I can call myself the boss. I've done the bossing, and I've done some of the work and fighting, too, as you'll have to admit. Jeff was a help in giving us the idea to start off with . . . the kid kept us in found while we was planning and waiting and working. It would have all failed but for Pug chipping through the rock that way . . . while we all remember that it was Boston that finally turned the trick for us. Here it is the last one of us . . . the dog. He saved our hides after we got the loot into them."

That was the way big Jake talked. He said that we had run out of all of our bad luck now. There would be nothing but easy sailing from that time on. We would skin out of that marsh and find our troubles over, nothing to do but to spend the money that we had raked in.

He went on talking that way until, along in the middle of the afternoon, we came to the edge of the swamp and tried to sneak off up a gully. We hardly got started when three rifles started knocking up the dirt around us, and Boston got a bullet through the crown of his hat.

That was enough. We turned back into the swamp pretty silent, and big Jake didn't have any more to say to us for a spell.

That night we made a sort of a camp on the driest ground that we could find—none too dry, at that. We wrung out our clothes, took a half hitch in our belts, and tried to forget how hungry and how weak we was.

Only Smiler seemed easy and comfortable. He had his stomach tucked right up against his backbone, but it didn't seem to worry him. I wondered what I could do to thank him for what he had done for all of us.

That last night with Lefty, I had picked up his pipe and carried it when we scooted out of the rain into that old, ratty house. How I wish that we had never seen it! Anyway, I had kept that pipe with me all the while. That evening I showed it to Smiler.

He gave a yelp when he smelled it, and he

swarmed all over me—begging terrible hard for it—and licking my hand and my face as though he loved me. I knew what he meant, and I gave him that pipe. He carried it off for a spell like it was a bone, then he lay down and guarded it. If anybody came near him, even me, he would give a terrible growl and show every tooth in his head. He lay there for hours, pretty near. When he thought nobody was looking, he would lift his paw a little and sniff at that pipe. Then he would cover it up again and guard it just as hard as he could, and love Lefty, and hate all the rest of the world.

Where was there another dog like that, I ask you?

The morning came, somehow, and we saw another day ahead of us. Just as that day started, a gang of searchers—there must have been thirty of them—went beating through the swamp. And they had dogs. We could hear the dogs yipping, and we could see the men through the trees, here and there. We knew that our time was short. They only had to get a few dogs with good scents used to our trail and we were goners!

We worked along the edge of the woods that day. When the evening came, we were pretty spent and sick, without food for twenty-four hours, and no water to drink except that marsh stuff that was so bad.

Just at the edge of day and night we found a chance to get away.

Chapter Thirty-Seven
LIKE A HERO

There was a big skeleton of a railroad bridge being built across the river at the edge of the marsh. That was what gave us the ghost of a hope. There was no sign of people guarding it at all.

We waited until it was completely dark, and then we started down. We had to climb up the big pier that we came to first. Then we had to work our way into the skeleton ironwork that stretched along above us. Though it was very scary and hard to do, even to think about, almost anything was better than that marsh.

There was only one trouble—that was the Smiler. How could we get him up that pier and away to the place where he could walk along the iron beams like the rest of us—if he had good luck. I didn't see how that could be done. I suggested that they leave us behind, but Jake said that the finest dog in the world and the best fighter was a lot too good to be left to a gang of thugs like the people from Crossman.

He took off his own coat, he did, and slashed it into strips, making a good, long rope out of it by knotting those strips together. Then we made a slipknot and harnessed it around the body of Smiler. After that, Jake swarmed up that pier.

With those big arms of his and those big hands, he could climb better than any monkey. When he got up there, Pug climbed up, too, and handed Jake the end of the rope he had made. So Jake pulled up the dog and fetched Smiler onto the iron beam beside him.

Smiler pretty near went crazy when he saw that I had stayed down below. I think that he would have dived off, or sunk his teeth into Jake, who was holding him, except that he saw me begin to climb up *pronto*.

There we all were, at last, the bunch of us straddling beams not more than six inches wide, most of them, and made mostly of new, slippery iron. Oh, what a long ways down to the water! We worked along. Behind us was the marsh, and we hated that a lot more than we feared the bridge, so we came right out onto the high, middle curve of the bridge with the Smiler walking along before me, just sneaking like a cat. He knew that I was there behind him, and he never got so busy that he wouldn't wag his tail—just one waggle—when I spoke to him encouragingly.

When we came out there to the big central arch of the bridge, the wind got in a strong swoop at us. The tug of it was hard on all of us, but hardest on Smiler, of course, till pretty soon he was just crawling along on his belly. I hung on with one hand and both legs and squirmed along, but I kept a free hand over on his back to show him that I was there to steady him along. Every time that the wind gave an extra tug at him, and my hand helped him to stay on his beam, he would give that tail one waggle to say: "Thank you!" He never shook any, and he never stopped, and he never whined. Only he was thoughtful and quiet, the way a brave man would have been in a time and a place like that.

Pretty soon we got over into the far edge of the river, where the wind didn't yank at us so bad. After that we made a pretty good passage down onto the firm land beyond.

When we all stood together, we gave each other a look like we loved one another. It made you feel that way. Everything that Jake had done to Lefty and Jeff and all the men that he had shot down that night hardly seemed more than enough to weigh up against the way that he had lifted Smiler up onto the bridge! The danger that we had all gone through together made them seem like almost my best friends in the world.

Of course, we didn't waste any lot of time worrying about friendship and such. The first thing that we did was to get on down the railway line that was built up to the point of the bridge. When we climbed the rising ground beyond the foot of the bridge and came to the view of what lay beyond, our hearts dropped down into our boots, for we soon saw another river right before us! Rather, it was another chunk of the first one that we had passed. It was easy to see everything from where we were. We could see where the land that we were then standing on ran up to a point. The river cut around on each side of it, ran down, and in about a half mile joined together again, making this an island. I suppose that was why the railroad picked out this point for the building of their bridge, so it wouldn't have to throw such a big span across the stream. Right here it could go across the river in two jumps, instead of one. I suppose that it was cheaper and easier to build two little bridges than one great big one.

That was why we hadn't found any guard on the first bridge. There wasn't any need of a guard, because they had put a jim-dandy at the *second* bridge. We could see that guard from where we were. There was a little campfire; in the light of it two were sitting. Closer to the bridge, we could see two more walking up and down like sentinels in an army, you know. There never was a picture that we wanted to look at less. It shut the door in our faces pretty good and quick. Naturally what we thought of first was to go down the river in a boat, or something, where it ran under the incompleted bridge.

We went back and stood there, looking at the water. It was running so fast that it fair hummed. We hunted up and down the shore, but there wasn't any sign of a boat—because they had all been fetched across to the farther shore.

Then Pug said: "Boys, I'm gonna strip and try to swim that old river and get across to the boats. If I do, I'll try to cut one of them loose and bring it back to you."

He was a good swimmer. They told him that he was the best fellow in the world, and he stripped and gave his wallet and all of his money to Boston to keep for him. Then he dived in and headed across.

Where he was at the time was the head of the island, away upstream. That current carried him downstream about as fast as you would want to run. It was ripping along at such a rate. Pug was such a good swimmer that it looked like he might have a pretty good chance to get across to the boats on the far side. But that old river was just full of things. There were snags sticking up here and there; down the water floated trunks of trees, driving along as straight and as fast as anything, with a cream of foam around them in the night. Pug had to watch out for those things, too.

He just about got to the boats, and we thought that he would be reaching for the gunwale of one of them in another minute, when he had to stop for fear of a log that was driving past him. Before he could make headway again, the current had brought him well below those boats. He could still land and work up the shore, if he had any luck.

Just as he was about to strike off toward the far

shore again, we saw a dark streak with white edges go over the spot where Pug had been. The streak went along, but we didn't have any more view of the shadowy body of Pug working in toward the shore again. We knew that he was dead! He had been hit by that log.

I can't tell you how queer it was to be looking at that river with a man in it, fighting for his life and all our lives, you might say. The next minute there was the old river the same as ever, but the man was all gone. Somehow it didn't seem to matter so much. What with the queer things we had been doing, the night, and the rush of the river in your ears, it seemed like something you were dreaming about, or reading in a book, even. But it was real, all right. Poor Pug was gone.

There's no doubt that he was the best of that three. He didn't have as much strength as Jake, or half as much brains as Boston, of course, but he had a sort of good nature. He didn't mean so bad.

The way I figured about Pug was that he was sort of stupid, but liked to have other people look on him as being bright. He was always talking about somebody being "ignorant," and I suppose that was because he was afraid that he would be called it. I think that was what turned him into a tramp and a yegg, because you can wonder at a criminal and you can shudder at him, but you can't very well laugh at him. And Pug might've been a sort of foolish person any other place, but, when he was mixed up with the breaking of safes and swimming rivers. . . . There wasn't anything foolish in that—and there wasn't anything foolish in his dying for our sakes as much as for his own. It was sort of grand.

After a minute we all begun to look at each other, and we each knew what the other fellow was thinking about—that Pug had been a pretty good fellow—always ready to do his share of the work and even a little bit more. That he had died for us like a hero. Yes, sir, that made us feel pretty blue, but I guess that, if the truth had to be told, we didn't feel half so sorry for Pug as we did for ourselves, because we saw that there wasn't much more than a ghost of a chance for the rest of us.

Suddenly Boston gave a groan and pointed. On the side of the land toward the marsh we saw the flicker of a new-lighted campfire. They had come up behind us from that direction. Now we were surrounded for fair.

Chapter Thirty-Eight
THE WATERFALL

There was enough to keep us worried before this happened. That flare of fire from the far bank about finished the last of our hopes. We looked completely stranded, because, if Pug couldn't swim to the other shore, what chance would any of us have, who weren't half such good swimmers? It was pretty plain that the water was the only road away from the island.

Jake got into a terrible stew right away, and Boston seemed mighty upset for a time. Then he took Jake aside and I could hear him telling Jake that there was only one thing for them to do—that was, of course, to bury all the money they had. Then Jake asked: "What will the kid do when they talk to him . . . if he knows where the money is?"

"You can't bump off the kid now."

"Why not? The river is pretty handy."

They were so desperate that they talked up careless and wild like this, hardly caring whether I heard or not. I knew, by what I got from them, that they meant business and bad business for me. I sloped down for the shore, walking along very casual as if I didn't suspect nothing, Smiler at my heels, as usual.

Now, when I got down by the water, watching a big log heaving down through the river, wallowing and thrashing, I saw Jake coming along after me, walking very fast. He was so squat and his walk was so rolling that at a little distance, particularly that night, he didn't look human. He looked like death coming straight at me on two legs.

I listened to the roaring of that river with new ears that second, because I saw that it was better to die in the water than at the hands of Jake. I gave him one more look, then I whirled around and yelled: "Help! Murder!"

The sound of my voice was sure to go across the river, and it was sure to get to the gents waiting on the far side around one of the campfires.

"You little fool! Sammy, don't make a noise like that!" cried Jake. "I don't mean you no harm!"

I wasn't fool enough to trust to him a single lick. I had heard Boston say that Salt Creek was waiting for him, and with my own eyes I had seen Jake do murder. I knew that all those scoundrels could depend upon was to hire fine lawyers with a lot of money. If they buried that money with me on that little dinky island, how could they ever be sure that I wouldn't see and betray the place to the searchers for the coin? I would have done so, too; I hated them both so bad.

Jake came closer and closer, and I saw that I couldn't wait any longer. I turned and ran to the edge of the water, jumping in as far as I could. Then I struck out, swimming with all my might to get to that big tree, floating down the stream— the same one that I spoke of a little while before.

I saw in a minute that I couldn't reach the trunk. It was shooting down the stream so fast. . . . There was a *plump* into the water behind me. I could see big Jake against the stars on the island,

276

trying to make sure of me by heaving rocks into the water—ten- and twenty-pound chunks that would have pushed me right down to the bottom of the stream. I saw something else, too. Smiler was streaking out after me, coming along fast and fine, with his head stuck out straight over the top of the water. I only thought, just then, how much better it would have been if old Lefty, Smiler, and I had died in the fight against Jake and his men. There would have been something sort of grand in that way of dying.

Yet here was Smiler following me to die. . . .

Just at that minute something hit me in the stomach, and I grabbed—a limb of that tree trunk—a limb that had stretched far out into the water and caught at me like a hand. I worked out to the bare tip of the limb and let my body stream out on the surface of the water. That way old Smiler was able to get a grip on my foot. He pulled himself in just like a man and came in on top of my body until he was riding up on my shoulders, just the way that he had always done when we finished off one of our little bags of tricks. You couldn't beat that dog. He just thought things right out. That was all there was about it.

I worked my way into the main body of that tree trunk, and there we sat as snug as you please, because that tree was a regular whopper. You would hardly believe how big it was. It must have been growing very close to the edge of the river and been sawed away from the banks by the last flood.

It was cold, riding there in the river. Smiler was shivering with the cold of it. Just the same he seemed pretty happy. He sat up there on the rough bark of the log between my knees with his ears all pricked, his head turning from one side to the other, watching everything that passed along the shores, or else just lowering his head and smelling of the water. Every once in a while he would turn his head around real quick and give me a look as much as to say that he had almost forgot that I was out there with him, but he was mighty glad to have me along.

He was company, Smiler was. He was so brave that you couldn't lose hope while he was along with you. He always seemed to be figuring things out so that it would start you thinking.

We went sailing down that river, kind of wondering how it could be that we were free from those rapscallions on the island behind us, wondering, too, at the speed of that current. Most of all, I wondered why it was that the guards who were watching the island hadn't set a boat below it and anchored it there to keep us from getting away in just this fashion. I wondered at that until we came swinging around the next curve like a train going around a turn. Then I saw why they had left the river open.

I guessed, first of all, when I heard a booming

and a roaring ahead of us before ever we turned the curve. I sort of thought maybe it was the beginning of a windstorm off among the trees. When we came around the bend of the river, there was no doubt left. The roaring jumped at our ears ten times stronger than before. I saw a white line across the river from bank to bank, nearly, and I knew we were headed straight for a fall.

Even Smiler knew it. His ears went back, then forward, as though he were afraid that I might suspect him of losing heart a little. He stood up, too, and gave that line of foam a look. If fighting could carry us through, he was ready to fight.

All you could do was to sit there and wait. How awful long that wait was!

I looked up, sort of wild, and I saw the stars. They seemed to be watching. . . . Closing my eyes, I remembered that I would be having plenty of darkness pretty soon. It was a pretty poor way of dying—drowning, in the night!

The roar of that waterfall smashed into my ears so hard I couldn't think. It sort of numbed my brain; I was glad of that in a crazy, sleepy way. It was like the anesthetic before the doctor took my tonsils out. You get sleepy, and you just don't care.

Then came a *whang,* and with the bellow of that fall right there under my nose, I found that we were sitting still on the tree trunk with the water curling and foaming up all around us.

Of course, what had happened was easy to understand. The butt of that trunk was so big and heavy that it had sunk down under the surface and caught on a projecting rock. It began to stagger and to turn as hundreds of tons of water sloshed along against it. It turned the lighter end of the tree toward the bank. That meant my chance. I was down at the end of that trunk in a minute, sitting there, waiting, forgetting that I was cold even. I could see where that tree was washing in toward the bank. It was only a twelve-foot gap from the tree to the bank. And then the butt of that tree slipped off the rock and jumped for the falls.

I jumped, too, and hit the water, and grabbed a trailing branch of a vine at the same minute. The current was so dog-gone fast that it pulled me right out sideways with a mighty strong tug. Smiler was right on top of my shoulders, grabbing me about the neck with his forelegs. His weight sank the two of us under the surface. I thought it was the end.

That branch that I had ahold of was the toughest stuff that you ever saw. A minute later I was pulling hand over hand to the edge of the bank, then I was wallowing my way up the bank and to the dry grass above.

When I got there, my strength melted out of me, and I just lay there, wet and cold and muddy, looking up at the sky where the stars had been watching me a little minute before, as cold and as mean as the eyes of cats. They were changed now. They were dancing and laughing, so that it was good to see them, you can just bet! Smiler stayed by me, shivering pretty bad, but forgetting his troubles to stand by and lick my cold face and my hands.

Chapter Thirty-Nine
SMILER'S HEAVEN

I was hungrier than I was tired. After about an hour of lying there and coming back to myself, I got up and started along. There wasn't much strength in my knees until I saw the light of a house. Then I remembered that, where there is a house in the country there is sure to be a lot of chickens.

It didn't take long to find them. I got two fat young roosters off the perch, because I've never been too hungry, I'm proud to say, not to be particular in the sort of chickens that I've swiped. I wrung the necks of those chickens and was back in the woods before you could say Jack Robinson.

One of the things that Lefty had taught me was never to be without matches in a water-tight safe or a little salt done up in a twist of oiled silk. I got outside of one of those chickens, while it was still only about half roasted. Smiler absorbed the other one.

After that I was sleepy, and Smiler could keep only one eye open. Another thing Lefty had taught me was never to sleep wet, if you could help it, and here was I more than half sopping.

Pretty soon I found a barn, and the smell of that sweet, clean hay that I burrowed into—well, it was about the best thing that ever happened in the whole world. I slept and didn't even dream. When I woke up, it was the next afternoon, and there were a lot of pigeons in the loft of the barn, talking and fussing. There's nothing sillier than a pigeon—nor more fun to watch—because they are always doing something. Everything they do is more foolish than the last.

I wanted to get outdoors, but I didn't want to get out bad enough to risk being captured, because I couldn't tell what would happen if they caught me. If they only sent me back to Aunt Claudia, that would be terrible enough. I knew that there was a lot of other things that they could do instead—reform school, for instance.

Half asleep and half awake, I laid up there in that loft, letting the smell of the swamp and the misery of it sort of work out of my brain. There was always in my head, too, like the ringing of a bell, what Jeff had said just before Jake finished murdering him. Lefty was alive!

When the day got thick and shadowy I began to think of getting down from the hay. Just as I started, I heard a couple of men drive some cows into the barns. First they shut their heads into the stanchions. After that they climbed up onto the mow to throw down feed. I heard them coming and rolled into a corner with Smiler, putting my hand over Smiler's nose, which was the sign that always made him keep quiet.

They threw down the hay and climbed down, and, as they started, I felt a terrible sneeze coming over me. There are sneezes that you can swallow, but there are some that give you a stab right between the eyes at the start. That kind you can't handle. That sneeze busted out, and, though I near choked myself, I couldn't swallow more than the half of it.

"Hey, Sam! Was that you that sneezed?" sang out one of them.

And Sam bellowed back: "Look at that fool brindled heifer, if she ain't got her head out of the stanchions again!"

They got so mad and excited about her that they forgot about the sneeze. Just when I thought they were quiet and that I could start down from the loft, I heard milk begin to go humming into buckets down there. They had that whole string to milk. I was mad, and I was getting hungry, too. There was Smiler asleep and that I had to keep from snoring, because he would snore very loud, just exactly like a man.

They were talking about how young Harkness was back in the town and said that he was going to sell off his farm, about what terrible goings on there was between a girl named something and a young gent named Perkins. Then one of them said: "Wouldn't you know those blockheads from Crossman would let the worst of the two get away?"

You better believe that I heard that, and sat up.

So Jake was loose! I heard the rest through a sort of a trance. The two on the island had surrendered the next morning, and Boston had agreed to confess everything to save his hide. They had started them back toward Crossman this very day. On the way Jake managed to beat over the head the gent who was driving the automobile that he was in. Two others, who were guarding him, were so scared that they jumped right out of the car. Jake with his manacled hands had managed to drive that car right away and get free, though there were a hundred guns shooting at him from first to last.

Well, I believed it! Here he was like a mad dog turned loose—with the money that he had stolen taken from him—with a lot of brand-new murders on his head, maybe heading right for this very same barn that I was in! That was enough for me. I scooted out of that barn the minute those two milkers were gone. South, straight ahead of me, I saw a row of lights, and I knew that the railway was not far off.

I got to it in under an hour of walking, and I

rambled right on down the track. On the siding I found a freight train taking things easy until a passenger went by. The passenger train went by with a whoop and a snort. Then the freight began puffing to get the cars started rolling. By the time that happened, Smiler and I were lying on the rods, me with a chilly prickle between my shoulder blades for fear lest Jake might be aboard of the very same train. Nothing could have been more likely, you got to admit.

That train went along pretty good, though loaded. I stuck by the rods for nearly three hours, when it stopped and a fresh brakeman stuck his lantern under the car and ordered me out.

I had to come. When he got me by the collar, he gave me a yell and a shake. "You're Sammy Moore, of Crossman . . . and I got you and the reward. . . ."

Where he made his mistake was in shaking me. Smiler wasn't bothered caring too much about me, but he had it fixed in the back of his head that I sort of belonged to Lefty, and that meant that he had to take some sort of care of me. Smiler sank his long fighting jaw in the leg of that shack.

The shack let out a yell and grabbed himself. By the time he got himself untangled from his emotions, Smiler and me were in the woods and gone.

We had no plans. We just jogged along for about an hour, and then found another prime hen roost to visit. We finished a rooster apiece. This time it was harder to get the last bits down—for me, not for Smiler. He was just like a boa constrictor. That night was clear and pretty warm; we just slept it out by the fire, staying under cover of those woods until the late afternoon, when we started on.

We kept to the trees until all at once I got a broadside whiff of jam and pies and coffee and bacon and frying beef and everything else that is good to a hungry stomach. In another minute there were the back yards of a village right at my hand. Nothing was ever more crazy, of course— nothing was ever half so crazy! I just couldn't help it. The smell of the cooking was so good that I decided I would sneak out and just get a nearer whiff of it.

I was standing, leaning against the side of the woodshed of a little cottage, when I heard a poor squeak of a violin playing a tune in the village. It was about the worst playing that you ever heard. What made it worse was because that I had heard it played so many times by about the best violinist that ever drew a bow—I mean, by Lefty.

It was the same Irish jig tune that he and I used to open up with usually—I mean that one about Molly who was waiting for you with blue eyes, and all that rot, you know. It made me extremely blue to hear it.

There was nobody around. It was just the sleepy

fag end of the day, when you want nothing but your supper and peace. And there was that violin to hurt your nerves. Well, I knew what would happen. I sneaked out between the cottage and the next street to see if I could spy the player.

And there he was! No kid, but a gray-haired man, with bent shoulders, sawing away at a violin—with his hat on the ground. Even though his back was toward me, I could see how hard he was working.

I was sorry for him, mighty sorry. I saw what would happen, and I wasn't wrong. In another minute a door slammed and a man came running out, singing: "What are you trying to do around here? Wake up the dead?"

The beggar made an apologetic gesture and said something. I didn't understand what the words were, but I knew the voice. Yes, I knew the voice; it went through me, sick and sharp and quick!

The tramp moved along and put down his hat at the next corner, not fifty feet from me. He was half facing me, and he started sawing again on the same old tune. I could see what was wrong with his playing now. His left hand that had been so supple and smooth, more flexible than a girl's, was just a twisted-up claw. I remembered how he had grabbed the knife of Jake's.

Here he was, really that which he had pretended to be back in that first town we had worked together. That hair of his was really gray now.

Even if his eyes weren't blind, there was no need to make them up—they were so hollow and blackened. No, it wasn't Lefty. It was just the wreck of Lefty. I didn't wonder that Smiler stood there, fifty feet away from his boss, and didn't let on to know him.

There was the violin scraping along very tired through that Molly tune. Another man yelled out from a door: "Shut up that noise, you hobo, and move on before I send for the constable!"

Then something in me opened up, and my eyes were closed with tears. But the song came just busting out and rang and sang up and down that street. The violin staggered, went out, and then came in again on the note—or pretty near the note. Something that was a little more like the ghost of Lefty's old playing was in that music.

There was a crowd gathering when I got up to Lefty. Smiler gave a whine, and in a flash he was there at Lefty's feet. Lefty told him—"Down!"—in a very wobbly voice.

Smiler was mighty hurt. He stood up and begged, which was his way of saying to Lefty that he was sorry if he had done anything wrong and would Lefty please forgive him. Lefty didn't pay any heed to him. He just laid his hands on my shoulders and looked and looked.

"People said that the river had you, Sammy," he said. "And I had given up the last hope, partner."

He was so busted up and so shaking that he

forgot all about his hat on the sidewalk, where the folks were dropping coins now. I scooped it up, and we broke away for the woods. Every step of the way he was shaking his shoulders back farther and farther and walking with a brisker step. When we were in the trees, he sang out for me to brisk up a fire. I did it while he got out his knapsack with some provisions. I don't know what we cooked or what we ate. I only know that Lefty did, and what he looked like, and what he said. He kept jumping up and looking around him, saying: "Why, this is not so bad, eh, Sammy? All I have to do is to supple up this old hand of mine and we'll be as good moneymakers as ever, eh?"

Then he would start in rubbing that left hand of his that had been so wonderful that it seemed like his whole soul could talk through it. Well, one look at it was enough for me. Lefty could say that he had a hope, but I knew in my heart that he didn't. He was just lying, because that hand was done for, with all the fingers withered up and drawn together. Only he wouldn't give up or admit out loud that he was beaten, that wasn't Lefty's way.

I couldn't stand it any longer after a while, my heart was swelling and aching so bad. I said: "Lefty, won't you give Smiler a word?"

"Aye," said Lefty, "there's Smiler. And he doesn't see any change in me, do you, boy?"

Smiler was busting to swarm all over Lefty and

tell him how he loved him, but all that he dared to do was lie down and brush the leaves with the waggling of his tail, raise his head, and worship Lefty with his eyes, and say with them how grand and wonderful his boss was.

Lefty began to laugh, and it made me jump to hear him, because it was the same rich sounding laughter as ever. It would have made anybody jump to hear such golden young sounds coming out of such an old-looking man.

"I tell you, Sammy," said Lefty, "Smiler has a better head than any of the doctors. He knows that I'm not so badly off. He knows that I'll change and be my old self some of these days. Why, that dog is a prophet, Sammy. Aren't you a prophet, Smiler?"

Smiler whined, saying as plain as day: "Only give me a chance to die for you. That's all I want to do!"

"A prophet! That's what he is," said Lefty.

He began to stroke the head of Smiler. It was very rare for him so much as to touch that dog. Every touch made a quiver of joy run from the tip of the Smiler's nose to the tip of the Smiler's tail.

I saw that Lefty had forgotten what he was doing and what he was saying. The happiness that he had brought up into his face on my account all died out. It left his eyes just dark hollows with no light in them. He didn't see me—or the Smiler— of his own will. He was looking at a time to come, and what he saw there I didn't even dare to ask myself. Well, I couldn't stand it. I got up and stretched, saying that I was going to go to sleep. He said that he would do the same.

So I curled up near the fire and closed my eyes. I began to breathe regular and slow, and pretty soon the glare of the fire that I could feel right through my closed eyelids was blocked away by a shadow. I knew that Lefty had put a rock between to shade me from the light. Yes, and I could feel him leaning over me. I only prayed that I could hang on to myself and keep lying still, and not bust out crying like a fool. Nobody could ever know how hard it was.

I lay there I don't know how long. Pretty soon I did go to sleep, right when I was thinking that I didn't care if I never slept again in all my life— and I didn't want to do nothing but die. The last thing that I could remember was the whisper of Lefty, extremely soft, as he talked to Smiler. I remember thinking to myself that Smiler was in heaven—pure heaven. Then I went to sleep.

Right in that sleep I heard a scream that brought me up standing.

There are two most awful sounds. One is the scream of a horse dying with pain. The most terrible of all is the scream of a man, and a real man, when fear has snatched all of his manliness away.

Chapter Forty
A DIFFERENT MAN

The fire was near out. It only lifted a very weak head of light showing the tallness of the trees and the blackness of them, without being strong enough to put out the light of the stars. There was light enough to show me Lefty, kneeling and cowering right beside me—holding one hand sort of before his face as if to shut out something that he was seeing. It was his awful twisted left hand that he held there. In his right hand he had a revolver that was shaking and wobbling from side to side.

He asked: "Was it a dream, Sammy? I saw him there as plain as day! And . . . it must have been a dream, because . . . I was grabbing the knife again. But there's no blood on my hand. . . ."

Then the whole horrible truth hit me. That dream of his was bad enough, but it was nothing to what came into my head, then, for I saw the truth about Lefty.

It wasn't his hand only that was gone, and all his skill and his cleverness with it. There was something gone out of Lefty's heart that couldn't ever come back. Think how grand and big and easy and sure of himself he had been, always sort of liking me, but sort of pitying me—laughing at me, and taking care of me. Here he was crouching at my feet like he was asking me to help him. . . . Oh, there was nothing so horrible as seeing Lefty changed like that!

Smiler didn't have to be told. He went ranging around through the shadows trying to find the thing that had dared to scare his boss so bad. The sound of his growling pulled Lefty together—but only part way. He beat out the fire, saying that we would sit up for a while together, if I didn't mind.

So we sat there, back to back, watching the dark. I could feel Lefty trembling and shaking. I knew, then, how many nights he had sat up watching the black of the night with not even a kid like me to guard his back. What kept shuddering home in me was that Lefty was so far gone that he didn't even care or feel ashamed that I would feel him shake and know how frightened he was.

I saw, all at once, that our jobs were changed. It was my place to be a man, but all the time treating Lefty as though he were the boss, still—and I swore to myself that I would keep care of him and never once let him guess that I saw the facts. Because grown-up folks are like that. They always seem to think that children are sort of blind in handy places. We aren't, not half.

After a while he reached a hand back and gave my arm a squeeze.

"Shoulder to shoulder, kid," he said, "and we'll beat him yet. It's good to have you back."

I said: "Lefty, he'll never bother you again. He's done you enough harm."

"Ah," said Lefty, "the more you harm a man, the more you hate him. It's always that way." A minute later, he said: "Smiler doesn't seem to think I'm so much changed, Sammy."

You see, my back was to him, and he couldn't see my face, which made it easier for me to say: "Why, Lefty, you're not much changed. You're gonna be all right. You're just a little tired now. And when you get all rested up . . . and then when that hand gets fixed . . . or even if it doesn't . . . because you've got a fine right hand, Lefty. . . ."

He caught at that with a gasp of breath. "That's it!" he said. "With patience and work, I could learn to use my other hand, couldn't I?"

"Of course," I said.

"And *then* I wouldn't seem so queer to people. So sort of disgusting to them, Sammy?"

He wasn't asking me. He was *begging* me.

"Gosh, Lefty," I answered, "there'll never be a time when you won't be twice as good as the average man."

"Do you think so, Sammy?"

"I know it."

He made a little pause. "Sammy . . ."

"Well?"

"Considering what you say, and how the Smiler acts . . . do you suppose that if I was to see Kate . . . that she could stand it?"

The tears were pouring down my face, but how could he tell? I managed to say: "Why, it wouldn't make any difference to her."

He took in a long breath, and he said: "I wonder . . . if it really would . . . make . . . no difference?"

Only you can't write down the way he said it.

After a while I could feel him weakening with sleep behind me. I guess maybe it had been weeks and weeks since he had had a really good sleep, you know. Now he slumped until finally his head fell back. I turned a little, got his head in my lap, and there he slept. Every minute of the night he would jump and start. There would be a groan and then a gasp. His hands would rise up—a terrible thing to see in the starlight—and grapple in front of him.

What I mostly thought of was if he would really want to go back to Kate. Would he be weak enough to want to drag her down and ruin her life by tying her to a man like him?

I never loved him more than I did right then—when I saw that even the grandness of Lefty, that had been his strength, was gone from him. Yet I knew he would never be any good any more after this. I saw it and I knew it. I knew, too, that the more worthless he got, the more sure Kate would be to marry him to save him. She would think that the real Lefty was still in him; she wouldn't know that man had died under the knife of Jake, and that all the doctors in the world could never bring him back to life.

Smiler came and sat beside me. He didn't like the way that I was holding his boss, and he gave me a wicked look. You can lay to it, that no matter how much Smiler and me had been through together, I was no more than a dead leaf in his life, compared with his boss.

Morning came. I slipped away from Lefty when the red came over the tops of the trees, and I lay down and pretended to sleep. I heard him easy enough when he woke up a little later and sneaked away. I heard him cutting brush in the distance for fear of waking me. I turned over and held my head in my arms and cried like any fool kid. Only I couldn't stand it, you see.

What I had guessed was the fact. Lefty wanted to start right back for Perigord. He didn't say where, but he wanted to travel, and when he took that direction, I knew.

All that day his spirits were growing pretty big. Every minute he was working at his ruined hand, trying to liven it up. That evening, when we came near to a town, he said that it felt almost like his old fingers had come back to him. We went into that town and he said that he would try a violin solo.

He tried it.

A woman jerked open a window and yelled at him to be off.

You would have said that her voice knocked the violin out of the hands of Lefty. He picked it up and went out of the town with his head down. That night he sat by the fire with the violin in his arms for a long time, not saying a thing. I was saying nothing, too, because I could see that Lefty was beginning to realize.

The next morning, though, he was hoping again. And the next evening I found myself singing my best and my loudest, trying to drown out the squawking of that violin as it played the Irish jig tune about Molly and her waiting blue eyes.

Then we came to the valley of Perigord. I knew that Lefty was going to do a thing that was a lot worse than murder—letting Kate see him like that—and then letting her marry him.

Back in the woods a way he stopped to get himself fixed up, brush his ragged clothes, wash his face, and be as fine as he could. Then he went on with me until he came to the lights of her house, shining across the fields. There he stopped as though he had been hit in the face.

Suddenly he grabbed me and he said: "Is it right, Sammy?"

I couldn't speak. It would have choked me to tell him that it was wrong, and it would have killed me to tell him that it was right. I just said nothing, and he finally said: "Yes, I suppose you're right. The old Lefty wouldn't have done this, eh? Well, you go on ahead, kid . . . take a look at her, and don't let her see you. Just see whether or not she is happy or sad. Just see that . . . and then you come right back here and let me know. Will you do that?"

I started off.

He said: "Take this dog along with you."

I said: "He'd a lot rather stay with you."

"Maybe he would," said Lefty, "but I have no time for a dog just now. I've got other things to think about. Go on along . . . get, Smiler."

That was how it was that Smiler was with me when the time came.

I went straight on toward the house. Right away quick I saw her out there in the back yard sitting in a chair under a tree, talking with another woman. I waited until the other woman went inside the house for something, and then I went out.

It was Smiler that she saw first and recognized. She jumped up without a sound and came running to find—only me.

She was too fine to show how much she was disappointed in that. She even put an arm around me and said how glad she was. You couldn't beat that girl, I tell you.

Then, when I didn't speak, she said: "Now, Sammy, tell me what's the matter. But come here, first, under the light of the window, and let me see your face . . . because there's something strange about you."

I said: "Maybe there is. But I can't stand that light. You'll have to hear me out in the dark."

There was only one thing to do; I told her the whole truth!

Chapter Forty-One
LEFTY'S TRIUMPH

It is queer how a big thing can be boiled down small. It only took me two minutes to tell her about the fight, and then about how I had found Lefty again—and what he was. I didn't leave out a thing that was worth being said, and, while I talked, I watched a big, broad moon climbing through the trees.

Her answer was: "He is out there waiting. I must not keep him in such sadness, Sammy dear. Come, show me the way."

The first thing I knew was I was walking along with her. She said: "Not that I doubt anything that you've said, or your judgment, but don't you think, working together, that you and I could bring him back to himself?"

Well, hearing her talk like that, you would hardly have doubted anything. We trudged along there through the night and climbed the stile into the horse pasture, coming to the edge of the woods where I had left Lefty. I stopped.

"Lefty!" called Kate.

There wasn't any answer. All at once a terrible fear jumped in me, and I ran forward until I came to the place.

Lefty lay there on the ground, only half alive. Jake lay crumpled in a heap, face down at the feet of Lefty. Lefty's old dream had come true, and Jake had died in his hands. Jake, being a devil, must have known that Lefty would come back sooner or later to Perigord Valley, and to Kate.

Well, I turned around and got back to Kate in two winks. I told her that Lefty was only half alive, and that he needed assistance quick. She said that she understood what had happened, and that nothing mattered so long as Lefty was still alive, and that she would nurse him back to health again. She said she knew that he had killed his man in self-defense and that everything would come out all right.

I could only follow along behind her until she came to the place where Lefty lay.

Smiler was there, of course. After all the petting and talk he had had from Lefty that night before, I guess he couldn't make things out. He was sitting up and begging, that way that he had when he wanted to be forgiven.

Well, Kate and Lefty have stayed together since. You'd be surprised to know how quick Lefty got well under Kate's care. And it was a fine wedding that Smiler and I were the chief witnesses at, you may be sure. Smiler padded around as big as life, and, if anybody so much as looked wrong at Lefty, he was met with a warning growl from the dog who worships his master as much as Kate and I do.

About the Author

Max Brand® is the best-known pen name of Frederick Faust, creator of Dr. Kildare, Destry, and many other fictional characters popular with readers and viewers worldwide. Faust wrote for a variety of audiences in many genres. His enormous output, totaling approximately thirty million words or the equivalent of 530 ordinary books, covered nearly every field: crime, fantasy, historical romance, espionage, Westerns, science fiction, adventure, animal stories, love, war, and fashionable society, big business and big medicine. Eighty motion pictures have been based on his work along with many radio and television programs. For good measure he also published four volumes of poetry. Perhaps no other author has reached more people in more different ways.

Born in Seattle in 1892, orphaned early, Faust grew up in the rural San Joaquin Valley of California. At Berkeley he became a student rebel and one-man literary movement, contributing prodigiously to all campus publications. Denied a degree because of unconventional conduct, he embarked on a series of adventures culminating in New York City where, after a period of near starvation, he received simultaneous recognition as a serious poet and successful author of fiction.

Later, he traveled widely, making his home in New York, then in Florence, and finally in Los Angeles.

Once the United States entered the Second World War, Faust abandoned his lucrative writing career and his work as a screenwriter to serve as a war correspondent with the infantry in Italy, despite his fifty-one years and a bad heart. He was killed during a night attack on a hilltop village held by the German army. New books based on magazine serials or unpublished manuscripts or restored versions continue to appear so that, alive or dead, he has averaged a new book every four months for seventy-five years. Beyond this, some work by him is newly reprinted every week of every year in one or another format somewhere in the world. A great deal more about this author and his work can be found in *The Max Brand® Companion* (Greenwood Press, 1997) edited by Jon Tuska and Vicki Piekarski.

Center Point Publishing
600 Brooks Road ● PO Box 1
Thorndike ME 04986-0001 USA

(207) 568-3717

US & Canada:
1 800 929-9108
www.centerpointlargeprint.com